Alegria

Alegria

Emi Wright

MADVILLE
PUBLISHING

Lake Dallas, Texas

FIRST EDITION

Alegría is a work of fiction. Names, characters, places, and incidents either are the products of the author's imagination or are used fictitiously. Any resemblance to actual events, locales, businesses, companies, or persons, living or dead, is entirely coincidental.

Requests for permission to reprint material from this work should be sent to:

Permissions
Madville Publishing
P.O. Box 358
Lake Dallas, TX 75065

Cover Design: Jacqueline Davis

ISBN: 978-1-948692-40-3 paperback,
978-1-948692-41-0 ebook
Library of Congress Control Number: 2020941263

Alegria

1.

When Alegría was born, no one in the little town of Prudent smiled. Not the mother, too tired to control her facial muscles; not the father, worried about the future cost the new baby would incur; not the unprepared delivering doctor, seeing a new face pop out for the twentieth time in his life; not the attending nurses, just holding on until the break at the end of their shift; not even Alegría herself. In fact, she came out with eyes wide open as big as the saucers Grandma Tracy had given her mother for Christmas and a countenance as red as Aunt Mary's worn Santa sock; her eyes looked on frightened under hairless furrowed eyebrows as a white nurse took her like a sack of flour and wrapped her in a pink blanket.

The nurse said "She looks rosy." And the anxious father took that as a sign that his daughter's name should be Rosie. But the fatigued mother interjected with a "NO. Her name will be Alegría, after my sister." The father thought naming a daughter after a sister drowned before she turned four bad luck, but not wanting to fight with his wearied wife, said nothing. As for the mother, the name Alegría meant she'd done her penance. Marisol had always felt a slight guilt at having egged her sister to go into the water when neither of them knew how to swim. At her funeral, she'd promised to name her daughter after her if she ever had one. Having lost her resolve with her first daughter, June, she'd pushed her husband for a second pregnancy to fulfill her once-broken promise. As she looked upon Alegría wrapped up like a taquito, Marisol hoped she would bring her family plenty of laughter and joy—as well as the removal of a thorn from her heart. It was with this hope that she smiled the first smile since Alegría's birth, and seeing her smile, Alegría's puffy face smiled also, her eyes becoming moon crescents.

Leading up to Alegría's birth, Aunt Teresa had advised Marisol to eat bananas for a quick and clean delivery, and the whole family had shrugged their shoulders and concurred. Knowing the wishes of Aunt Teresa could not be ignored—lest a curse fall on his progeny—Daniel Cana bought two big crates of ripened bananas. Along with these yellow spotted packages of potassium, Alegría's mother had balanced her diet with pomegranate seeds, *pan dulce,* grilled cheese sandwiches, and goldfish crackers dipped in everything from peanut butter to *cajeta.* And indeed, just as Aunt Teresa had said, Marisol had not been in labor for more than eighteen hours when Alegría came out headfirst on the sixth of January, the bluest month, at 6:03 p.m.

Once the nurses and doctors perceived that everything was in good order, they shipped Alegría and her parents out first thing the next day with a complementary teddy bear. For the next hour, Marisol hugged her daughter protectively to her chest as they passed the ice-cold Mipared River, the blonde fields where the hard red spring wheat would be planted come late March, the familiar flat beige houses on their way to Pinnacle Street in soporific southern Prudent.

It might be said that no one in the family was as excited for Alegría's birth as her big sister, five at the time. For as soon as June saw the old jean-blue sedan parked, she slipped out of the house, where she had been entrusted to the care of her Aunt Mary. "Can I see her? Can I see her? Does she look like me?" June's questions bombarded her mother as soon as the car door opened with a "Yes, yes, all in good time."

When they entered the house, Aunt Mary was cooing and awwing in Alegría's face and June, being no taller than 43 inches, could not sneak a peek behind her abundant backside. "Let me see! Let me see!" she said. Once allowed a look at the wonderful gift her mother had brought,

June was disappointed to see a flushed little raisin with eyes too big for its face. With arms and legs tiny as those, the little raisin would be incapable of playing mystery pretend or tag or even hopscotch. The small look alloted June was soon taken away as all three adults in the room cooed and awwed over her. Feeling she was of no more importance than one of the houseflies brought by the ripening bananas, June soon became disillusioned with her new baby sister and hoped her parents were not intent on keeping her.

Much to June's disappointment, they kept her through her terrible two's and horrible three's—even when she cried and wailed and screeched at the top of her lungs and pooped in her pants on a regular basis. All of the undivided attention on Alegría, which she got without doing much else than breathing, made June resent her for taking the love that used to be hers away.

When Alegría was taking her first steps, helped by the edges of the coffee table, June secretly hoped that she fell, would be deemed a broken product, and taken back to the baby store for a refund.

Alegría grew up pampered with a love for sweets, especially *cajeta*. However, advised by Aunt Teresa that too much sugar would stunt her growth, Marisol decided to make *cajeta* sandwiches off-limits to her. But rules could stop Alegría's cravings and so it was on these crack of dawn-trips that Alegría would find herself in the kitchen, climb up on the kitchen counter, slide open the breadbox for a slice of whole-wheat, and squeeze half-a bottle of the readily available caramelly goodness on the bread, fold it in half, and stuff it into her salivating mouth.

Upon finding the remains of the *cajeta* bottle on the kitchen counter and Alegría passed out on the couch in the living room, her parents decided that Alegría's room needed to be locked from the outside-in every night.

When the prospect of preschool every Monday, Wednesday,

and Friday of every week was introduced to Alegría, she accepted it with all of the good-heartedness with which she accepted mandatory bathing. On the first day of preschool, she held on to her mother's warm hand as fiercely as if it were the only thing keeping her from falling into a pit of slimy sea monsters.

However once she saw that no one was going to try and eat her, Alegría good-naturedly released her mother from her captive grip and walked into her class by herself on every consecutive visit that followed.

Once she turned five, Alegría attended kindergarten with Miss Gables. Independent and confident in her abilities, Alegría would walk the half-block to her school singing half-coherently to "Old MacDonald Had a Farm" and *E-I-E-I-O*-ing to the tunes she would hear her mother hum in the shower. Arriving at school, she twirled and waved to all of her classmates, for she believed the world was her friend.

Such was the idea implanted in her by Grandma Susana, who was a very wonderful grandmother to her thirteen grandkids. Were it not for the distance, she would've cooked and baked for them all day. Grandma Susana had the twinkle of a secret in her eye and a quiver in her lip that would often turn into laughter. And boy could she laugh! Everything about her was musical: the lilt with which she spoke, the perfect pitch in which she hummed, the steady tempo with which she handled her kitchen—in short, everything but her laugh. Her laugh was one to make new acquaintances wonder how such a laugh could come from someone who was otherwise so graceful; it was a mixture of chortles and gurgles that would build-up into what Uncle Tim had rightly described as the sound a witch-donkey hybrid emits when kicked in the rear end. The laugh, when it built up inside Grandma Susana, would take over her youthful body, bending it forwards, then backwards, then forwards again. When she found something really funny, Grandma Susana would stomp her feet and clutch at her aching belly and exclaim "Oh dear!" (Thankfully) not one of her four daughters had inherited her infamous laugh, which she believed was the cause of all but one of them managing to keep a husband.

Grandma Susana had—as she called it—salt-and-pepper hair, a drooping bosom, and a slim figure that made the other grandmothers on her street jealous. Her face was the shape of a peach and the color of a date; in it were two chocolate-brown eyes framed by prominent eye bags and a round nose resembling a pear. Her teeth she still had, pearly white as the day she received them, and was quite proud of them. Although perfectly at home in her face, when she laughed her lips pulled back to reveal them so they seemed too big for her face, like horse teeth.

On the first day of spring, Marisol received a phone call which brought her hand to her lips and red to her eyes. Alegría, who had been playing with Legos on the kitchen floor knew that something was wrong and instinctively got up to hug her mother. "Mother passed away?" she repeated in dismay, now stroking the top of Alegría's head. Alegría knew that mother's mama was Susana, and that Susana was her grandmother, and that passing away was something people said when you couldn't visit a person anymore. The thought of not being able to go to her grandmother's house every month for a cooking lesson made Alegría stretch her arms around her mother tighter. "Okay, I'll stop by later this afternoon ... You too."

"Mama what happened? Is Grandma Susana alright?" Alegría interrogated her mother with a deepening sense of foreboding as she sat down at the kitchen table.

"Your grandma was really sick, Alegría."

With a knot in her throat, Alegría thought of her last visit to Grandma Susana's house. It had been but two weeks ago. "Let's go sit down by the TV, *mi Grillita*," had said

Grandma Susana. But Grandma had promised to teach her the secret to her churros, and hadn't she said that too much TV was bad for the brain? Grandma Susana thought for a moment and replied, True, true. But the Powerpuff Girls were on and surely she did not want to miss the rerun? Alegría quickly consented and found a spot next to Grandma Susana on her pink and yellow camel-backed couch with the big flowers on it. While the evil monkey with white boots was laughing his abnormally big head off, Grandma Susana had gotten up with many complaints by the old couch and returned from the kitchen with two big blue bowls—one filled with sugar snap peas and the other empty. "Here, help me snap the ends off, if you please," she'd said.

After a while of snapping the ends and dunk-shooting them in the now partially-filled bowl, Grandma Susana had slid one into her mouth instead, finishing it off with a satisfying crunch. "Grandma, can I try?" Alegría had eagerly taken a sugar snap pea, plucked the end with the white string off, and followed her grandmother's example. After a few moments of careful chewing and the deliberation of a seasoned wine taster, she'd said, "It tastes like sweet grass."

Grandma Susana had laughed her infamous laugh and said, "And how would you know what grass tastes like? Don't tell me you've actually turned into a *grillita*? The sight would give me fright."

Somewhere in the wake of the colored streaks the Powerpuff Girls left behind from their day of fighting crime, Alegría had lost track of time and it had soon been time to say goodbye. At the door to her house, Grandma Susana had said in that bursting way she had about her "Don't ever stop smiling, *mi Grillita*," and pinched Alegría's cheeks affectionately. She had seemed fine then—one hundred and five percent healthy.

"She didn't seem sick last time we watched Powerpuff Girls together."

"Sometimes people are sick in ways that are not so visible to others. They're sick in here." Marisol pointed to her heart.

"Can't you take pills for that? Lily's mom takes orange-flavored pills when that hurts, when she eats too much pizza."

Marisol twiddled her thumbs. "No, Alegría. That's a different kind of sick."

"Can I go see her now?"

"No, Alegría. She's—she's dead."

Dead was a final word, one that was a gavel in the courtroom of life, one that pronounced the person unfit to live in this world with all its sugary churros and flowery couches anymore.

"What's going on? What happened to grandma? Did she finally—you know." June's sudden appearance made her mother slightly jump.

Alegría jumped from the brown, smooth kitchen chair and went to hug June. "She's dead," she answered for her mother.

June slithered out of Alegría's iron hug and said, "Oh."

"I'm going to call your father," and with that, Marisol excused herself out of the room.

When Daniel Cana heard the news of Grandma Susana's death, he tried to suppress the twinge of relief in his heart. "Mm. I'm sorry to hear that, honey. Are you okay?" Once the formalities were over and he'd done his duty as a faithful husband, he couldn't help but question, "And the house. Did she say who she left it to?" Marisol said that she did not know, that she was meeting up with her sisters that same afternoon to discuss all the details. The crackle and echo of the telephone line made her seem farther away than the past. With that, she hung up before her husband could get in his last two dutifully comforting cents.

Although Alegría's parents were not poor, they were not rich either. Her father's bookbinding line of work was not doing too well in the economy, not that it had ever done particularly well, and maintaining a wife and two daughters accustomed to female comforts was more than he could manage at the moment. That was why when news of Grandma Susana's illness had reached him, the thought had skidded across his mind before he could fully stop it. What if Grandma Susana did die? Would they be able to get her house? Of course, that was not the proper manner of thinking for a caring son-in-law. But was it entirely wrong if after Grandma Susana's death, he could hope for the house as a blessing in disguise?

When Alegría was told that she and her family were going to be living in Grandma Susana's house, she had mixed feelings about the prospective move. She liked visiting Grandma Susana at her house, cooking and baking and smelling her wet-corn-flour scent—but Grandma Susana was not there anymore. She was "passed away," gone into some other world Alegría could not enter. Marisol had explained that moving into Grandma Susana's house would mean switching schools, which would mean not being able to see her best friend Lily anymore, which would mean that Lily, in a way, was passing away too. Alegría mentioned as much to her mother. However, her mother did not share that point of view.

Alegría thought long and hard about her house, the one her family had lived in since before she was born. The important rooms were the ones with the dining room table, the TV, and the bathroom. But her favorite room was her own. It was a nine-foot-by-nine-foot square with walls the color of fresh sourdough bread. Facing the only window in the room was a brown canopy bed her father had found on the side of the road a few years back with a "free" sign taped to its dismembered frame. She liked laying on the pink butterfly bed covers overflowing with her collection of stuffed monkeys and pretending she was trapped under the wooden bars by the evil monkey Mojo Jojo, having to figure out ways to escape his evil schemes. The small desk flush against the right side of Alegría's bed held her princess coloring books and Crayola art supplies. It was here that she'd spent countless hours coloring and playing house with her stuffed monkeys like she'd seen in the movies her mother liked. It was in this room that Señor Monkey had married Señorita Monkey and they'd had seven monkey children: Bob, Joey, Juan, Jorge, Jimena, Matilda, and the most-recent, Mon-mon.

Even with all these memories, Alegría decided she was okay with moving homes—as long as she was still able to attend her old school and play with her friend Lily, and she said as much to her mother.

"Ha! That's not how moving works, *Grilla*," said June, over-emphasizing the e sound enough for Alegría to see her sister's tongue trying to escape against the prison bars of her bottom teeth.

Alegría liked the nickname her grandmother had given her because it had love when she said it. "My Alegría when you visit, the questions you bring! Every two seconds you chirp them up like how the crickets sing. When you talk, the sounds they flock and flitter around the room, filling it up like crickets' sweet serenade before a monsoon. My Alegría, I think I'll call you my *Grillita*."

Alegría couldn't quite put her finger on it, why her nickname sounded so dissimilar when pronounced from two different mouths. Maybe without the *-ita* at the end, "little cricket" turned into a plain, mirthless "big cricket." Whatever it was, when her sister said her special nickname, it was like she was violating some deep bond between Grandma Susana and her. Now when June said her nickname, it was like she was mocking Alegría's naïvete and lack of knowledge.

"Why not? Why can't I go to school like normal?" Hit with the sudden spark of an epiphany, Alegría shouted, "I could take the bus! Mama, mama, I could take the bus! You wouldn't have to drive me to school, I could go by myself."

"You can't take the bus," said June, matter-of-factly. "The bus doesn't go that far. Grandma's house is in Manteca. You know where that is, right? Across the river." June gave Alegría the same look that the worker at Loony Lottie's Amusement Park had given Alegría when she'd told her she was too short to ride The Zipper.

"Well then I can take a boat," said Alegría, crossing her arms and sticking out her lips.

"You can't take a boat."

"Why not? Mama."

"Mother, she can't take a boat."

"Mama please, I can go by myself."

"Mother, tell *Grilla* over here she can't take a boat, she'll fall and drown."

"Why do I have to fall and drown? Mama please—"

"Mother—"

"*Basta. Cállense.*" Their mother silenced the two girls' chatter. "Alegría, you can't take the bus or a boat to your old school."

"See? I told you." June's voice died down as her mother silenced her with a look audible as silver slicing through air.

"But going to a new school will be fun, you'll see. You'll make lots of new friends and get a nice new teacher to start off your second year. It'll be like an adventure. You like adventures, don't you?"

A half-hearted "yeah" was all Alegría could muster. Had she opened her mouth a tiny bit wider, a flurry of bitter words at her sister would've ensued, but these had to be avoided in the presence of her mother.

In two weeks' time, Alegría's family had packed up all of their belongings in garbage bags and cardboard boxes and thrown them inside a white delivery van borrowed from a close friend of Daniel's. Themselves they jammed into their jean-blue sedan. As the car drove away, Alegría scooted up against the window to see the house in which she'd grown up. It was as empty as if she'd never lived there.

2.

Manteca was a suburb to the town of Prudent, prideful in its rich history and good bread. Back when the clove-colored land was devoid of Grandma Susana's house, Josefina's grocery store, and tulip poplars, the first pioneers had settled on the sun-rising part of the land.

They had been led by Anthony Delgado and true to his name, he was a stick of a man. His shoulders were so narrow and his hips so wide and his hunch so deep that it was as if his creator had taken the log of tree, carved out or scraped off a long strip of wood like butter and called him a man. Long and willowy, tall as a one-year old Brazilian Fern tree, his arms seemed to forever be stretching to the ground. The first things one noticed about Anthony Delgado were his hunched height and his two cat-tails-mustache, which shook and quivered tremendously like hypothermia when he talked. He had six brothers and seven sisters, being born dead-center of them all. Though his was a relatively small family, Anthony Delgado could see that there was not enough room in his native Oregano for all, where women gave birth to upwards of twenty children in their family, so he had organized an expedition with three of his brothers, four of his sisters, and all of their wives and husbands.

Sailing longer than Don Quixote went exploring, Anthony Delgado and his family made it to the land of Manteca, settling on what Anthony called the chosen land, the first dry land available by the edge of the water. His people listened to him because of his few, albeit pretty, words and unshakable demeanor. With his serene way of talking, he'd whispered into the wind the name of their new home: Prudent, after his wife, Prudencia.

An industrious folk, they'd set to work cutting trees and planting seeds, building up houses and tearing down weeds to pave the way for future generations. Before two years were up, the Delgados and their people had populated the eastern, bean-shaped part of the land. In harmony, Anthony Delgado and his wife Prudencia had birthed two sons, named the elder Thomas and the younger Joaquin.

Born wailing, it seemed that whatever talent for talking had been allotted Joaquin was stolen by first-born Thomas from the womb. While neither inherited their father's height, it was Joaquin who inherited Anthony's narrow shoulders and calm demeanor.

Countless winters and springs later, Anthony Delgado had breathed his last breath. On the first of a fated August, Anthony Delgado had stepped into a puddle formed by the nail-seeping rains of Manteca, slipped and fallen down on the big knot in his back. With this fatal blow, Anthony Delgado was dead a week after the thirty-first birthday of his twin boys.

Still in mourning, Joaquin set to work preparing the festivities that were to take course after his father's funeral procession while Thomas took to the preparation of his burial ground. While turning up the land for his father's grave, the elder Thomas had paused for a while, leaned on his shovel, wiped the sweat from his smooth brow, looked on as the blood-orange sun settled down on the western part of the land, still as yet unbroken, and thought how much that clove-colored land needed a bakery.

And so, after the prescribed period of mourning, elder Thomas had proposed his plan to younger Joaquin. Joaquin had simply said "Mm," which Thomas took as approval and began preparations for the move. He prepped building materials, farm animals, and every type of seed to be had. In six short days, he had convinced a few of his friends to bring his families along and had wooed a girl enough to unite with him in holy matrimony. Within ten days, Thomas Delgado, his mother, his wife, and his friends had left the town of Prudent for the untraversed land of the west. Seeing their departure, Joaquin, forever a man of few words, had only grunted in response.

Upon arrival, Thomas's group was quick to build buildings and turn over soil. Within a year, not only had they established their houses, they had also established a street lined with shops selling anything from hand-woven jewelry to dairy delicacies made from the strong herd of cows who produced their weight in milk every day. Right in the middle of this street of shops was Thomas's dream bakery, a mere two inches taller than all the other square buildings on the street and colored in a guajillo red. Past the white sign reading *Thomas Delgado,* one could see into the windows of the bakery, whose walls were painted with the Delgado family history in intricate murals and adorned by adjacent rows upon rows of baked goods.

The item best known in elder Thomas's bakery was the scored bread. Having taken his wife's secret family recipe for bread and adjusted it to his own liking, Thomas's scored bread had a crunchy thin crust on the outside and a soft, airy crumb on the inside. Known as scored bread for the designs carved on top that Thomas himself would come up with to direct the rising of the bread in the oven, its secret ingredient was lard rendered from pig fat, which made the bread puff up into flaking layers that could be taken apart or eaten together.

People came from far and wide to try Thomas's bread and whenever they asked what the secret to its puffiness and airiness was, Thomas always simply answered: lard. So many visitors came and so much was lard the takeaway answer that people started referring to that part of the land as Manteca.

Now in the prosperity of the year, both Mantecanos and Prudentos were blessed with children. But as it happened, the Joaquins had remained on the much more fertile part of the land, hence their children grew up faster and had children of their own, a great of part of which had heard of Thomas's bread and wanted to visit his bakery. Therefore, they constituted a not-small portion of those visitors who came to the bakery to ask the scored bread's secret.

Some of these children, seeking to remain closer to the many wonders of the street of shops, moved to Manteca and became part of its community. And for a while, all was well.

One night, elder Thomas had a dream in which Delgado bakeries sprouted up everywhere like little weeds. Upon waking up, he decided to expand his bakery's business to the surrounding areas of Manteca. Thomas hoped his sons would step up to the plate and look over the other bakeries. Alas his sons were more inclined to frolic with the young dames that came from the east than to be burdened with the affairs of a bakery business. In the heat of an argument, Thomas's sons pranced away from his threats to take away their allowance. Several young men from Prudent witnessed the argument and came to ask Señor Delgado if he would be willing to hire them in his sons' stead at the bakeries sprouting faster than weeds.

At this simple question, Thomas Delgado became inflamed, and still furious redirected his anger at the visitors from the eastern Prudent. It was one thing if they wanted to come visit the bakery and buy goods, but it was another thing entirely if they wanted to stay for good and meddle in family affairs.

For the first time in a very long time, elder Thomas went to go visit the younger Joaquin and counsel with him as to the affairs of his people and business. Thomas asked not-so-cordially if Joaquin could keep his people on his side of the land. Unsatisfied with Joaquin's grunted response, Thomas decided to take matters into his own hands.

In order to defer any further movement of Prudent's ever-expanding population into Manteca, Thomas decided to pour the money from his steady bakery business into the formation of a physical barrier between Manteca and Prudent. When finding a mountain and transporting it to the land where Prudent meets

Manteca proved a too difficult and risky business, Thomas settled for building a river between the two lands. The never-lacking supply of young men in need of work from Prudent constituted the labor that endeavored to build a natural formation where none before had existed. After the initial excavation and the latter transportation of the sea's water in buckets pulled by oxen, a few trees and rocks were planted for an aesthetic flavor and Thomas's "river" was complete. They called it *Mipared*.

Thomas's people, forever led by his glibness, celebrated the hindrance of further eastern invasion. A big feast was held to commemorate the completion of the river, with bread and milk abundant for everybody. Of great pleasure to the celebration were the young men from the east who'd helped build the river. They toasted and danced and joked to the expulsion of those who had once been their people.

While Thomas's exuberant celebration was going on, on the other side of the river Joaquin smoked his pipe, stared thoughtfully at what had once been undisturbed clove-colored land, and said nothing.

The next day, Joaquin's people, undisturbed at a river which had nothing to do with them, built makeshift bridges to get across it and kept their travel eastward moving as sure as the water from the river flowed north. However finding themselves unwelcome at Manteca, decided to settle on the surrounding areas of Manteca. Thus were establishments other than Manteca and Prudent created. Nevertheless, the Prudentos never forgot the unwelcoming gazes of the Mantecanos, which pierced their souls, from which wounds' bad blood flowed; the Prudentos promised to make the people of Manteca one day rue the day they'd turned them away and deprived them of the fluffy scored bread.

Peering through the glass window, Alegría could see the weather changing. She imagined there was a Big Painter in the Sky, with his watercolors dictating the weather. In the before—when she still lived in her old house—the sky had been a piercing electric blue. But now the Big Painter had sullied his canvas with milky tears, turning his electric blue into a muddy gray. Alegría didn't know why the Big Painter was crying, letting bulbous drops fall on the car window. Perhaps he was moving houses too. As for herself, Alegría felt not like crying, but like the stillness and emptiness after a heavy rain. She had subjected herself to moving and in her mind, was already there.

From behind the curtain of streaks, Alegría saw the dirt road of Prudent muddy. Up ahead she could see the famous Mipared River, gorging itself on the rain, rising up around the raindrops to suck them from the sky as they fell. The manmade body of water was lined by heavy rocks and trees too-purposefully spaced-out to be natural.

"Why did you agree on the bottom floor?" said Marisol. "You know we have two daughters, we needed the extra space."

"Count your blessings, the way the meeting was going, we were fortunate even to get the house. You have three sisters and not one of them would I describe as selfless," said Daniel Cana.

"This isn't about my sisters. You shouldn't have agreed so readily," said Alegría's mother in the way which she had about ending conversations.

In a short time, Alegría's family had reached grandma's house. Warm orange, with the dimensions of a super-sized gallon milk jug and two windows or more on each side, the three-story house was known as the pumpkin house by her neighbors.

Welcoming visitors was a facade of bright green and meticulously cared-for rows of flowers surrounding the porch. A big cyclops window watched over the house from the third, upmost floor, different from the smaller, rectangular windows that decorated the sides. A wooden fence turned green as the growth on it sprouted like vines from each side of the house to encapsulate a big backyard.

Getting out of the car and walking up the front porch steps with her father in tow behind her mother, never before had the white front door seemed so daunting, so foreign to Alegría.

Directly behind the door was a single square space with a coat closet door to its right; this space served as connector between the top and bottom floors of the house. Instead of walking up the stairs in the front leading to the open area that was Grandma Susana's living room with its television set and flower-patterned couch, Alegría's mother led the group down the stairs to the left, which made an abrupt right to descend parallel to those ascending upstairs. Here was a place that Alegría only vaguely remembered, having preferred to stay upstairs with Grandma Susana's cooking and comfy presence.

At the bottom of these stair steps was a hall running to the back of the house where a door opened to a bathroom. Along the left side of the hall were three doors, the first of which hid the garage; the other two doors opened to bedrooms, with the farthest on the left having its own bathroom. On the right side of the hall, a single arched doorway led to the big space that was to serve as living room, dining room, and kitchen.

After a quick look-around and a murmuring of "big enough," Daniel Cana went back upstairs to start moving things in with the help of the white-truck friend. Alegría followed him to serve as the door-holder while her mother and sister stayed downstairs. From her position, she could hear her mother say "Oh, I forgot this was a pantry," as she opened the door to the laundry room in the kitchen and "Oh, I forgot this was a closet," as she opened the door to the boiler room in the living room. Marisol could not hide the bitter disappointment in her voice at the effects of her husband's cowardice.

First, there was the problem of the shared bedroom. The first and smaller bedroom on the left was the bedroom that the grownups had decided would become Alegría and June's shared living space, to which June had wholeheartedly objected. Although big enough to park a car in, the two beds that would have to be fitted in it would make it seem much smaller, with barely any room for anything else. The walls were a grainy yellow, textured like undissolved sugar. June wasn't sure if that was an artistic choice or something gone wrong with the plastered walls. Upon entering the room from the door, the first thing one noticed was the basement window too high up to be of much use to anyone, surrounded by the three walls of the window well and a pebbled floor.

"But I used to have my own room. I'm twelve years old, I can't share my room with a—a messy kid." Alegría understood that she was the messy kid in reference, but thought she was really quite tidy for her age.

"Look, if it makes you feel better, we can try to fit both of your beds in the same room. Though Alegría's canopy bed is a bit big…we might have to get you both bunk beds." Mother shrugged.

With this possibility came the second problem. "Bunk beds! No. Oh no, I'm not sleeping anywhere near that drooling monster," said June.

In the end, Alegría's parents had scrapped the sisters' previous beds and gotten them plain white twin beds that Aunt Teresa's daughters had outgrown. The beds were placed perpendicular to the door, with their heads against the wall. No sooner had the beds been assembled and the first two problems resolved than June raised the third and final problem.

"I need my privacy. I don't want Alegría bothering me every two seconds. Can I get a room divider? We can go to that grocery store, Josefina's. I saw one on the drive here." But with the suffocating night already fallen and the weariness of moving day, June's question was pushed aside without mention.

"We'll get you guys new mattresses but for tonight, just sleep on top of your cousins' mattresses. Goodnight," said Alegría's mother as she turned off the lights on the self-tucked girls and put the bottom house to rest.

"I'm really not that messy," said Alegría. "And I only drool sometimes."

June sighed. "Whatever. I just don't like being able to look at you. Turn around." And with that, June turned towards the window, away from Alegría.

Staring straight up at the textured ceiling and then down the walls, the bright yellow of the morning turned sickly like jaundice in the night. Grandma's house smelled different. Stale, dry, cold, dead. Grandma Susana had packed up all of the life, spice, and warmth from the house and taken it with her when she left.

The newly installed clock in the living room broke the otherwise calm quiet, its apathetic ticking serving as a heavy reminder of the passage of time. Alegría wondered if Grandma Susana was angry with her for never noticing that she was sick. Had she silently suffered in pain while Alegría had been carelessly laughing? Alegría's insides clenched as she thought of the ghost stories cousin Nico had told her, about the things that came to get you on dark nights like this if you were bad. Had Alegría been bad? Would Grandma Susana come back, wrathful and unrecognizable? No. No. Ghosts only came back if they had unfinished business, some bone to pick with someone.

Although Grandma Susana had left many unanswered questions in her wake, she wasn't revengeful. She didn't even get angry when Alegría dropped the eggs on the floor. Still, maybe she was different now. Did people change after death? People's bodies changed. That's why family put them in the ground, because they changed so gruesomely into cottage cheese-flesh—at least that's what Nico had said during the funeral. Alegría squirmed underneath the bed covers. She hadn't been allowed to go to Grandma Susana's funeral. She'd been made to stay at Aunt Teresa's house with all the other kids as the adults went to go bury Grandma Susana. Why didn't she get to say bye? Why had Grandma Susana's back-bending laugh been buried into permanent silence, her mouth covered with dirt like chocolate cake?

The clock ticked one.

Alegría didn't sleep a wink.

3.

Around the kitchen table sat the four Canas, breakfasting.

"Pass the eggs, June." Marisol stretched her hand out expectantly.

The air was thick with the smog of frying oil, the kind that caused Alegría's spent eyes to itch and burn with reddened rims, and the smell of freshly squeezed oranges.

"Don't forget we have the family gathering next week. Teresa wants to have it here—as a type of house welcoming party—and Mary wants to have it at Teresa's house. She doesn't think holding a party at our recently deceased Mother's house right."

"We'll have the party here. As long as everyone agrees to bring a dish. We can't afford to feed those gluttons," said Daniel Cana, serving himself orange juice.

Marisol shifted in her chair. "Now listen carefully, girls. You remember the stairs leading up to the top two floors? Don't go on them. Also, don't be so loud. Whatever you do, don't disrupt Aunt Mary. Okay?"

Alegría remembered Aunt Mary faintly from when she was younger. She used to babysit June and her when their parents needed to run an errand. But a few years ago, she'd stopped coming. All that Alegría could remember about Aunt Mary was that she was quiet and smelled like bar soap.

When neither of the two girls answered, Marisol repeated herself, emphasizing the second syllable. "Okay?"

Jolted into action by that second syllable, June and Alegría affirmed their mother's okay and muttered apologies.

"Next time answer your mother when you're spoken to. I don't know where we went wrong to have two such disrespectful daughters. Perhaps we've pampered them too much." Daniel Cana laid a fried egg on his dry toast and doused it with *salsa verde*. He took a sip of orange juice from a clear glass and punctiliously wiped his mouth with a clean napkin. "When do you start school?" Daniel's question was directed at June.

"I start next Monday," said June curtly. Recently, her clothes were becoming uncomfortably tight and eggs dripping grease on fattening toast were not doing her any favors.

"What about Alegría? Does she start the same day as you?" Alegría's father chose to ignore June's blaringly bad mood and kept on walking the tightrope of June's emotions.

"I don't know, I'm not Alegría." June tried to downplay the bite in her voice as she gingerly nipped the edge of her dry toast.

"But you start school on the same day? Since you both go to the same school…" Alegría knew her father had stumbled and lost his footing on the rope. She sank a little in her chair, her pounding head making her more susceptible to June's outbursts.

But June didn't whine. She simply colored like a red pepper and not-so-politely said, "We don't go to the same school. I'm starting middle school this year." Her father didn't know anything about her, she thought. June was sure he didn't even know her birthday. Not that it was important to anybody.

Alegría's mother swooped in to save Alegría's father from further blunder, from tangling his legs in rope as he fell. She wanted to avoid any loud confrontation, tired as she was from Alegría's insomnia keeping her up at night. "Alegría starts school on Monday as well. Did you like the butterless toast I substituted with the eggs? I was trying to be healthier."

"I miss the fried tortilla," muttered Alegría.

The round kitchen table was of a tulip poplar wood, the color of slow-toasted marshmallows. Though it was hard to determine which blue-cushioned seat was the head of the table, Alegría's father had determined that the seat closest to the kitchen would be the head seat and so made a point to always occupy it.

On his left sat Alegría, grumpy and disheveled from a lack of sleep. His wife sat across from him, tired from staying up with Alegría and sulky from the oil stain that now adorned her shirt above her heart. June sat on his left, with the fury of a thousand volcanoes repeating to herself that it didn't matter to her if she didn't matter to others, and how other tweens' parents not only knew their kids' birthdays, but also their favorite colors and foods and hobbies.

However, for all the irritable mood of the room downstairs, thick and tangible as the smoke of the fried eggs, Alegría's father only saw a family eating together like it should. As long as everyone was at table and the table was covered with a mantle, everything was as it should be.

The days leading up to Monday slipped away in the restoration of habits and furniture. The third problem constituted by June was resolved not in the buying of a wall divider, but in the buying of a shower curtain and a package of ten stick-on wall hooks. The ugly deck-of-cards color scheme highlighted by the rows of abstract squares would've been enough to make the Jack of Clubs stare in shocked disgust at the murky shade of black and the flippant King of Clubs gossip to the indifferent King of Hearts about the scandalous position of the red squares within the white squares while the Queen of Diamonds curled her lip in disgust at the whole scene; it was presumably the reason why the curtain was on sale for $1.95 at Josefina's.

Hanging the shower curtain on the wall hooks stuck on the low ceiling, Alegría's father thought that as long as it shut up June's whining, he was willing to put up the black-and-red abomination.

The night before school started, Alegría lay in bed thinking about who her new teacher would be and if she would make friends. She had never doubted she could make friends before.

She was determined to disturb her mother no more and to have a full night's sleep for the first time since moving into Grandma Susana's house. Alegría closed her eyes and tried to put all thoughts out of her head.

The needle on the clock in the kitchen moved with a fluttering click. If she strained her ears, she could hear the distant hum of the refrigerator. Her mother shifted on the bed in the room next to hers, the bed creaked in accommodation. The clattering of a marble against a table sounded from somewhere in the house. The door slightly groaned, announcing a slight shift in the air around it. A light shuffling sounded by the door. Each step sounded like sticky hand toys being ripped off glass surfaces, only magnified. They got closer, squelching to the left side of her bed.

Alegría could feel a presence there as tangible as her mother's breath near her ear the past nights she'd stayed awake with her.

She was afraid to open her eyes. Alegría could feel the shuffling thing's weight on the air by her left side. It leaned over her, radiating cold instead of heat, like Aunt Mary's once-attempted macaroni casserole. Getting closer, it was like being forced to eat that macaroni casserole, all the disgust of the dense, clammy macaroni slithering down your throat.

It was too unbearably close. Alegría wanted to open her eyes and shout to the nearest person for help, her sister, even if she got angry. But trying to push the sound between her teeth, she found that she couldn't. Her eyes were glued together like the dry macaroni in the casserole. A pressure was exerted on the bed by her left wrist, making her cousin's used mattress sink to its left. The thing was pressing on her bed. Alegría wanted to scream. But the sound was trapped inside her head. She wanted to pry her lips open to release the sound but they wouldn't respond. Just when the pressure on the air and the pushing of the unformed scream in her mind reached their pinnacle, her eyes snapped open with as much ease as if they'd never been glued shut, releasing with them her whole body. Alegría sat upright in her bed like a board. The cold thing was gone, leaving no trace of itself on the carpet or on the bed. With wide-open eyes, Alegría trembled violently like a frightened chihuahua. Then sobs escaped her body and tears spilled from her eyes like the rains on the day she and her family moved in Grandma Susana's house. She was crying. Loudly.

Everyone else in the house simultaneously woke up, Alegría's alarm echoing in their ears. Marisol was the first to move. Getting out of bed and going into the next-door room, she felt for the light switch in the dark and squinted at Alegría crying in bed. She flew across the carpet to sit on her daughter's right, her back to June and the curtain. Hastily shushing and caressing, lest her crying disturbed Aunt Mary upstairs, Marisol asked her what had happened.

The only things intelligible from Alegría's blubbering were "there was a thing" and "it was next to me" and "macaroni."

June broke in. "That's not true. I was here and I was awake the whole time and I never heard anything."

"But it was really here!" said Alegría. Looking at her mother for signs of belief and seeing nothing but dark circles, she said, "It was on my bed. I'm not lying."

Seeing her daughter's eyes welling up with tears again, and fearing her sister upstairs, Marisol said "Okay" and stayed awake next to Alegría for another night.

As the rising sun replaced the cowering moon, it turned into the fateful first day of school.

Knowing she was a transfer student, Alegría's new teacher had called Marisol the weekend before the start of school to find out more about the child. "Oh, so you came from Prudent? I see, I see…" Alegría's new teacher had said. While the new teacher had been trying to politely extract whatever information she could about Alegría from her, Marisol had been busy trying to prepare dinner and juggle the new teacher's questions simultaneously.

The phone conversation hadn't ended until it came out that

"Oh? Her grandmother died? That's unfortunate. Yes, yes." With the purpose of her call a success, Alegría's new teacher had quickly said her goodbyes and hung up.

Remembering the conversation as she buckled Alegría in, Marisol regretted having said so many personal things to her youngest daughter's newest teacher. She hoped that her daughter would fit in at her new school and that life would soon get back into its normal routine.

Feeling a twinge of guilt at Alegría's pitiful crying yesterday, June didn't complain about being dropped off to school last—always after Alegría. Instead, she buckled herself into the passenger seat and stared out the window silently.

As for Alegría, she stared at the back of her mother's seat, feeling artificially jittery and exhausted at the same time. With drooping lids, she wished for the day to get on a move on so that it would be all the more quickly over. Although the sun was bright, the Big Painter in the Sky had drawn his clouds too big, giving the wind confidence to blow fiercely under their cover. Easing into the back parking lot of her new school, Marisol told her to enter through the closest door, and that her classroom would be the first one on the left. She apologized internally to Alegría for not walking her to her class on the first day.

Crecimiento Elementary School resembled a big sheet cake, only its walls were covered with red bricks instead of fondant. Next to supporting metal posts that looked like candles was a light metal door, its red paint chipping away to reveal the original gray. Opening the door, Alegría heard her classroom before she saw it on her immediate left. She looked inside tentatively. The walls were slathered with alphabetical posters, numerical posters, and motivational posters with sayings as inspirational as the dead deer Uncle Tim had killed on the road. The single desks were pushed into four rows of three pairs.

In front of the polka-dot-bordered whiteboard was a young woman of medium height and a slim build. Her short hair rose up in small ringlets like meringue. Her features were peppy and hard to match with her personality. Underneath her lime-green cardigan, eagerness at molding the kids' infantile minds and trepidation at losing authority in the classroom swirled around in her stomach. As the wayward children laughed and hummed and stomped and whooped with the excitement of the just-past summer vacation, she tried to reel their attention in with all the struggle of a novice fisherman against an Atlantic blue marlin.

Upon seeing Alegría peering in, the second grade teacher's eyes had sparkled; she knew immediately that she was the student from Prudent. "Come in, come in," she said as Alegría reluctantly walked into the outstretched arms of the teacher. Resting her perfectly-manicured pink nails on Alegría's shoulder, she cleared her throat loudly. The children, seeing someone new in front of the room, finally quieted down. "We have a new student. She is from Prudent. Her grandmother recently died so be extra, specially, nice with her." Eyes from all four corners of the room moved from the second-grade teacher to the girl who just reached her waist.

Alegría didn't think that these pieces of information were anything that her classmates needed to know. The scrutinizing stares of the other students made her feel as uncomfortable as the unnatural smell of cupcakes emanating from the person behind her. "You can go sit down in that empty space by the window, next to Bo in the blue shirt, he doesn't have grandparents, too" said her new second-grade teacher.

Alegría headed to the third row, the desk closest to the right wall and window, flush against the boy in the blue shirt. She sat down and looked around the classroom. Some of the other kids met her stare, others had already lost interest in favor of other students. The boy in the blue shirt had his head, covered by mangy black hair, down on the desk. He sneaked a glance at her, met her eyes and swiveled his head back to staring at the yellow-streaked wood of the desk.

With the confidence of having successfully obtained the students' attention once, the adult in the front of the room decided that now was as good a time as any to start the school day. "Settle down, everyone back to your seats." The second-grade teacher introduced herself as Miss Turtle. She was young and inexperienced, this being her first year teaching. She said she had two cats at home and that her favorite color was green.

The day ensued with more introductions and get-to-know-each-other games. While singing the frog song, Alegría witnessed blue-shirted Bo dig his left index finger into his nose and squelch it around. The sight gave her a bad taste in her mouth, but she swallowed it and turned to look at Miss Turtle once more.

During recess, a gang of students approached Alegría, who couldn't decide whether to play on the swings or play on the slide. The apparent leader of this gang of forty-eight-inchers was named Paolo. His cronies and henchmen swarmed around him. "So you're here from Prudent, right? You can tell right away."

Alegría wasn't sure what he meant at all. She had on blue jeans and a rainbow-striped jacket that was a hand-me-down from June to protect her from the wind. Her thin, brown hair was pulled back in a ponytail tighter than Uncle Tim's belt to prevent any of her unruly hair from curling out, though a few wisps around her temples had already escaped the iron hold of the pink scrunchie. "What do you mean?" she asked, wrinkling her nose in confusion.

Paolo scoffed and looked back at his fellow troublemakers, who opened their mouths too widely in mock shock and raised their eyebrows to their hairlines. Satisfied with their supportive response, Paolo gave Alegría the once-over and said, "It's obvious. Your shoulders are so narrow, you have to be from Prudent."

Now it was true that Alegría's shoulders were a bit narrower than those of the Mantecanos, but this difference was no more significant than two inches and imperceptible to the eye unless one was looking for it.

"So?" She raised her chin and stuck out her bottom lip, trying to look like the scary dogs that ran loose in the dark alleys of Prudent. Her fleeting sleep had taken with it most of her patience.

Paolo said, "Don't you know that Prudentos and Mantecanos don't get along? My big brother told me that you Prudentos are thieves and unhonest folk, that you're opportunists." His mouth wouldn't form the word correctly, making it sound like "apple two knees."

His words evaporated into the clouds overhead, staining them a light gray. They were part of the storm that would one day break over Manteca and Prudent.

4.

A full two weeks had passed since the first day Alegría and her family had moved into the pumpkin house. Nights were too often spent sleepless in the arms of a mother who was more distant when awake than when asleep, next to a sister who grew irritable when provoked by noise from the other side of the curtain, in the adjacent room of a father who noticed his wife's absence at his side only enough to ask why his buttered toast was burnt. It was then that Alegría developed one-touch-one-sleep syndrome. Whenever Alegría would lie on her cousin's bed, or rest on the green couch with broken springs, or sit on the poplar chairs of the dining room table, she would get the irresistible urge to close her eyes, curl up into whatever position was most comfortable, and sink into a heavy sleep.

When Miss Turtle assigned each student thirty minutes of reading guided by a parent, Alegría found that she could simply not stay awake long enough to get through the thinnest of storybooks. Instead of being guided reading, these thirty-minute sessions would turn into half-asleep listening sessions for her. Marisol would say, "It's time to read, Alegría," and pat a spot on the green couch next to a stack of books June had fought to keep as hers and hers alone.

Dragging her feet to the couch, Alegría would sit next to her mother and try to keep awake as monotone sounds came out of her mouth clicking together like magnets and swirling in the alphabet soup of the pages before forming a chain around Alegría's neck and pulling her head down hypnotically towards her curled up legs. Sometimes Marisol felt pity for her child and let her sleep. Other times, she acknowledged the necessity of completing at least a few minutes of the prescribed reading homework and shook Alegría from the shackles of sleep at every turn of the page, even though she would've preferred to take a long nap herself.

As to the issue of bedtime, Alegría grew too tired to care much about some shuffling thing coming when the lights were out. Rather than play with Bob, Joey, or any of the other seven monkey children, Alegría opted for the feel of her pillow behind her and the brush of the bed sheets on top of her. While the shuffling thing didn't show up next to her bed every night before sleep, it sometimes showed up while asleep as a smudge darkening the edge of her periphery. Her vivid dreams grew so lifelike, they sometimes startled her awake so that while she had no trouble falling asleep, she had trouble staying asleep.

At school, Miss Turtle noticed a head in her class more often down than up. She could not understand why a child's head would droop so often during her lessons. Was her teaching style not captivating, not enticing enough to the bright minds of her students? No, that could not be the case. All her other students' eyes were on her, stuck on like glue—except, of course, for those of the troublemakers. So Alegría was a troublemaker. Not that she openly defied Miss Turtle, she was too careful for that. It was only that Alegría seemed annoyed with Miss Turtle. Yes, she didn't adhere to her teachings, didn't open her mouth in a wide enough "o" when she taught them all the does, Joes, and tiptoes, didn't gasp in amazement at the story of the bat in the trap, didn't do her reading homework like she was supposed to. Miss Turtle didn't know why Alegría had to oppose her.

On the last Friday of August, Miss Turtle noticed Alegría's coloring of a "Color the World" worksheet she had spent so long deciding on during that week's lesson planning; Alegría had been coloring the hair of the smiling African character a dark purple, but now her crayon strayed to adding senseless loops that were straying off the paper in a lazy manner. "Alegría," she said, adding a smear of sympathy to her voice, "I know that you're having a hard time adjusting to life in Manteca. I know that it can be hard getting used to all the shops here. But if you don't start showing a little teensy bit more effort, then I'm going to have to contact your parents." Miss Turtle raised her hands palms-up.

Bo watched from the corner of his eye as Alegría looked up under crescent lids at Miss Turtle. He heard Miss Turtle sigh in disapproval at Alegría's messy coloring, or maybe her indifferent stare. He went back to his own coloring and didn't say a word, waiting until Miss Turtle was far away to taste the salty reassurance of his snot.

"Okay, is everyone done coloring?" Not waiting for an answer, Miss Turtle continued. "Good. Now we'll have each one of you come up starting from left to right and snaking down the rows. Show us your colored picture and present your country. You can read the description on the paper about the country that you've chosen and compare it to your own culture. Milo, you can start."

The more classmates finished their presentation, some stuttering through their reading, others flying through it like Milo, the more Alegría wished that a giant tornado would rip the cake-shaped elementary school apart, throwing Miss Turtle and Paolo into the air like swans so that her name wouldn't be called and she wouldn't have to present. But the Big Painter stubbornly kept his canvas clear and no tornado ever appeared, though Paolo did crane his neck in a way swans would've found natural to look back at Alegría as Miss Turtle called her turn to present.

Alegría made the trek from her seat by the window to the front of the class by Miss Turtle. She turned her paper so the rest of her class could see the picture of an uneaten kid surrounded by lions and leopards and antelope all under a setting sun. She thought the harmony of the scene unrealistic. Having read aloud the accompanying description without really understanding it, Alegría struggled to think of similarities between her culture and Botswana culture. She didn't really know what her own culture was, much less what it had in common with a foreign culture.

"Well you're from Prudent, aren't you? What do you have in Prudent?" Miss Turtle asked with the sweetness of her perfume. Alegría answered that she didn't know and Miss Turtle, being unable to think of anything about Prudentos except their lack of respect for boundaries and abnormally narrow shoulders, told Alegría to continue thinking and to sit down.

As Alegría passed Bo on his way up to present, he gave Alegría a small nod. His eyes were two grains of black sweet rice under his blue oval glasses.

Once recess came, Alegría headed to the small, grassy field so that she could rest for a bit and stare at the clouds in the Big Painter's canvas until her lids closed on their own. But she wasn't able to look up at the clouds. A forty-eight-inch shadow covered any sight of the canvas.

"I can't believe you don't know anything about where you come from. I bet you don't know anything about your family. I bet you're so dumb you don't even know what your father's profession is." Paolo italicized the word profession and held unto it so long a loopy border and stars were added around it.

Alegría was stunned into silence by the truth of Paolo's words. She really didn't know what her father's profession, as Paolo had called it, was. She just knew that he left in the mornings and came back in the evenings. She'd asked her mother about it before but couldn't remember what the answer had been.

"My father's a lawyer," said one of Paolo's followers.

"Mine works with computers," said another, and pretty soon, everyone was naming the type of work the provider of their homes had.

On the drive home from school, Alegría wanted to ask her mother about what her father's work. Looking across the sedan's center console at June, Alegría thought it was best to wait until they got home. She didn't want her sister to remind her of Paolo.

Entering quietly near the coat closet and stepping down the stairs, Alegría followed her mother to her parents' room. The bed was supported by a yellow wood that reminded Alegría of the kitchen table. Two matching bedside tables adorned each side of the bed. The symmetrical flower pattern of the bed covers reminded Alegría of an insect, with two small red flower-eyes separated by a huge nose flower with outstretched petals that reminded her of a mustache. Alegría was glad the stretched-out stem-arms were covered by clothes that had half-tumbled from a purple laundry basket.

"What is dad's profession?" Alegría did her best to pronounce profession in the same way Paolo had.

Marisol made time to think by folding her husband's shirt with the collar adorning the face of the shirt like a crown; that was the way her husband liked it. "Your father works with books. He helps bind them." She picked up a pair of June's pajama pants, unfurling them like a banner to get out the wrinkles.

Alegría remembered having received this answer before. She played with a black sock, putting it over her hand like a puppet and seeing the rough fabric, thin around the heel and the sole, move with the whims of her invisible hand. It had the soft lavender scent of her mother's fabric softener. "Oh. What does bind mean again?"

"It means," Alegría's mother snatched the sock from Alegría's hand, killing its short life instantly, and twisted it into a ball with its pair, "to hold things together."

"Oh," said Alegría. It was clear as mud that her father's work involved books of some type. And that he held them together with stuff. But she didn't really know what that meant. Fingering the powder pink flower of the insect's abdomen, Alegría asked how books were held together.

"They're held together by glue." Marisol meant to signal an

33

end to the conversation by getting up with a basket-full of neatly folded clothes to put away. But she had conjured up images in her daughter's mind of her father pasting the edges of pages together with a special strong glue stick and she wanted to know more.

"Is that what he does all day?" she asked. It made sense if that's what father did all day.

Some books had a lot of pages. But her father's job wasn't like a police officer or a lawyer. There wasn't a name she could put to it. At least with a police officer or a lawyer, she knew what they meant and what kind of outfits people like them wore. Someone who works with books was a title that raised questions rather than answered them.

Looking up at the lack of response, Alegría noticed that she was alone in her parents' room. Her mother had already gone away, too far to reach.

It was true that Alegría's father had worked as a bookbinder, that he had experience with printing and binding tools. But that was something that he did only sometimes, when his work was needed. To fill in the space between jobs and put food on the table, Alegría's father had gotten a commercial driver's license, which he used to do small delivery jobs for small companies. Now that they had moved to Manteca, Daniel Cana's scarce work as a bookbinder had all but ceased existing. No one wanted to hire a bookbinder from Prudent. Thus was his side job turning into his full job, something that he was sure Aunt Teresa and her dentist husband would mock if they knew.

Marisol stirred the boiled water in her aluminum pot that passed for soup. She added more vegetables to the bubbling water, watching the peas bob up and down as if they were drowning. She grimaced. Aunt Teresa had been the most vocal about her marriage to her husband. "Mari, why didn't you say anything? You should've talked to us first," she'd muttered when Marisol had called home to invite her mother and two surviving sisters to a wedding they had no idea was taking place. "And in Prudent? You're getting married in Prudent?" Aunt Teresa had spit the capital P in 'Prudent' like she spit the hulls of sunflower seeds.

Marisol knew that her marriage to Daniel Cana had been too fast to be a good decision. But she'd gone along with it anyway because he'd provided a way out from her family. As a child, she'd been quiet. Her mother, Susana, had been too carefree, too lively for her taste. Her exuberance was annoying, her laugh ugly, and her love suffocating. She'd wished for a stricter mother, one who had rules to enforce. Grandma Susana had given birth to Teresa at twenty-one and to Marisol at twenty-three, an age Marisol had thought too young until she'd had June at twenty.

When she was eight years old, Marisol had been told to take of her younger sister, nicknamed Ría for her laughter, while her mother had left with the crying Teresa to clean up her scraped knee. It had been their first time going swimming in the big, sparkling-new pool donated to the community by some man in a suit with green-tipped fingers. A glittery, shimmery day with the promise of cool relief from the blistering heat of that summer's unexpected drought—until Teresa had tripped over herself and scraped her knee on the concrete surrounding the water. "Don't try to go into the water until I come back," Susana had said over the shoulder of her bright red one-piece bathing suit.

But Marisol had wanted to taste rebellion. She'd known her mother loved her too much for anything to happen to her in the pool. "Hey Ría, the water looks nice and cool, doesn't it? Let's go in for a little." Marisol had moved to the stairs at the edge of the pool, sat on the first step, and kicked her toes in the water. It felt freezing. Pasting a big smile on her face, she'd sighed as if the water had felt nice. "Wow, you should come feel it too." She'd held out her hand to her three-and-five-sixths-year-old sister. Ría had approached the pool but recoiled at the cold touch of the water. "Come on!" Marisol tugged her sister's arm, coercing her into the water until she was firmly on the second step, the icy ripples up to her belly. Then Ría had calmed down a little and they'd gone deeper into the water, holding on to the rail at the edge of the pool. But Ría had gotten scared again. She'd swallowed a little of the salty chlorine water, spluttered and thrashed in disgust, gone under. It'd been out of Marisol's control. She couldn't feel Ría next to her anymore. It'd been too late. The water too greedy. It had blinded her, opened her mouth and gone too far inside.

There were a lot of people that Manteca could blame: the inattentive lifeguard who'd been flirting with his classmates, the careless mother who'd left her late daughter in the care of her eight-year-old daughter, the onlookers who hadn't noticed or bothered to act on the panic of the two young girls. Nevertheless, Marisol felt that the guilt belonged only to her, a personal parting present from her late sister. Susana's lack of anger at her, who she'd understood was in as much pain as she was, only made Marisol angrier at her. Marisol already felt resentful towards her mother because she hadn't been there in the one moment when she'd most needed her, and the comfort Susana tried to wrap around Marisol only made Marisol hate herself because she knew she didn't deserve it.

Marisol added chicken bouillon to the pot. Using the wooden spoon, she gave the soup five stirs and then tapped it to her palm, shaking off a few droplets of the soup to taste like Teresa had taught her. The only flavor was boiled water. She added more chicken bouillon. Marisol accepted that her soup would never taste the same as that of her mother or older sister.

"Mom! Alegría's acting funny!" June's shout startled Marisol out of her soupy reverie. She set the spoon down on the counter and turned the heat down on low. Exiting through the living room doorway, she went down the hall to the source of the shouting. Something had to be done about the lighting in the hall. The bulb in the light fixture was going out and it was too dark to see well. If only Daniel Cana could secure a truck driving contract.

Entering the room, she came upon June shaking like a bobble

head and sticking her tongue out at Alegría, who was on her knees in her bed with her hands on her hips.

"Did not. I didn't," said Alegría. She huffed like a bear.

"Did too. I saw you. You can't lie to me!" June's arms disappeared into the folds of her brown shirt. Noticing her mother in the doorway, she called out to her. "I saw it with my own eyes, Alegría's tongue."

Turning around, Alegría jumped off the bed and ran to her mother, clutching the folds of her jeans. "Mama! Mama! I didn't mean to do it!" Alegría looked up with eyes rimmed like the cups in the sink after the chocolate milk has dried up in them.

"Aha!" June raised her chin slightly in triumph. "You admit that you did it. Tell mom what you did."

Alegría kneaded the fabric around her mother's thighs. "I— my tongue was alive in my mouth." She could see her mother's confusion in her face.

"You could see it by her bottom teeth," piped in June, coming closer.

Marisol sighed. It was always the same between her two young daughters. Some little thing that was probably causing the vegetables in her soup to overcook. "Come help me set the table Alegría, utensils and napkins. June, cups and plates." With that, she shook off her youngest daughter's grip and walked back to the kitchen. She could smell the flat, salty chicken odor wafting up over boiling tap water from adding too much chicken bouillon to her soup.

5.

It was the week of the family party. Preparations, like everything else, came last minute. On Sunday, it was finally agreed by everyone that the party was to be held at Grandma Susana's house—just as long as everyone stayed outside and didn't disturb the house from the inside. On Monday, people called out suggestions for what others should bring to the party. On Tuesday, no one talked about the party to show that their life was busy and filled with more important things than a tatty tradition so old no one remembered how it'd started. On Wednesday, Daniel Cana grumbled to himself about seeing Aunt Teresa and her husband at the party while he tucked a blue checkered shirt into his black jeans for work. Come Thursday, the near-adults had crossed their i's and dotted their t's in secret combinations for the upcoming party. On Friday, Aunt Mary had second thoughts about the location of the party, having had a strong premonition that her upstairs bedrooms were to be torn open and her late mother's china broken.

The morning of the party, Marisol woke up with a start, having remembered that Uncle Tim and whoever else was coming had strong stomachs to fill. At precisely 5:58, she turned over from the right side of the bed and shook her husband from his shoulder awake. "Daniel. Daniel, wake up." Feeling a shudder and a groan, Marisol continued, "we have to buy meat and sausages." "We can do that when the sun's up," he said, raising his head ever so slightly to look at his wife with closed eyes, and laying his head back on his pillow, he proceeded to ignore the laundry list of things his wife told him needed to be done before that evening.

After a brief period in the still dark in which Daniel Cana thought Marisol had fallen asleep, she said, "I'm glad Alegría's sleeping again."

His eyes snapped open in the ensuing silence. Staring into the dark void of the open bathroom door, he said, "Me too."

Around noon, while Daniel went out to buy meat and sausages, milk for Jacob Ramos, sodas and juice for everyone else, plastic cups and plates, a 6.3 lb bag of *tortillas*, and enough fruit and *chiles* to satisfy even the picky Prudenta, Grandma Tracy, Marisol began the call network among her family to get some idea of what everyone would be bringing. Cousin Toro agreed to bring *tamales*. Granduncle Elliot promised *pambazos*. Aunt Teresa volunteered the scored bread before anyone else could beat her to it. Cousin Salome sighed and said she'd bring the only thing she could think of: *gorditas*. Aunt Mary said she didn't want the party to go on too long and disturb the neighbors, and that it was best to start it early. Everyone agreed with Aunt Mary that to party earlier meant to party longer (except Aunt Mary) and the starting time for the party was settled as five thirty.

In the kitchen downstairs, Marisol began prepping the *huaraches* she thought to bring to the party. In a big green plastic bowl, she mixed corn flour, warm water, salt, and lard to the sticky, putty-like consistency of *huarache* dough. "Girls, come help," she said.

June and Alegría came from across the living room like two porcupines. Both were cranky at being disturbed, one from sleep and the other from talking on the phone with her cousin Stacy.

"Wash your hands." Marisol directed her youngest daughter in scooping out balls of dough and June in shaping them into elongated balls the size of banana passion fruit. The cool dough bothered June's sensitive skin and she complained about her sticky hands, so Marisol told her to go help Aunt Mary set up outside instead. June decided to risk the sticky dough. She passed on the balls of dough to Marisol, who put them on the wooden contraption known as the *tortilladora*. Consisting of three parts that folded up like a game board on hinges, the *tortilladora* worked by sandwiching the ball of dough between two pieces of plastic wrap on the thick middle wooden square of the contraption. This ball of dough was topped by a wooden square of similar size and width on the right side of the contraption. Taking the lever on the left and resting it on the second wooden board, Marisol placed her hand on the lever and pushed down with her body weight, her shoulders heaving up, applying the same pressure that her mother and that her great-grandmother had once applied. Unfolding the *tortilladora*, Alegría and June looked on in hypnotic wonder as the now flat piece of dough was handled by its plastic wrappings and flipped on its other side to repeat the process. The trick to a good *huarache*, as taught by great-grandmother Lolita, was to abstain from sticking the dough to the plastic by applying too much pressure and from making a *tortilla* instead of a *huarache* by applying too little pressure. Removing the dough from its plastic, Marisol put it on the hot broad flat surface of the metal pan, where Daniel Cana watched over it until the wet sand-like dough dried and cooked in the heat. After a few seconds, he would drop melted lard on the pan and fry the *huarache* on both sides until it crisped up. While the dough was cooking, Alegría, June, and their mother continued the assembly line of *huaraches*.

The end result was a stack of vessels resembling the woven sandals they were named for—which Grandma Susana had vowed never to be caught dead in when she had seen them on Great-grandma Lolita but had grown to like for their comfort until she had to give them up for her joint pain in cold weather—ready to carry refried beans, red salsa, green salsa, sliced steak, chicken, cilantro, fresh cream, cheese so soft it fell apart like creamy powder, and whatever else the Ramos family could think up to pile on.

The wet corn flour smell of the *huarache* dough filled Alegría's nostrils with the essence of Grandma Susana. That other place, the one where Susana now was, that was separate from the now, was she okay there? Alegría wondered if anyone made *huaraches* for her there. Remembering cousin Nico's words again, she felt icky. Maybe she should put some *huaraches* out for Grandma Susana, steal them when no one was looking during the party and put them outside in a place where no one but Grandma Susana would look—like by the garage door. Yeah, that was a good idea. Then Susana wouldn't be hungry anymore.

Outside, Aunt Mary was busy setting up all the chairs she could find around the house along with the ones Jacob Ramos didn't bring over until around six. As everyone knew when planning for five thirty, the family party always found a way to start later than agreed upon, but the hope to start the party on time was renewed yearly. Cousin Salome, Granduncle Elliot, Aunt Teresa and all the others were still busy prepping the dishes they were going to bring over to the party around the time the party was supposed to start, and it was no surprise to anyone that they, the life of the party, didn't arrive until a little after seven. Entering with paper bags full of scored bread and other goodies, Aunt Teresa would lean her head to the side and wink, "better late than never."

Aunt Mary was happy at the reliable tardiness of her guests, for the late Grandma Susana's backyard was a bigger mess than she had originally imagined. Although the front of the house was a well-manicured garden of flowers, the back of the house was like the bunion toe with a fungal infection that one hides from the sights of others to avoid their gagging. The grass was gasping its last breath, parched and yellow like hay. The war the weeds had gleefully waged on the flowers in Grandma Susana's absence was terrible. Devastating. Luckily the family feet weren't discriminating in any way; they didn't mind whether they trampled crisp-green grass or brittle-yellow grass. Tables were set in two long strips, one of which reached from the middle to the end of the yard and the other of which extended the full length of the yard, with as much care and planification as Aunt Mary used when vacuuming the carpet with her crosshatch pattern, though by the end of the evening, some tables were turned upside down, legs dangling like a crab unable to get up, and no pattern was more recognizable than that of chaos.

Five white plastic folding tables were placed near the back entrance to the pumpkin house, next to a grill smoking with meat. They were packed with so much food and drink, including thirteen different types of sauces, five different styles of meat, two big pans of rice, and seven kinds of tamales, that Daniel Cana's soda and juice had to be moved inside in lieu of the jugs of tartly sweet tamarind juice and creamily sweet *horchata* brought by Uncle Martin.

Once Aunt Teresa got there, the pumpkin house became hers. She had a type of commanding presence inherited from her late mother. When she entered the backyard, the serene self-confidence and natural authority that exuded from her in waves like the smell of freshly baked bread's crackling crust and curled in tendrils got under people's scalps and made them nod in acknowledgment of her power as she walked by. Her dentist husband followed in her wake, supported by the splendor of his wife, nodding back to all who looked at his wife so fervently that he resembled a distressed chicken with a vitamin E deficiency. Their eleven children broke out like fairies, going every which way in the spirit and joviality of the occasion.

Newly arriving family members greeted family members who had already arrived, going all around the table before sitting down, so that people were constantly getting up to greet others in an endless cycle until the last person arrived. More chairs had to be added. Once the descendants of Great-grandmother Lolita and Great-grandfather Lewis were all there and the crowd had settled down, the confusion soon started again as people got up to load their plates with the familiar food. The children were separated from the adults, waiting until the adults had gotten their food before serving themselves, and designated to the separate, shorter, smaller table. Cousin Stacy whispered to June their plans for later that night. "We'll sneak away when all the adults are rubbing their bellies, talking of dancing, and drinking their milk." Cousin Rico and Cousin Yolanda made eye contact with each other and smiled with a secret spreading back to the birth of Cain and Abel.

An essential component of the tremendous reunions of Great-grandmother Lolita and Great-grandfather Lewis's descendants was the superfluous conversation and the determination by family members of other family members' business; carried on the air made thick by the smell of cooking meat, the tangy, rich smell of the dying grass, and the hum of the ever-present mosquitoes' wings biding their time at the edge of the yard until the meat was done cooking, the milk-drinking, tradition-upholding Jacob Ramos, who everybody called so to distinguish his indirect grafting into the family tree and his solitary nature by choice, could be heard to remark on the sudden splendor of Uncle Martin's teeth, before ravaged by his persistent habit of sucking on halved-limes with salt, and attributed the magical transformation of his smile and confidence to the powers that be and a trip to the fancy office of Aunt Teresa's dentist husband while at the same time, Uncle Martin could be seen to say to Cousin Salome, who was born on the same day as he from the womb of his mother's sister, "Doesn't your brother have anything better to do than to listen to that backwards Jacob Ramos?" to which Cousin Salome's only comment was to ask him to please stop needlessly baring his teeth and picking fights and to eat his *gordita* filled with shredded pork, re-fried beans, and a seven-*chile* salsa, which she hadn't spent all morning making just so he could lose his dentures in the steaming mess of Prudent-style *pozole* sadly attempted by Grandma Tracy who, in the middle of whispering to her husband, Facundo Cana, the dangers of coming to a party that was filled with *Mantecanos* greasy as Granduncle Horace's thinning locks, heard everything said of her *pozole* with her elephant-like ears and accidentally dropped her *gordita* onto the dead grass as she made eye contact with Cousin Salome, eyes blazing like the sun that was setting on the hills of Manteca and taking with it the melted melancholy that Alegría perceived in the burning glow of its receding rays that first Saturday in September.

Cold. Despite the warm air and even warmer company, Alegría felt empty. Before, family parties were events of the year, flashes of something great and alive that broke through the river of forgetfulness and scarred the memory until the next reunion. But all the voices around Alegría were too loud and too clear. They went through her like glass and echoed in her mind so forcefully that Alegría couldn't find her own voice among the shards. She struggled to think, but that wasn't possible with Cousin Nico's jabbering about the newest spy film and with Uriel and Muriel's daring each other to see who could hold the most *horchata* in his mouth at a time. So Alegría resigned herself to let the different voices bounce around inside her without really understanding or engaging with any of them as her *huarache* on the table got cold.

On the north side of the adult table, Aunt Teresa, who'd caught a glimpse of something strange in Alegría, changed the course of the conversation like a seasoned navigator. Avoiding the rants of Grandaunt Elena over her crazy children who were all going to grow up to be doctors and lawyers one day and steering herself clear of Granduncle Elliot's endless recollections of his youth and of the time Great-grandmother Lolita had killed eighteen chickens with an old hickory knife and shown him the true meaning of life, Aunt Teresa reached Marisol and with a honeyed smile asked her, "So Alegría has been having trouble sleeping?" Marisol said that that had been the case a few weeks ago but that now, Alegría couldn't get enough sleep and that she was doing just fine and that her grades were fine and that her eating habits were fine and that her friendship-making qualities were just as good too; she stuttered, unable to curtail the conversation with Aunt Teresa like she was able to with everyone else because Aunt

Teresa held more of Grandma Susana's power. Aunt Teresa's eyes crackled with calculation. "I hope she doesn't turn out like Uncle Dominique," she said. Because everybody was always simultaneously in everybody else's conversation, everyone around the table grew silent like the chickens under Grandma Lolita's hands so that Cousin Stacy could hear from the children's table and ask Aunt Teresa without shouting, "Who's Uncle Dominique?" Aunt Teresa gave a short summary on what everybody knew about Uncle Dominique. He was a strange man from long ago, from the founding of Manteca, who'd been a lazy and idolatrous man. He'd foolishly sold his wife for a few warm *tamales* and had thus been cursed with a frog tail and a terrible sleepiness the rest of his days. Uncle Dominique had been one to wake up in the night and fall asleep in the day. Worse than a sleepwalker and an insomniac, he'd died in the in-between of sleep and awake.

A brusque snort ripped the silence. "That's only a fable. Go back to your *tamales*, children," said Aunt Mary, and shoved a forkful of chicken-and-*mole tamales* the size of the moon in the darkening sky into her mouth. The laughter and chatter quickly resumed, with nervous shifts in seats and tugging at collars; people didn't like talking about Uncle Dominique in case they were cursed with a frog tail, too. In the quiet and serene voice of advice, Aunt Teresa told Marisol so that no other ears would hear, "If you want what's best for her, take her to see Great-grandfather Francis." Marisol pretended that a leaf had blown into her ear and that she was incapable of hearing whatever it was that Aunt Teresa had said. Though later at the party, Marisol made eye contact with her husband and saw what he knew reflected in his eyes. Aunt Teresa was always right.

As the grill ceased smoking, plates cleared, bellies rounded, and pants were unbuttoned, the hum of the mosquitoes moved in on the yard getting ready to feast. The children were called to move the tables to the sides as the adults took seats on the chairs and moved the food in their stomachs around to make room for the traditional scored bread and milk of the evening. As soon as they were finished, the children were allowed to take one piece of scored bread and a glass of milk before being let loose to play. Those in their late childhood went inside the house, led by June to her downstairs bedroom, and the younger children followed in curiosity, including Alegría, who had lost knowledge of herself and of her plan to leave a *huarache* out for Grandma Susana.

While some of the younger children went into the prohibited upstairs, banging bedroom doors and checking the cupboards for chocolate, Nico took Alegría's hand and led her to her bedroom, where the rest of the older children were. The light in the hall cast a yellow glow of boiled eggs on the walls and the light in Alegría and June's bedroom was turned off. The only real source of light came from a flashlight someone had placed in the space between the two beds where the deck-of-cards curtains had been pulled back. Creaking the door, Nico put a finger to his lips to quiet the silent Alegría, and slipped into the bedroom. Nico and Alegría were quickly discovered, but allowed to stay there because Nico was turning ten at the end of the year and was mature for his age; Alegría was quiet.

The children were telling stories of any encounter they'd had with the supernatural. "I knew Grandma Susana was dead before mom told me," said Cousin Stacy. She began telling the story of how she'd had to go to the bathroom at 3:09 in the morning and how she'd forgotten toilet paper (at which Cousins Uriel and Muriel giggled) so she'd whisper-yelled at her sister Genesis to get her a roll. She'd heard some type of grumbling and shuffling by the door. Having assumed it was her sister, Genesis, Cousin Stacy had opened the door a sliver, and a hand had passed her the toilet paper. Having blurry eyes from sleep, Cousin Stacy hadn't seen the hand well, but she'd felt it when she'd grabbed the toilet paper. It was weathered and had a scar on the thumb like Grandma Susana's. Cousin Stacy hadn't thought much of the incident, except that she needed to get Genesis moisturizer for Christmas, until later in the morning, when she'd told Genesis to stop washing her hands so often, that they were getting wrinkly. But Genesis had shown Cousin Stacy her hands, and they were as smooth as a 14-year old's. Cousin Genesis, who was also in the room, nodded and put her hands near the flashlight so that everyone could admire the smoothness of someone who didn't wash dishes without gloves and moisturized daily. Then Cousin Stacy said that in the afternoon, her mom had found out about Grandma Susana's death and told them. That's when Cousin Stacy knew. It had been Grandma Susana who had passed her the toilet paper on her way to the other side. Those listening with rapt attention to her nodded in earnest agreement.

Alegría rustled her eyes. She started coming to, in the dark silence of the bedroom.

Some of the other children started telling their own stories about encounters with Grandma Susana and other beings, as well as those they'd heard from adults. Cousin Nico joined in with his tale that he'd overheard Jacob Ramos say to Uncle Martin. "I think it was about that guy mom was talking about earlier. Uncle Dominique." The children murmured assent. "Jacob Ramos was saying how one time his great-grandpa had to deliver something to Uncle Dominique. Uncle Dominique liked birds and had his house full of them in cages. When—"

"What kinds of birds?" asked Cousin Jonathan, who was a year older than him.

"I don't know. All kinds," said Cousin Nico impatiently. "Macaws and blue jays and parrots and all kinds. Anyway, when Jacob Ramos's great-grandpa went inside, he saw Uncle Dominique had two dark purple stains that looked like teardrops below his eyes. But when Jacob Ramos's great-grandpa looked inside Uncle Dominique's eyes, he saw something so dark and scary that the birds starting flapping their wings in their cages and cawing and singing like crazy. Jacob Ramos's great-grandpa got so scared that he dropped the package on the ground and ran out of his house faster than a horse." The children got quiet because they knew that stories like that were true and scared even the adults; they were not bedtimes stories or fairy tales.

The door broke open, almost hitting Alegría who was sitting close by it. An invisible hand turned the lights on. It was Marisol. The spooked children got up and ran outside faster through the front door faster than Jacob Ramos's great-grandfather could've run out of the house like a horse, leaving Alegría and June alone with their mother. Someone upstairs had broken one of Grandma Susana's china cups.

6.

The day after the family party, the pumpkin house seemed to quiver quietly in recognition of its sudden emptiness. Gone were the smells of pork and chicken, the sounds of the invading mosquitoes and Grandma Tracy's complaints, the tastes of fried *huaraches* and sweet *horchata*, the sights of shadow puppets reflected on the walls in the light of a flashlight. The secret transaction between June and Cousin Salome plagued June's mind the night after the party so much that it seeped into her dreams and woke her up at precisely the same time Aunt Mary upstairs woke up startled at the eerie chirp of a solitary cricket outside her upstairs window.

Peeking out behind her door to check if her parents in the other room were asleep and determining that the stress of last night's party and the strength of Uncle Martin's *jamaica* had sufficiently knocked them out, June returned to her room and tapped Alegría gently, once, twice, thrice. Only with the last tap did Alegría shift, and even then, it was ever so slightly. Satisfied that the house was left to her alone, June eased her cousin's mattress off her creaky bed frame. She slipped her hand in the space in between, ignored the three-year old crinkly sheet of paper, and pulled out the the push-up bra and and crop top that Cousin Stacy had agreed to give her for half of June's Halloween candy come October. Creeping past her parents' bedroom, she tried them on over her pajamas, looking into the bathroom mirror. The bra looked unnatural, and the crop top was a flowery thing consisting of more frills and ruffles than late Grandma Susana's cooking apron. June lifted her shirt to show her bare belly button as the shirt was designed to do. It looked like a keyhole. It looked like a mushroom. It looked like anything other than what other girls' belly buttons looked like. June shivered and let her shirt fall back down.

Staring at her reflection in the mirror, she saw something that didn't match. She had the thin shoulders of the Prudentos and cheeks round like the scored bread of the Mantecanos. She pinched her thighs, which had started to grow bigger, despite her attempts to eat less. And her chest was growing two domes like cakes that have been baked at a too-high temperature. Her body parts didn't seem like hers. It was like someone had taken body parts from other people and replaced her own with theirs, forming some type of Frankensteinish freak. Under thick eyebrows, June had the small eyes of her father, the kind that Aunt Mary said looked like the angled-up brush strokes of a thick brush. When she smiled, her eyes became even smaller and her round cheeks pulled to the sides of a her lemon-shaped mouth.

It was these round cheeks that June had heard compared to her mother's at the party. There was not a single family party where the parents didn't compare their children to their relatives' children, and where the children weren't compared to their parents and great-grandparents.

"Wow, June is looking more and more like you each day, Mari. She has your cheeks. And that bathroom loofah-hair," had said Grandaunt Elena, before mentioning her son for the fifth time that night, who looked just like his father and was destined to be a lawyer.

When she'd first heard the comparison being made at the party, June had scowled. She didn't want to look like her mother. Marisol had married her father and he wasn't handsome, so she must've not been pretty. However, the severeness in her mother's eyes at hearing her daughter compared to her had made June's cheeks redden as they did now in the mirror so that Cousin Stacy had asked her what the matter was. June hadn't dared to say that her own mother didn't want her daughter compared to her.

"Oh, and I see Alegría is behaving," had said Grandaunt Elena. "But she does seem more quiet than usual. Is she having trouble at school? Did you chastise her too much? You know, you have to let children be children sometimes. Anyone else who saw Alegría here might think her parents' beat her at home. Look at her, she looks miserable."

June soured as she saw a flicker of wakefulness in her mother's eyes. It was only Alegría that could make her mother shiver with life from the lost sea she was in.

June heard a bed nearby creak. She fumbled to take the shirt and bra off and ran past her parents' bedroom back into her bedroom. She shoved it under her cousin's mattress, accidentally pushing the crinkly sheet of paper closer to the edge of the bed frame so that an edge of the paper was visible underneath the mattress. In her hurry to feign sleep, she pulled the paper out from underneath the mattress and threw it onto her bed, protecting it underneath her body and bed covers. With the stress of one who holds onto secrets, June tried to control her breathing.

The paper nestled underneath her seemed no different than any other crinkly sheet of paper to Alegría when she found it a year later, but to June, it was sacred. The sheet of crinkly paper with handwriting too big and squarish to be anyone's other than hers was a memory, a reminder that she was who she was and would never be any different in her parents' eyes or anyone else's. The letters written on the sheet formed a string of words that connected into the hopscotch of verses known as an acrostic poem. To June, they contained everything about her.

She had written it as an assignment for school and her fourth grade teacher had found it so wonderfully full of emotion that she had sent it home to her parents with an excellent mark and a written note exclaiming her praises at June's talent. On the ride home, June had excitedly bounced up and down in her seat, dripping with the inquietude of baring her work in front of her mom.

Not waiting for her mother to set her keys down in the little compartment by the kitchen she had designated for just those jean-blue sedan keys and Pinnacle Street-house keys, June brought her paper directly in front of her mother's face. "Look, look!" she'd said. June had proudly shown her mother and father the poem, graced with a circled letter grade that meant "Amazing. Absolutely Astounding. You have a brilliant daughter." Much to June's disappointment, her mother had looked at the poem without a trace of shared excitement; she wasn't really seeing it. She'd given it back to June with an intelligible mumble as an answer.

"Look at it," June had said, persisting in her need to feel validated.

"I did," Alegría's mother had said with a dazed confusion and slight disinterest.

"No, I mean really look at it. My teacher said my poem was the best in class."

At that moment, her father had entered the room. Finding no evidence of recognition in her mother, June had snatched the paper from her mother's all-too-willing hands and shoved it into the hands of her father. "Behold!" she'd said with her eyes.

Her father had taken the paper, moved it closer and farther away from his face as if to put the words into focus. "You need to work on your handwriting. I can't read a thing. Your letters are chunky, too much like a boy's," he'd said, each of his words pounding June until she was no bigger than a number 2 pencil.

June had snatched the paper from her father. "But my teacher could read it! She said it was the best poem in the world!" June felt unloved and misunderstood by her parents. Why was it that when Alegría did something other than breathe, everyone eulogized her? But when June did something well, no one so much as batted an eye. She'd felt her chin slacken and her heart tighten, until each heartbeat hurt. Crumpling the paper, she'd swallowed the pain down. "But Alegría's handwriting! It's bad, too! She always writes her 'd's backwards!" That would show her parents. Alegría wasn't the perfect daughter they thought she was.

"Alegría is barely learning to write. Besides, you're five years older than her. You should know better," had said her mother.

People always said she should know better. But how was she supposed to know better if they didn't teach her any better? Her mother never talked to her unless she really needed to, and the only reason her father ever talked to her was to tell her how much she wasn't meeting their expectations. More than she wanted it from her father, June wanted approval from her mother.

Curling her body around the crumpled sheet of paper, she thought how much her mother wasn't her mother. Although she looked the same, her real mother had shrunk away from her long ago, and she'd only kept shrinking ever since.

The first time Alegría saw her mother in the same way June saw her was also the first time she was sent to the office as a troublemaker. She had been in Miss Turtle's class like any other regular weekday. She'd come in and sat down in her chair by the window; the seat next to her had been empty. Bo that day, was absent. Looking at the skip-counting math worksheet in front of her, Alegría had felt a sudden tickling on her neck. She'd swatted at it to get it away and felt a little pea-sized ball roll from her neck and land on her paper. She'd thought that she hadn't been so long without a shower as to start growing little balls of dirt. Getting closer to the pea-sized ball, Alegría saw that its colors shifted from a gray-purple to a murky-white. She blinked twice at it and it blinked back. Startled by the opening of the pea-sized ball to reveal a small, chocolate-brown-colored eye, Alegría jumped backwards from her desk, bumping Bo's empty desk beside her. She looked up to meet Miss Turtle's questioning stare then looked quickly back down to avoid suspicion. Alegría had the idea that Miss Turtle didn't like her and Miss Turtle had confirmed her idea that Alegría was indeed a troublemaker.

Looking back down at her paper, Alegría saw the pea-sized ball was gone. Looking around to see where it had rolled off to, Alegría found that there were many pea-sized balls all around her, and they were bouncing closer to her. She didn't really notice anything wrong with the balls until they touched her exposed skin and gave her a small shock, the kind she received when she touched the static-y shopping cart at Josefina's. She got up to get them away and found that the classroom had transferred into an open space of clove-colored dirt. She smelled the sweet-earthy scent of wet corn flour.

"Hello, *Grillita*" said a voice behind her. "What are you doing here?"

Alegría turned around to find an adult-sized orange lump. It looked like a sweet potato, except that between two lines of imperfections, there were located a pair of brown eyes, the same shade as the chocolate eyes on the pea-sized balls. Those balls had followed Alegría into this primitive environment and they bounced onto the orange lump, sticking themselves magnetically on the rough skin, they disappeared into it, like how the knob on a tree would disappear from its bark if Alegría stared at it long enough, becoming nothing more than wrinkles on the adult-sized lump.

"I don't know, I was in second grade. And Bo was absent," said Alegría.

"I know what you're doing here," said the orange lump with as much certainty as with which Alegría knew Aunt Mary's macaroni casserole was inedible. "You're here to help me find my dear," said the sweet potato.

Not knowing who her dear was, Alegría questioned her ability to find the sweet potato's dear, but she didn't have the opportunity to say much else. The ground in her dream turned lime-green, and she smelled the unmistakable intoxicatingly sweet smell of cupcakes. And then she wasn't in her dream anymore. She was staring at the front of her teacher's lime-green sweater in her seat by the window. After Alegría hadn't responded the first few times she'd been addressed by Miss Turtle, Miss Turtle had felt that it was time to call in reinforcements. She sent Alegría to the office with a note saying to call her parents to come pick her up, that their daughter was falling asleep in class.

Alegría never thought that she would be sent to the office. Rumors of children leaving the office crying and of being chastised by means of a big, black stick belonging to a dead police officer had floated around the elementary school since its opening nearly twenty years ago, reaching Alegría's ears no later than her first week in school. But being in the office, she noticed that it wasn't as scary as other people had said. There was a child with tear-stains sitting a few chairs away from her, but his reason for crying was a stolen crayon box, completely unrelated to the office. Looking around at the big, wooden front desk with its middle-aged desk ladies, black phone with a loopy cord, stapler, bell, and cups filled with pencils, the big, black stick was nowhere to be seen. Frankly, Alegría thought that even if the big, black stick were in the office, she wouldn't really care much about its presence. She was grumpy that she'd been interrupted from her sleep in the middle of a very important conversation with a sweet potato and been made to stay awake while she waited for her parents to pick her up.

After what seemed like a year and four days to Alegría, her mother finally did arrive at the elementary school office. She took one look at Alegría and then moved her attention to the middle office lady, the one with big hair dyed too light for her heavily contoured face holding the sticky note written by the personal pink ink of Miss Turtle. Alegría had looked on while the words "sleep" and "disruptive" and "problems" were thrown around by the office lady and reiterated by her mother.

Now that her mother was in the office, Alegría felt slightly more awake. She wanted to talk to her mother and to go home. She got up from one of the office chairs whose seat felt like carpet and moved to hug her mother from behind. Her mother did not hug her back. Finishing her talk with the office lady, Alegría's mother walked out of the office in silence. Confused at the lack of address, Alegría looked back at the office lady to see if she could follow her mother outside. The office lady gave her a single nod in an aura of artificially-blond hair, so she hurried to catch the door her mother didn't hold open for her. On the walk to the family jean-blue sedan, Alegría kept looking from the ground to her unresponsive mother back to the ground. Finally, her mother looked at her as she opened the car door for her seat in the back, but she didn't say anything.

Alegría got a sickening feeling in her stomach, like when Cousins Uriel and Muriel had made her try Cousin Salome's seven chili salsa. She started to think that maybe sleeping in class was really something bad kids did. Before, she'd been annoyed by Miss Turtle, who made her stay awake during the school day, but now Alegría realized that it was necessary to avoid whatever state her mother was in. The only discernible sound was that of the car motor as it pushed through a bad case of indigestion. The sky outside had been mostly drained of color, leaving only a faint reminder of the indigo blue from the night before. Stretching against the seatbelt to catch a glimpse of her mother's face turned away from her, Alegría saw that it, too, was drained of color and emotion, the corners of her uncolored lips relaxed into an easy frown. This pallid person wasn't her mother. She was a bad impostor in place of the egg-frying, sock-folding, hair-caressing mother who stayed up with her at night when she couldn't sleep. Alegría wanted that mother.

Uneasy, she tried to think of something to say to her mother but no ideas volunteered themselves to go into her mouth. The only thing her opening-and-closing mouth did for her was make her look like a fish struggling to breathe.

From the princess sticker-decorated rearview mirror, Marisol could see her daughter struggling to speak in the backseat. It made her uncomfortable. "We're going to the store," she'd said stiffly, filling the car momentarily with sound other than the car motor. Hearing the cold voice of her mother, Alegría's eyes flickered back to her mother's hair, and she waited to see if her mother was back.

The quietness from the car moved with them through the store as Marisol looked for milk, peanut butter, rice, paper towels, chicken bouillon, eggs, sour cream, and vegetables of the frozen and fresh varieties. During other shopping trips, the store was an island with trees of canned green beans, crabs, fish, red and white onions, sand floors of shiny polymer, and hoards of candy booty. Marisol's shopping list would serve as a treasure map, and they'd have to find all of the items on the list, leading themselves only by the symbols on the bright white signs that advertised prices as low as $12.99 and store sections like "Bakery." But for the daughter, the store that day was simply a store, so big it was suffocating, and for the mother, a place that made her heart rate speed up and her hand unconsciously clutch her brown bag with its wallet inside, a place she wanted to leave as soon as they'd entered.

Walking as quickly as her thin legs would allow through the aisles, Alegría started to feel a faint pressure on her head. It clamped the back of her head to the roof of her mouth and tried to convince her that the polymer floor was as soft as it was smooth. While she waited for her mother to decide between the paper towel roll that would give her the most uses for her dollar and the paper towel roll that was economical enough to buy the pack of 18 eggs instead of the 12 pack, Alegría's head started bobbing back and forth, as if held by a calm current. By the time they reached the fresh vegetables, Alegría couldn't resist the temptation to lay on the floor thousands had tread on before her.

"Alegría, what are you doing?" said her mother. She shook Alegría awake into a semi-standing, semi-leaning position and decided that she didn't need green tomatoes after all. They went to the check-out counter. The assistant wasn't much of an assistant. Dressed in a green vest that emphasized the skinniness of his arms against the rotundness of his belly, he was working the store's cash register only to sustain his bowling addiction. While trying to keep Alegría upright, the mother counted every penny on the cash register screen. As the paper towel rolls were scanned, the mother felt the beep go through her very heart. The lights in the store flashed. She realized she'd gone over her budget. Looking at the remaining items, the frozen vegetable mix and the eggs,

Marisol said in a small but stony voice, "I don't want the frozen vegetables anymore." She stared at the eyes of the paunchy store attendant, daring him to comment on her statement with what power she still had. He simply looked at her suspiciously and removed the frozen vegetables from the counter. Checking the eggs out, the bowling-addicted store attendant asked for the total cost. With slightly trembling hands, Marisol unzipped her bag, pulled out the money from her wallet, and reluctantly handed it over.

"Two cents is your change. Have a nice day," said the store attendant. Marisol put the items back in her cart in such a hurry that she broke one of her eighteen eggs. The sleepy daughter and anxious mother exited the store, leaving behind them a place that in spite of its racks of vegetables, dairy, and candies, seemed as empty to them as if it'd been a lonely island.

7.

On the three-month anniversary of her death, Grandma Susana decided that she had had enough of the other world. At first, the other world had seemed like a repose, an eternal sleep on a soft bed of damp, downy white soil that glowed like the white calla lilies she had kept in flower pots by her front door until the unprecedented snowy winter the year her daughter, Marisol, and Daniel Cana eloped. But then she'd woken up. The culprit was the discordant symphony of laughs, sneezes, sighs, gasps, titters, and coughs just outside her final resting room. With a prickling in her bosom, Grandma Susana had risen from her downy bed and gone to investigate. Finding a multitude of people, dressed in a plethora of colors, hairstyles, shapes, eyes, and noses, she'd asked them not who they were but where the kitchen was. She was feeling a little peckish. Once the people of the other world had discovered the delicacies she could conjure up with just oil, flour, eggs, salt, and water, they'd furnished her with an ethereal apron of frills and pockets like no other in hopes that it would motivate her to stay in the kitchen and cease her proselytizing tendencies.

It was this same apron that she donned as she made her way through the misty veil that clouded people's eyes to the inhabitants and deeds of the other world to check up on her three daughters and fourteen grandchildren. Walking through her front door and down the flight of stairs to her basement, she'd crossed the hall in silent footsteps and peered through the first door on the left. Surprised to see to Alegría's moony eyes boring holes in the ceiling, she'd come into the room for a chat with her granddaughter. "Hello, *mi Grillita*," she'd said, "it's been a while." Alegría, who had not seen her since they'd watched the Powerpuff Girls fighting crime on television, mistook her words for those of the shuffling thing that had tormented her during the first nights she'd spent in the pumpkin house until she realized that no shuffling thing could ever be so warm, so soothing, so euphonious as Grandma Susana's voice.

"Grandma! Grandma!" she said as she got up from her stiff, plank-position on the bed and jumped towards her grandmother's outstretched arms by the doorway.

"Shh, not so loud," said Grandma Susana, "you'll draw a crowd, and you know how being wakened would make your sister frown." Embracing her felt like drinking hot apple and cinnamon tea to Alegría, the toasty liquid warming her from the inside-out as it passed through her throat and settled in her stomach.

Having inhaled as much of Grandma Susana's wet corn-flour-scent as she could until she felt lightheaded from the lack of oxygen, Alegría asked her where she'd been and why she hadn't come sooner. Grandma Susana replied that the people in the other world, which was really on a different dimension of the living world, had kept her cooking and baking until she'd started to lose track of the outside world behind the stacks of *taquitos de papa*, pots of *esquites*, plates of *pastel imposible*, and bowls of *menudo*, and asked Alegría why she wasn't sleeping at three o'clock on a Monday morning. Alegría, who up until that moment had forgotten the frustrations of the night, relayed to her grandmother the strange disturbances in her sleep that had kept her awake in spite of her tiredness so heavy it could pull down mountains.

"I know what can make you smile again, *mi Grillita*. Let's go to my kitchen and make *arroz con leche* together." So Alegría followed her grandmother up the two flights of stairs to the kitchen, thinking that if her mother accused her of disobeying orders not to go upstairs, she had the backing of her grandmother, of whose kitchen and house it was, after all.

Entering the familiar pink and yellow tiled kitchen that matched the flower-pattern camel back couch in the living room, Alegría set to work under the direction of Grandma Susana. The painful lead in her head had disappeared and she felt at peace. She stepped onto the black stool under the sink and held the red mesh drainer loaded with rice with both hands over the sink while Grandma Susana opened the tap to unleash the river of water over the rice. Alegría shook the drainer to get rid of the excess water and with her grandmother's help, dumped it in a pot with four cups of water, a cracked cinnamon stick, lime zest, and a dash of salt to boil. While the rice cooked, they chatted about everything from the bouncy chairs in the other world to Bo's nose-picking habit.

Looking for the lid of the pot to cover the rice when they added the milk later, Alegría bumped into the other lids, pots, and pans inside the cupboard, causing a momentary ruckus that awoke Aunt Mary from an impossible dream in which she couldn't find one single accursed bathroom with an urgent desire to relieve herself.

On the way to the bathroom, she noticed the dim shadow of a glow that came from the opposite end of the hallway. Putting her bladder on hold, Aunt Mary followed the shaft of light to the kitchen, where she heard the murmur of boiling water and smelled the sweet, dry heat of cinnamon. Upon seeing her dead mother and seven-year-old niece quietly chatting and boiling rice in the kitchen, Aunt Mary deduced that in her hurry to get to the bathroom, she'd simply forgotten to wake up. Not taking the time to address the characters she thought were in her dream, she turned on her heel and made a beeline for the toilet.

Aunt Mary, who had a mole near the left side of her nose, resembled her father the most out of her three sisters. The one thing she'd inherited from her mother was her drooping bosom. She had a thin mouth, and an even thinner smile, which even those closest to her sometimes found indistinguishable from her lopsided grimace. Though the youngest of her three sisters, she had one of those faces that often got her confused as the same age as her oldest sister, Teresa, who was her senior by seven years. She had a full figure and thunderous footsteps that shook the ground so much so that her position could be determined by Alegría's family downstairs at any given time from where the thuds fell on the ceiling. Quiet like Marisol, though not quite as irritable, she'd become stiff as stone when a boy in high school had cornered her in a classroom and touched her in a way that she didn't understand; unlike the Midas touch, his touch hadn't turned her to gold, but rather to steel. As a result, she'd not only had to get a special nail cutter to cut through her steel nails, but had also had to give up her dream of giving birth to children, the complications arising from having steel flesh being too great.

Unshakable in her demeanor, there were only two instances in her life when she'd doubted the reality of things. The first was when her husband, five months into their marriage, had confessed his affair with a fertile woman to her, confident that she wouldn't react violently. Aunt Mary had fallen in love with him five years prior, when he'd demonstrated that one plus one is eleven, and that there were eleven visible stars in the universe from his position, and that his position was exactly four feet from her, and that every four equal sides make a square, which at the time of day, when both the moon and the sun were present, could be arranged with the two extraterrestrial circular bodies to form a heart, which represented a love between them stronger than any diamond ring could buy, for which he did not have the sufficient funds to profess his love by. Twelve women and countless nights of senseless waiting up, Aunt Mary had finally begun to grasp that reality which had formerly seemed so inconceivable. The day he'd come back from a month-long holiday with the wench Margarita, she'd wordlessly repacked up his clothes and his toothbrush, and placed them outside the front door. He had refused to leave. They'd stayed together for two more months. When she grew tired of supporting him and his pleasures on the meager pay of a teacher and he wouldn't agree to a divorce he knew she wouldn't dare ask him for (he knew she still loved him and had held onto the last shred of hope that he would change), she began looking for another place to stay. It was around this time that Grandma Susana's timely death had provided her with an inexpensive way out while her husband sorted his things out; she left him their house and still sent him monthly checks.

The second instance came years later, as she struggled to understand what she viewed as the nonsensical division between Mantecanos and Prudentos with the violent confrontation by the Mipared River, to reconcile the idea of her innocent, young niece with the fierce, passionate activist she saw before her.

For the most part, however, Aunt Mary remained steadfast in her beliefs, one of which was that the supernatural and natural worlds had nothing in common. So when come midnight, the bubbling smells and clanking saucepans coming from the kitchen would make her halt mid-step on the way to the bathroom, when she would wake up to find the sink, glistening empty the night before, unexplainably full of dirty, soapy dishes in the morning, and when she opened the door to the fridge and discovered bowls and Tupperware filled with familiar dishes, Aunt Mary still attributed the inconsistencies to dreams and sleepwalking.

Grandma Susana kept up her visits to Alegría until the birth of her first child, when she knew that Alegría had learned enough not to burn the rice for her own family. She visited her nights so frequently that it was a true testament to the sleepiness of her family that no one noticed except Aunt Mary. Once she'd established a nightly path back to her house to keep her granddaughter company, Grandma Susana could not keep from visiting the other rooms and inhabitants in her house at all hours. When June was brushing her teeth, she thought she saw Grandma Susana's face reflected in the zinc alloy faucet as she put her face near it to spit. When Marisol scrubbed the stove top clean of all imperfections of the past, she thought she smelled her mother's wet corn flour scent trapped underneath the flakes of burnt grease. When Daniel Cana buttoned the top three buttons of the white-red pinstripe shirt he had prepared for his interview later that day, he thought he heard his mother-in-law's melodic voice by his ear whisper, "you look like a candy cane."

It was the beginning of December when Christmas made itself known in shops and houses. Nobody could remember when the tradition of Christmas had started, or who had lit the first candle on a tree, or who had made the first Christmas punch, but people could remember the look of expectation on their family and friends' faces come the 25th, and they could remember the lightness in their wallets come the new year. People in Manteca and Prudent liked to have little pocketbooks made that told the roots of their family history intertwined with the origins of the towns; these were put in the children's shoes that were left out until the sixth of January, when the *Reyes Magos* had had time to visit every child's home in the area.

The production of these little pocketbooks was so popular in those years that they made it the only time of the year when Alegría's father had work ensured. Still, it was important to him that he made a good impression on the families that ordered these little pocketbooks. People had to know that whoever was binding the histories transcribed on yellowed pages was a trustworthy man. So, despite the annoyance he felt at hearing Grandma Susana's voice near his ear, he could not ignore the image of candy canes that swirled before his eyes while looking in the bathroom mirror, or the feeling of his mother-in-law's judging eyes peering over his shoulder. Irked at the time lost buttoning up a shirt that was not going to impress the Flores family, he ripped the buttons on the shirt off and threw it on the floor beside his bed. From there, it watched in a disheveled, abused pile as a crisp, clean, plain white shirt was taken gingerly from a hanger in the closet and its sleeves slid into. The buttons were done up with care not to wrinkle the front. Remembering the tender attention Daniel Cana had paid to its buttons only minutes before, and recalling the savage mistreatment they had abruptly received, the shirt in a fit of jealous rage declared to itself that it was glad it was not covering that over-cologned body. As Daniel Cana smoothed his white collar and remained still for ten seconds, unconsciously listening for the verdict of his mother-in-law's voice, the ravaged shirt slithered out of its pile on the ground and into its cunning position by his feet. Hearing no chiding remark from his mother-in-law on the dullness of his shirt, he nodded once and moved in confidence towards the door, not noticing the resentful shirt coiled in a crescent around his left foot. Catching himself on the door, he puffed air out of his nose and picked up the dignity he had dropped on the floor by the smirking white-red pinstripe shirt during his near-fall.

Passing his daughters' bedroom, he ignored the sleeping Alegría and the standing June who called out to him from within. Heading into the kitchen, he banged open a cupboard of glasses and took one out to serve as the vessel for the glass of milk that was to count as his breakfast. June followed him into the room, while her father was downing the milk, she noted with disgust the little drops that had made their escape along the sides of his mouth and down the curve of his chin. "Dad, someone from school invited me to a Christmas party, Can I go?" The only answer she received was the slam of the glass on the table. "Dad?" she probed again.

Flying past her on the way to the bathroom, he said, "ask your mother." Brushing his teeth violently, he thought about how little he could afford to be late to the Flores family interview. The previous September, he had driven the trucks for the *Estandar* cereal company, one of the big ones, transporting grains grown in Prudent and processed in Manteca to other parts of the country.

The hard red spring wheat grown in the fertile Prudent land was famous for its sweetness. While other wheat often carried a slightly bitter taste, the wheat grown in Prudent had mutated to be light as soft white wheat, so that recipients of the processed product would often wonder if their product had been misla-beled. This hard red spring wheat has remained one of the main constituents of the Manteca-Prudent economy.

However coming from Prudent and being new to the Manteca company, Alegría's father had had a hard time adjusting to the work. He was left the shifts at the most undesirable hours, which had made his already scant time at home virtually nonexistent, not that he thought anybody had noticed; nobody at his house seemed to pay attention to him or to the advice he would give. Indeed, his wife had probably only noticed enough to not set out an extra plate at dinnertime. But the long hours of driving had taken a toll on his body. After looking in the mirror and realizing that sitting for so long at such irregular hours of the day had made him shrink a whole five centimeters, he drove his borrowed truck back to the *Estandar* cereal company and told his manager that he could not keep such a schedule and that he needed a new one. The balding manager had looked him up and down and said, "Puh! I knew you were a lazy Prudento when I saw you." After that, Daniel Cana had been released from his schedule but not in the way he had intended. Despite not having to pay rent after moving to Manteca, he had somehow managed to put his family in a worse economic situation than the previous one.

Oiling his curly hair upwards to hide the lost five centime-ters, he hoped that the Flores family didn't judge him for being a Prudento. Back in Prudent, Daniel Cana wasn't a central figure to the community, but because of where he was born, he was ac-cepted. People didn't mind so much that he had married a Mantecana because he had stayed true to his origins and brought her over to live on Prudent land. But now that he was an outsider in Manteca, he was seen as the intruder who had corrupted one of the daughters of one of the finest families in Manteca; he was seen as indolent, as an incompetent who had failed at finding work in his hometown and was now scavenging for work where he was not wanted or needed.

"Dad!" He heard his daughter's whiny drawl coming from the hall. She couldn't understand that this Flores meeting was important if she wanted to have food on her plate for Christmas dinner. Bracing against the bombardment of June's whines that awaited him outside of the bedroom, he made his way upstairs to the front door.

June tried to reach him but no vocal inflection, no volume, no tone could stretch that far.

Her father slammed the door on her words with a final "ask your mother," and they bounced down the stairs right back at her, the "Mother's at the store," and the "she told me to ask you" pummeling her face with their rejection.

At first, she hadn't really wanted to go to the party; she didn't like Hector at school so much. But her father's insistent ignorance of her made her determined to go to the Christmas party in defiance of him. She vowed to make him pay attention, he and her mother, one way or another.

8.

In the Flores family, there were five family members, none of whom knew how to swim. The father, Jonas Flores, said that clean, calm, silky water was meant to be gazed at in admiration, not disturbed by dirty toes and vulgar bathing suits. Nobody knew why he and Hortencia had married, the one liking classical music and the other country music, but they had, within two months of their first date, which was a trip to the then newly opened Museum of Manteca. Not wanting to waste any time, they'd gotten pregnant with Hector not a week after saying their vows, leading some to believe it was this baby that had been the prime motivator in their quick union.

After having Hector, the mother had said she'd be fine if she never saw another delivery room again. But little five-year-old Hector, that fifth of February, had blown out his birthday candles and said in earnest what he'd most desired: a baby brother. Hortencia and Jonas Flores could not deny their little boy his innermost wish, so that same night, after putting Hector to bed and the remaining cake in the fridge, they'd gone up the stairs, closed the door, and done their duty as devoted parents in the magic of the bedroom. On October 28th, Paolo Flores was born. He was naturally small and could've been mistaken for a Prudento in his youth, so his parents tried to instill in him the idea that he was big, strong, commanding, regardless of what size he was. When Hortencia Flores was 34, she'd gotten six things simultaneously: a metallic taste in her mouth, sore gums, cramping, a cold, constipation, and an aversion to cheese. That was when she knew she was pregnant with Concepcion, named so that her pregnancies would be just as immaculate as her mother's. The fertility of Hortencia, even when it was least expected, was attributed to her great, great—exactly how many greats is uncertain, for Daniel Cana, in his haste, had bound the page with their ancestry too close to the center of the book, and they'd been cut off—Grandfather Nestor, who had been a friend of Thomas Delgado and one of the brave who'd moved out from Prudent and helped found Manteca.

When Daniel Cana paid his visit to the Flores household, he was captivated by the august glow that seemed to emanate from the mouth of the patriarch, Jonas Flores, whenever he spoke and lit up the family atmosphere behind him. After a firm handshake, Daniel had been asked to sit down in the living room that was made just the right temperature by a powerful, state-of-the-art air conditioner; unlike the slightly cold rooms of the basement he was used to, this room could afford to be heated by an expensive running air conditioner. The house was decorated by the kaleidoscope of purple, red, and gold lights that came from the Christmas tree decorated with sparkling burgundy ribbon and regal champagne ornaments that looked like pulled sugar. A posh black piano stood in front of a wall dedicated to family pictures. Everything was clean and in its place. The delicious smell of crushed maple leaves permeated the room from a plugged-in air freshener by the entrance.

Jonas Flores called his wife and two sons down to greet the man that was going to bind their family pocketbook. No sooner had their names emanated from his mouth than his family was down the stairs, hugging and kissing the provider of their livelihood and greeting Daniel Cana at his request. Sitting across from them on the leather couch, he listened to their family stories. The parents were affectionate towards each other and proud of their children. The children participated in good-natured banter and were grateful towards their parents for everything they had. They were grateful! From his position on their couch, he could see the ruby red mantle on the kitchen table.

It was glossy, caught the light with an attractive glimmer. That was a mantle on which some mighty fine *huevos rancheros* could be placed, around which a virtuous family could sit and talk and bask in each other's irreproachable light.

Jonas Flores shifted the conversation from past Christmases to their current Christmas and the Christmas party they were having on the 14th. "I'm sure my son has already invited your eldest daughter but I'd like to extend a formal invitation to your whole family." Daniel Cana shifted in his seat; the sound was like two balloons rubbing together. June had said something about a party that morning. He graciously accepted their invitation and promised that his family would be there. Apparently the Flores were the type of family to hold parties whenever they pleased. Like Teresa and her dentist husband.

When the topic became that of the family pocketbook, Daniel Cana tried his best to assert his authority on the subject of binding. He told them how before people read using flexible thermal glue-bound paperbacks, the first people in Prudent read using Coptic bound books. First, leaves were organized into signatures, stacks of leaves, which after careful planning, were punctured through their outer spinal creases and then sewn together using waxed thread. Back then, people didn't fill so many books with fiction meant to entertain; rather, they used them as a way to pass notes between family members and friends. Before cell phone towers pierced the ground like stakes and telephone lines hung like ropes from wooden crosses, books were printed blank and people wrote messages to neighbors in them like "Don't feed used cooking oil to the wild turkeys," and "I need to borrow Juan's baby blue shorts to make a pattern;" they were then delivered to front doors by a primitive form of post mail, which was never really popular in letter form in Manteca or Prudent, the singular sheets of paper becoming too easily lost. The Flores family listened to him with polite interest.

When Daniel Cana had exhausted everything he had to say and still the Flores showed nothing more than polite interest, the empty noise without words lengthened. He shifted in his seat again. The balloon noise followed. Daniel Cana wondered if the balloon would ever pop. The Flores were everything he wanted, and he didn't want to be pulled from the ideal reality that was within his reach but finally, under the towering pressure of that glowing patriarch's silence, he rose to his feet with a "Well I thank you" and a "Don't worry about a thing," as well as other reassurances about the binding of their family pocketbook. As they were closing the door on him and putting perfection out of reach, the glossy red mantle winked back at him.

At six o'clock on December 14th, the sky in Manteca had already darkened. The night was eerily calm. Not even the wind could be heard. Inside the orange house, the Canas had accepted that they were going to be late to the Flores family Christmas party. June had thought their Christmas party was going to be teens only but now that she knew her whole family was coming along, she didn't want to go. Moreover, none of her dresses looked good on her. Marisol Cana had spent the day planning what they would eat for Christmas dinner and mathematically trying to determine what she would need to spend at the store to make the dishes. Exhausted at the thought of having to give up dessert at Christmas dinner, she didn't feel like going to a party where they probably had three desserts and more. Alegría had been woken from a two-hour long nap just to put on a stuffy dress and stockings; she was not excited either. The only family member who was excited was Daniel Cana. He wanted to be back in that luxurious house, to admire the piano and to just graze the glossy red mantle with his fingertips. So he pushed the rest of his family to get ready faster. He yelled, to see if that would have any effect on them. June was already on her seventh outfit change. Marisol didn't even have her hair curled. Alegría couldn't seem to buckle her shoes right.

Her head kept leaning forward. Daniel Cana yelled some more while he oiled his hair.

Around six forty, the Canas exited through the front door and got into their jean-blue sedan. Aunt Mary could see them leaving from the big cyclops window. June had on her least flattering dress, a gray piece of cloth that gave her all the figure of a trash can. Alegría's black shoes and tights disappeared in the dark under her white dress so she looked like a floating ghost. Aunt Mary didn't know how their mother had let her daughters go out dressed like that. Except she did. Her sister had no style sense, as evidenced by the curls on her hair so tight they could break and the blush on her cheeks so loud it looked like she was suffering from heatstroke. They drove away towards what the father had promised would be a spectacular party. After watching them disappear around the block, Aunt Mary left her post at the window and went back to her television show.

Once at the party, the parents were taken on a house tour by the conscientious host, Hortencia Flores, and her husband. Marisol Cana put on her happy face, which was, if nothing more, at least as convincing as Aunt Mary's grimace. Daniel Cana resisted the urge to leave the tour and go back downstairs to rest his hand on the ruby-red mantle on the kitchen table. The children were corralled to the outside, where a *piñata* was being set up.

Alegría was left to the special care of her older sister under strict orders from their mother to stay together. When she tried to hold onto her sister's hand, June slipped her hand free. So Alegría tried to hook onto her sister's arm, but then June stiffened her arm against her side.

Determined not to be left behind, Alegría half-hugged, half-glued herself onto whatever part of June she could hold onto. She wanted to tell her sister she was scared of seeing Paolo at the party, that ever since she'd been sent to the office, his taunting had grown worse, but June was preoccupied with her own problems. People from her middle school were there and she didn't want anyone to see her with her annoyingly-clingy little sister.

Someone had strung red and green Christmas lights on the trees outside and laid tables laden with *empanadas* and cupcakes by a back corner where they wouldn't be an obstacle to any of the youths dancing in the middle of the yard. From somewhere, music boomed, a collection of Christmas songs remixed to have a catchy rhythm. "Santa's belly moves, to the right, to the left, ho ho ho..." sang a fast-talking man to the sound of trumpets and accordions. June led her sister by the edges of the fenced yard to the food table. Alegría was asking June why Santa laughed to the sound of the Hostess cream-filled chocolate snack cakes when Hector emerged from the crowd of dancing youths slightly sweaty and with eyes that reflected the Christmas lights in the trees.

"Hi" he said in what could have been interpreted as slightly shy. June didn't know what to do other than stare at him while she mouthed an unheard response. "Is this your sister?" he asked. Not waiting for a reply, he crouched down to Alegría's level and stretched out his hand. She took it with mistrustful eyes and clutched June even harder. "Would you like to dance? A bunch of us from school are here. There," and he pointed to a group of teens jumping like deranged monkeys in the center of the yard.

June looked at the sheen of sweat on his forehead. Hector had wavy long black hair that he scooped up with his fingers and threw back out of his eyes carelessly. She didn't really like him.

He was too excitable. He didn't respect other people's privacy. He talked when and where he wanted to. He had no respect for the unspoken social rules and talked to strangers like they were close friends he'd known since the intimate age of diapers. He intruded into people's line of sight and talked a string of words that encircled them and tied them up closer and closer until they found themselves nodding their heads to whatever he was saying. June's thoughts were interrupted by a small tug on her gray dress and she looked down to meet the eyes of her sister. They were big as saucers, big as when her parents had first brought her home, and they were sending a silent, desperate message: no, don't leave me.

"You can leave your sister with my brother. I think they go to the same elementary school. Over there by the tree. They're probably done setting up the *piñata* by now. It's great. It's fine," said Hector. *No, it's not fine,* said the eyes beside her. Alegría gave two quick shakes of her head. She willed her sister to remember what their mother had said about staying together. "It's fine," repeated Hector and stretched out his hand. June found herself prying her sister's arms off her and taking it. She thought she heard a sound like a trunk breaking.

"You'll be fine," she said, looking back at Alegría as Hector led her through the throng of people to his group in the center. She looked so small, and her shoulders were so thin, standing by herself at the edge of the food table.

After watching her sister disappear holding onto to her boyfriend's hand, Alegría turned to the area with the trees her sister's boyfriend had pointed to. There was something strange about that boy. Her sister wouldn't have gone dancing with just anyone. Maybe he was her boyfriend, and so things were different. Something shiny by the trees caught her attention. It was a star, with six different rings of color and seven horns with colored crepe paper hair pointing out in every which direction. Forgetting her sister's abandonment and her drowsiness, she drifted towards it.

Standing by the edge of the crowd of children that had gathered around the *piñata*, she could see where the star *piñata* had been hung from the biggest tree's branches. The three adults who had helped hang it were there, one was holding the wooden stick that would be used to hit the *piñata*, another was handing plastic bags to all the kids around the center, and the third was blindfolding none other than the evil playground lord Paolo. Alegría could see his gang of cronies standing at the edge of the circle, but they didn't scare her now. She could play the *piñata* game without them ever seeing her. When the first kid swung the stick, it was every girl for herself, and the kids were made equal in the frenzy of candy.

She smiled in anticipation. Children have to be smart to survive a *piñata*. Once its outer shell breaks and a few candies spill out, it's only the brave who dare dive under the wrath of the wooden stick to snatch the few treasures of peanuts, chocolates, lollipops, and sugar cane, and Alegría was one of the best seven-year-old candy snatchers there was. As she was handed her plastic bag, she hung it on her wrist and pushed it up her arm. Alegría didn't need a bag. She knew she could get one of the *piñata's* seven cones to store her candy in, and then use it as a hat later.

The man who had blindfolded Paolo spun him around three times one way, then three times the other way. The crowd of children and adults who had been attracted by the colorfully shiny star began singing the *piñata* song, the one that urged the wielder of the stick to hit the *piñata* being swung in the air by the two adults manipulating its ropes by the tree. The game had begun. Alegría saw Paolo move his head from side to side like a meerkat trying to sense where the *piñata* was by the whistles its tissue paper made through the air. She heard herself laugh and it was like myriad bubble wrap bubbles popping simultaneously. Paolo swung wildly and the crowd sang that he had hit the *piñata* once, twice, thrice, and that his time was up. The sacred power of the wooden stick was given to another child, and the game began all over again.

The new wielder of the stick had on a green T-shirt, was big for his age, and was one of the providers of muscle for Paolo's gang. On his first swing, a small wound was made to the *piñata* body, revealing its *papier mache* interior.

The sight brought Alegría back to memories of making *piñatas* with her grandmother. Grandma Susana would put white flour in a pan and mix it by hand with a spoon while Alegría added water little by little to avoid forming clumps in the batter. After the mixture was the consistency only Grandma Susana knew was right, she would heat it over the stove while vigorously stirring so that the goopy mixture wouldn't stick to the bottom of the pan. When the mixture had boiled and thickened, she would take it off the heat and let it cool while Alegría and she tore up pieces of smooth newspaper to cover up a blue balloon she'd blown up. Grandma Susana had reluctantly switched to using inflatable balloons instead of clay pots as the base for *piñatas* when Grandaunt Elena's son, who was destined to be a lawyer, was struck by a falling piece of *piñata*; luckily his head was as hard as a coconut and he hadn't suffered any permanent injuries, except for a banana-shaped scar he liked to tell people was a shark bite.

Next, they'd painted the newspaper strips with the water-flour mixture and glued them unto the balloon. While the *piñata's* newspaper body dried, Alegría would help Grandma Susana form cones out of cardboard paper to glue on the *piñata*. Grandma Susana would take a cone and put it on Alegría's head like a princess hat. She'd take another cone and put it on her forehead like a unicorn. Then the table would shake with her laughter. Alegría smiled again, remembering Grandma Susana's table-shaking laughter.

The boy with the green shirt and wooden stick struck one of the cones on the *piñata* with a swing like a baseball player and the trapped candy spilled out. The children swarmed everywhere like rats on a hunt, vigilant of the stick still in the green-shirted boy's hands. Alegría swarmed with them, and she felt joy. She felt like herself again, lost in the excitement of childhood and *piñatas*.

But then the world stopped and Alegría's body froze. She felt a swooping sensation in her stomach, like when she'd illegally ridden the roller coaster at Loony Lottie's Amusement Park. It was so cold it was wet. Alegría's spirit swam out of her body with her breath and paused to observe itself lying there. The grass smelled sweet; the stars in the sky twinkled as brightly as the Christmas lights in the trees; the ground felt like ticklish strands of jelly; and the children trampled the white dress and body on their way to the candy. There was a heartbeat that sounded in the chest and the ears and the neck and from everywhere. There was the whisper of a breath when it went in and out of the body. A voice called a name that was familiar, but it was distant.

The body began calling Alegría's spirit back to it. Using the currents of air that passed through its mouth, it began tugging at Alegría gently to get back inside. When the whirlpool of breath pulled her inside, her spirit stretched its fingers and toes, trying to get a feel for its body, and remember who she was. And it hurt because she realized that there were footprint-sized bruises forming under her skin. It wasn't until much later, a few months before her death, that Alegría found out that the separating of her spirit from her body was called cataplexy.

"*Grilla!* Didn't you hear me calling your name to get out of the way?" said June. She was standing next to Hector. When the singing had started, he'd grabbed her hand and pulled her to the crowd around the tree so they could witness the breaking of the *piñata*. They wouldn't participate, of course, because that was only for little kids, even though in her heart of hearts, June would've preferred to scuffle around the ground with her sister than hold the entangling hand of Hector. She didn't know why Alegría had dived to the ground only to stay there immobile while the other kids trampled her. She must've had the head of an egg to remain still for so long; it was annoying.

As June was about to stretch out her hand to help her, she heard snickering to her left. "She's dumb as a wood block. She just stood there while kids stepped on her," said Hector's little snot of a brother. His gang of hooligans wheezed air out of their lungs in twangs that were sorry imitations of laughter. June heard little twitters coming from the people in her middle school. She stayed her hand.

Alegría ignored them and set about to brushing her now-gray dress free of any stuck pieces of dirt and grass. Checking her sleeve, she noticed her plastic bag empty of any candy. "Oh," she whimpered. Surveying the scene, she saw that the ground was free of all of the *piñata's* booty. Not even a cone was left. "I missed out on the candy."

Hearing Alegría's whimper, Paolo guffawed. "She's worried about the candy? She needs to sort out her priorities." He pronounced priorities like "pie Oreo tees." His cronies wheezed louder in response. They wheezed until the goat-like sound came out their noses. "Betcha I could poke her stomach and she still wouldn't do anything," Paolo said and moved towards Alegría with a spindly stretched out finger. She dodged but no one else moved, not her sister or the other adults in the yard. The world was still stopped. Some time before, the speakers had silenced themselves and the night had returned to quiet, except for the hollow bleating emitted from the band of forty-eight-inchers.

The silence had alerted the adults who hadn't already come out into the yard and they spilled from the glass doors, bringing with them Hortencia and Jonas Flores and Marisol and Daniel Cana. "What's going on here? Why did the music stop?" said Hortencia Flores. Hector elbowed his brother to be quiet. That's when Marisol Cana spotted her daughter's ruined white dress. She didn't need to ask what had happened.

"She slipped," said June. Hector and Alegría both turned to look at her. She avoided their stares. Fact-of-the-matter was, her mother didn't need to know what happened, or her father.

Either way, she knew she was in trouble.

"I think it's time for us to go home," said Alegría's mother to everyone and to no one in particular simultaneously. Motioning with her head to her daughters, she pasted a smile on her face and thanked their kind hosts. They nodded politely in response but didn't raise any of the customary objections to their leaving so soon. Then Marisol Cana took her husband's arm and guided her family not through the house but through the fence door to their blue sedan. People's eyes followed them as they made their exit, waiting until they couldn't be seen anymore to start time back up again.

Marisol Cana said, "You were supposed to be watching her. You're the older sister, act like it," to June. She remained quiet but she shot her eyes at Alegría; there was a glint in them. Alegría also didn't say anything; she knew better than to contradict her sister at such an awkward moment.

Daniel Cana looked back at the Flores house as he started the car. The Christmas dance music could be heard to play again and the Christmas lights outlined the house in a red and green glow. If he concentrated closely, he could hear the faint echo of piano keys and feel the warm heat from the expensive air conditioner. From the front door window, Daniel Cana could see into the dining room and feel the wink of the glossy red mantle from the kitchen table as it promised what could've been and what could be.

9.

The first Christmas season spent in the pumpkin house was one which Alegría would remember with fondness when she was expecting her first child. It was a time of family and hope, of remembering and forgetting, of stuffed monkeys and white, plastic babies. During that holiday season, the house was decorated for festivities. Aunt Mary had hung her worn Santa sock with care outside the front door with a piece of duct tape. To her, it was as good as a sparkling new Christmas wreath, for it had been given to her one Christmas morning, when her then-boyfriend, now-separated-husband, had promised her that they'd spend the rest of their Christmases together. Even though the broken promise was now a bruise on her heart, she still put up the Christmas sock because it was good to remember. In the front yard, she placed an inflatable Santa patched up with some more duct tape and a snowman made out of stuffed white garbage bags because real snow was hard to find in Manteca. In the living room next to the late Grandma Susana's pink and yellow flower pattern couch, she placed a small Christmas tree she'd purchased on a whim at Josefina's.

Unlike her sister, Marisol Cana didn't begin decorating the basement for the holiday season until four days before the big twenty-five. Last Christmas, she had splurged on buying an expensive orange-and-clove scented candle and she brought it out now, placing it on the kitchen table with some ornaments as a makeshift table topper. Next to the TV and near the couch, she set up a Christmas tree that came with its own lights and wrapped a green tinsel garland around it strategically to make the branches look fuller. Although there was no door in the doorway leading into the living room area, she managed to hang their Frosty the Snowman door hanger beside the door using one of the stick-on wall hooks leftover from hanging the black-and-red curtain in June and Alegría's room; it had a bell dangling from it that Alegría liked to hit every time she walked through the doorway on her way to the kitchen and pretend that its ringing noise was that of wind chimes and that she was the whistling wind, formidable in its forces.

Three days before Christmas, Aunt Teresa called both Aunt Mary and Marisol to see if they wanted to join her for Christmas dinner. When they both declined, she didn't bother to invite them over for her New Year's or Three Kings' Day celebrations. Aunt Mary had decided to spend the holiday over at her old house by request of her husband, who said he had repented of all of his wrongdoings and missed her, and she, looking at the Christmas sock on the front door, agreed to go. So two days before the twenty-fifth, the pumpkin house was left empty of everybody except Alegría, her sister, her mother, and her father.

Around six p.m. on Christmas Eve, Marisol Cana took out the saucers Grandma Tracy, her mother-in-law, had given her for Christmas many winters ago and placed them on the mantled table. They were a simple white, with a golden rim that went around and around like time. The matching aspen cups were fragile and only to be taken out on special occasions like that day. She couldn't find the tamarind pods and *tejocotes* at an affordable enough price and so had resorted to making hot chocolate with mini marshmallows and candy canes to fill up the aspen cups instead of the traditional Christmas punch. Marisol knew that Alegría would miss the punch of past Christmases, but that she wouldn't remain disappointed for long. Alegría never stayed sad for long. June wouldn't be picky with the drink as long as the marshmallows were fat-free and the candy cane was sugar-free.

For dinner, she'd planned a simple red *pozole,* watered-down so that it would be enough to fill up all four hungry mouths. However, she'd underestimated the cooking time of the *pozole* and so it wasn't until about 7 p.m. that her husband and two daughters gathered around the table to eat dinner.

June made sure Alegría knew about the drool stain near her mouth, and critiqued her grossness for not washing her hands before dinner. Partly because she needed help and partly to stop all further confrontations between Alegría and June, Marisol Cana called her two daughters to help slice the radishes and wash the lettuce to put on top of the *pozole.* She did not call her husband resting in the living room with his feet up on the couch's armrests to help her with the salsa, though she needed help figuring out how much salt was too much. He had been touchy since ten days ago, when their attendance at the Flores's Christmas party had unexpectedly ended with Alegría's ruined white dress.

Since then, Daniel Cana's yelling was up forty-five percent from his normal yelling, and his mutterings were up by ten percent. But that Christmas, his wife wanted to keep all confrontations to a minimum. So she urged her daughters to be especially mindful of their father and to do everything he asked them faster than he could finish saying it. The Cana women were so successful in their endeavors that the father felt he could see a golden glow emanating from his mouth and imagined that their autumnal leaf-patterned table mantle was a glossy ruby red.

Normally, the only sounds heard during dinner were the clinking of forks on plates, the sipping and gulping of water, and the occasional small talk. On the days Daniel Cana was out delivering, even the simple small talk was absent. Nonetheless, during their first Christmas in the pumpkin house, happy, albeit strained, voices were heard coming from the Canas' mouths in the basement. The father asked his children to recall the blissful memories of past Christmases and to reflect on their gratitude for being blessed with such experiences. Alegría offered up that every Christmas was good. June shared a specific Christmas memory from two years before Alegría was born. Her parents had gotten her a pink play piano with a whole octave of tinny notes. Alegría wanted to know if she could play "Jingle Bells" on the piano and June told her that she didn't know, she was three and didn't know how to play piano and that it was all before Alegría was born so it didn't concern her anyway. Marisol Cana, upon the invitation from her husband, had sunk into the lake of childhood Christmas memories with her mother and two living sisters, though she peeked her head out of the memories long enough to give her eldest daughter her customary "look" and June's mouth obeyed and was silent. Daniel Cana, upon seeing his wife deep in contemplation, slurped up his soup, mindful not to make too much contact between the spoon and his open mouth.

After dinner, Alegría was impatient to get to sleep. She wanted to dream of sugar plums—whatever they were—like the poem she'd learned at school promised. She imagined they looked like regular plums, only they had sugar on the outside like sugared gummy bears, and that they tasted like sugar cane, cinnamon, apricot, and walnuts.

June wasn't ready to sleep, but their mother sent them off to bed anyway, with a strict warning that if they didn't fall asleep as soon as their heads touched the pillow, Santa Claus wouldn't come through their front door and walk down the stairs to the living room.

When the sisters got to their bedroom, they changed into their pajamas, brushed their teeth, and got ready for bed. When the toothpaste bottle accidentally touched her toothbrush and June didn't say anything, Alegría was relieved that her sister hadn't noticed her misdeed. But when she inadvertently sprayed a few droplets of water as she was cleaning her toothbrush and her sister didn't say anything, Alegría knew something was wrong. So she said the only thing that came to her mind at that instant. "That Paolo is a turkey."

June snorted. "And his brother is so ugly, he makes onions cry," she said with a small smile. And then despite the Flores

Christmas party, everything that had happened between them and everything that would happen between them, all was fine between them again. June thought how if only Alegría were born of a different mother, she would've been a nice sister to have.

When they got to bed, Alegría laid down upside down, making sure that no inch of her head would touch the pillow near her feet. Within seven minutes, she was asleep. But within an hour, she had woken up again. Calling her older sister's name and getting no response, she confirmed that she was the only one awake. Getting up off the spongy bed and opening the door with a groaning creak, Alegría peaked around the corner of the doorway hoping to catch a glimpse of Santa (of whom she'd made a special request), and making sure to avoid the loud bell sure to wake up anyone who heard it hanging from the felt snowman door hanger. What she saw surprised her.

After sending the kids to bed, Marisol began clearing the dishes from the table while her husband returned his feet to their rightful place by the couch armrest. Once the pot used for the *pozole* was scrubbed clean and the fall table mantle had been put away, she joined her husband in the living room. The lights on the Christmas tree cast a soft glow over Daniel Cana's face. His eyes stared at the blank, black screen of the TV; they were like pools of umber mud. Marisol had the feeling she was falling, sinking into memories that rose up around her and applied pressure like quicksand.

And then there was a lifeline. She felt the warmth of her husband's hand hover over hers before he took it. His fingers curled around her palm and he was pulling her up with the strength of the waxed string he used to bind books.

Daniel Cana couldn't remember why they had married or if they'd ever shared a passionate love between them. He could only think about what he wanted them to be, what he thought they could be if they fast-forwarded past the troubled present. As he led his wife in a dance, swaying from side to side and turning in place like two drunkards, he rested his cheek on her shoulder. He could sense her stiffness. Raising his head near her hair, he whispered a song from long ago, from the time before they'd been married and he still snuck out of his home to see her. "With my little donkey of the Savannah, I'm going to Bethlehem."

Marisol Cana stopped. Sixteen Christmases ago, when she was seventeen and Daniel was twenty-three, he'd come visit her at her home. She'd gotten into a fight with her mother and run outside to escape the suffocating smell of pineapple *empanadas* inside the house. Daniel had sung the Christmas carol *"El Burrito Sabanero"* made popular by the boy band, Los Chayotes, in both Manteca and Prudent. "If they see me, if they see me, I'm on my way to Bethlehem." He'd come wearing the head of a goat because he couldn't find that of a donkey to match the song at the only place that sold costumes in Prudent. That was back when he loved her.

Marisol smiled softly and hummed along.

Alegría gasped in delight, rushing through the doorway and bumping the door hanger bell on her way in. Her father never sang and it had been a long time since her mother had smiled. She hugged her parents near their legs, who were just as surprised as she was. "Tuki tuki tukituki, hurry up my little donkey, for we're about to arrive," she sang with her father. Her parents opened their arms up to include her in their circle of dancing. As the song ended, Alegría laughed at her happiness. Then, as abrupt as a hiccup, her body folded down on itself until she was on the floor. Daniel Cana thought she'd simply fallen down and helped his daughter up unto the couch. Marisol looked at her daughter with scrutiny. The way her daughter had fallen, she'd seen it before, but she couldn't remember where or when.

Hidden by the edge of the doorway, June looked on as Alegría's mother stroked her little sister's hair. She'd woken up to the sound of bells and checked behind the deck-of-cards curtain to find

Alegría missing. Hearing muffled sounds coming from the living room, she'd stolen a glance from behind the doorless doorway. Seeing the touching family scene ensuing without her, June looked down at the smiling snowman door hanger. It was ugly. She returned to her room and laid on her cousin's mattress without a word.

On Christmas morning, the sisters woke up to the smell of ginger tea and to the sight of small bundles under the Christmas tree. Everybody knew that the small bundles Santa Claus always brought contained underwear, clothes, socks, and miniature pocketbooks eerily similar to the ones Daniel Cana bound together. The girls would try on their new clothes over their pajamas and parade around the living room for their parents to see and say, "Wow, Santa outdid himself this year," with a smile on their face that reminded Alegría of suspicious fish lips. But that first Christmas in the pumpkin house, before tearing open any wrapping paper, Alegría had decided was the best Christmas ever, for Santa had already brought her the the gift that was most precious, seen in the freshly-brushed teeth of her sister's smile, heard in the deep song of her father's voice, and felt in the tender caresses of her mother's hand on her head as she asked her if she was alright.

However, had Santa not lived up to the jolly in his laugh and the benevolence in his beard, Alegría had prepared a back-up plan of Christmas cards to bring her family joy. She handed out the glittery, folded pieces of paper she'd decorated at school to her family while they ate a breakfast of sweet bread dipped in ginger tea. Sharing hugs with all of her family members, Alegría wished that she could stay in their safe embrace forever. After breakfast, the holiday was spent watching Christmas-themed dramas and a Powerpuff Girls holiday movie at the request of the youngest daughter.

Less than a week later, it was the evening of the last day of the year. The families in Manteca and Prudent spent the afternoon gathering in great, big block parties and cooking lamb meat in the pits they'd dug in the ground lined with red bricks. By then, most all people had ovens inside their homes, but cooking lamb using underground ovens was and has remained the most popular method of cooking because only then does the meat carry the deep-rooted taste of tradition favored by Anthony Delgado and those pioneers who had first settled the clove-colored land of Prudent.

Before her death, Grandma Susana would prepare a pot with a little water, vegetables, and herbs every New Year's Eve. Then she would take the seasoned meat marinated in a mixture of chilis, spices, and avocado leaves, and wrap it in green maguey leaves cleared of thorns. The wrapped meat was placed inside the pot, and then topped with the sheep's stomach, herbs, spices, and *chiles*. This pot was placed inside the dug pit, which had been heated with a wood fire for four hours, and topped with planks, metal sheets, or whatever was on hand. Grandma Susana made sure nothing was wasted, using the moist, tender meat to make *tacos* and *tacos enchilados*, for which *tortillas* had been fried in a *guajillo* sauce, and the broth infused with the soft flavor of the lamb found at the bottom of the pot to make *consomé*.

Because not one of her daughters had mastered the pit method of making *barbacoa*, though Aunt Teresa had come close, she felt the need to leave the other world and visit her granddaughter to teach her the family secrets that would be passed down long after Alegría had joined her in the other world. But the method of learning took so long, for the meat itself took eight hours to cook, that her granddaughter missed the rest of the New Year's Eve celebrations. When the children in Manteca and Prudent ate twelve grapes (or chocolate-covered raisins if no grapes were to be found) when the clock struck midnight to signify twelve months of prosperity and luck, Alegría was busy seasoning the lamb with lard, salt, and pepper. Not even the men in Manteca, who were eager to show off their bravado by shooting twelve bullets into the canvas of the Big Painter in the sky, could distract the young girl from the intricate wrapping of the lamb meat with the maguey leaves like a *tamale*.

It wasn't until a Sunday, six days later, that Alegría woke up to the goings-on of her family when Grandma Susana was summoned by the people from the other world; they were hungry and missed even her proselytizing. In the morning, she'd walked into the living room with her sister to find her and her sister's shoes by the couch. They were filled with the gifts from *Los Reyes Magos*.

The day before, Daniel and Marisol Cana had gone out to buy the toys and food necessary to celebrate Three Kings' Day and their youngest daughter's birthday. Because they'd waited until the last day, they'd had no choice but to leave their daughters to the care of Aunt Mary, who had come back from her stay at her old house with a kind of familiar sadness and resignation in her eyes. The 60 degrees Fahrenheit temperature was typical for January, which is the coldest and bluest month in Manteca, so it was no surprise to Daniel Cana when his wife had shivered and side-whispered to him as they were out shopping for toys, "I told you we should've gotten June the warmer sweater instead of the one with the buttons."

"The sweater with the buttons looks better. The other one looks cheap," he'd said.

"It's not about how she looks, it's about how warm she is," she'd whispered back.

Because the shopping had been done last-minute and because Daniel Cana wasn't willing to expand the budget for what he thought were useless, childish playthings, the only presents gotten for June were a pink, plastic, light-up watch, a gingerbread keychain, and a box of chocolates—none of which were things on her list to *Los Reyes Magos*. Alegría got much the same things, but with an additional stuffed monkey for her birthday collection.

On the afternoon of the sixth, the best part of the Three Kings' celebration according to Alegría occurred: the cutting of the *rosca de reyes*. Because it was her birthday, Alegría always got to choose first which part of the *rosca de reyes* was hers. She chose thoughtfully, for somewhere inside the crown-shaped bread, there were two white, plastic babies, and whoever found one in her slice would not have to make *tamales* for everybody the second of February like Manteca tradition required, but would rather get to make a wish, according to Cana family tradition. Unfortunately for Alegría, she chose wrong. The first baby wasn't found in the slice of sister or her father, but in that of her mother. Instead of making a wish, however, Marisol Cana gave the plastic baby to her daughter to use as a sort of birthday wish since there were no birthday candles to blow out. Seeing June's eyes twitch slightly with her mother's especially considerate gesture, Alegría pushed the baby back unto her mother's plate and told her she didn't want it. After staring at the little baby boy with his hands clasped in front of his chest blankly at a loss for all of fifty-five seconds, Marisol Cana put the plastic in her pocket and said she would save her wish for later.

After Alegría was done eating her slice of dried fruit-topped bread, she went to the living room to play with her new monkey. He was small, brown, with ears that stuck perpendicularly out of his head and glittery blue-rimmed eyes that caught the light. It had a simple smile and hands that rested on his four-toed plush feet. She named him Mateo and dubbed him the youngest member of Señor and Señorita Monkey's family. Alegría set the monkey down on the couch and went to go get the rest of his monkey siblings to play. As she came back to the living room with Bob, Joey, Jorge, Jimena, Matilda, and Mon-mon, she saw Mateo's eyes blink and then return to the blue-rimmed blankness he'd been born with. Putting down his siblings on the couch, Alegría picked up Mateo, wary that his glossy eyes hadn't really blinked. She brought her face closer to the monkey's and then she saw it again. Mateo blinked. She threw him back on the couch and scurried backwards.

Eating the leftover *rosca de reyes* in the kitchen, her father noticed her scampering and asked, "What's wrong? Is it a bug?"

"He blinked! He really blinked!" said Alegría.

The father asked who it had been that blinked and she asserted it was the monkey, Mateo. June poked her head through the living room doorway to clarify that it had not been the monkey and that Alegría was losing what few marbles she still had.

Just then, Alegría saw the sewn mouth of the smiling monkey move and heard his kazoo-like voice in her head, "Did you find *el cielo*?"

"There—he just did it again. He just talked." said the eight-year-old who no one believed. June scoffed and returned to her room. The father stood there, eating his bread and watching his daughter, and warned her that she should not make up stories.

Too focused on the monkey's mouth to care too much whether anyone believed her or not, Alegría continued to talk to the furry Mateo. She asked him what he meant and Mateo reiterated that he meant the sky. Alegría asked him what the sky was and the monkey said it was not a what, but a who. She asked him who the sky was and her most recent birthday present answered it wasn't his but hers who had already left.

Daniel stood there as they conversed and became concerned with the determined look in his youngest daughter's eyes; it was like she was actually conversing with someone but the only thing that answered her questions was the voiceless, static monkey. It wasn't right. It wasn't proper. The more she talked, the more uncomfortable he became. "That's it," he said, cutting off Alegría's fourth question to Mateo, "we're taking you to see Great-grandfather Francis."

10.

Great-grandfather Francis was the most honest witch-doctor in all of Manteca. He was a self-proclaimed *chaman*, an invoker of spirits, a seer of prophetic dreams, and a practitioner of cures for the mind, body, and soul. Using the knowledge of ancestors more ancient than Anthony Delgado, the powers of song and dance, and the assistance of herbs, eggs, and other natural products, Great-grandfather Francis was able to solve any unsolvable problem and answer any burning question—for the right price. Nobody knew his lineage, date of birth, nor the origin of his supernatural powers, yet his startling sharp memory and wit could put any doubters of his abilities to shame. Apart from his curative business and professional counsel, he had a curiosity about the other world and explored any mysterious phenomena for free. He also enjoyed a good cup of *atole* and three-minute packets of instant ramen, but never together.

When Marisol Cana had been younger, she and her three sisters had accompanied Grandma Susana on a visit to Great-grandfather Francis. People visited him for rain, for cheating husbands, for back problems and wisdom teeth pain. She'd never known why her mother had made the visit, but while she was waiting for her to exit the bathroom, the aged *chaman* had approached her and said closely, "don't dwindle in the waters of yesterday too long."

"I didn't." Marisol had taken a step back. Who was this old thyme-smelling man to scold her for something she hadn't done only a few minutes after he'd met her? He had disturbed her the same way Alegría and Mateo had disturbed her husband. For that reason, when Daniel had suggested they take Alegría to see Great-grandfather Francis, of whom he'd only heard rumors before, Marisol had said no. With that power of hers, she'd silenced any rebuttals and encased Alegría's interaction with Mateo in a box entitled "imaginary friends."

It took a whole month and a half for Marisol to agree to a visit with the old *chaman*.

Alegría's weight gain, suspected Daniel, was the main instigator to her agreement. The long nights spent with Grandma Susana cooking and eating their creations had caused a sudden weight gain in Alegría. Seventeen pounds later, June was tormenting her sister about the roundness in her cheeks and the squishiness of her belly. Apart from the incurred cost of buying clothes a size bigger, the low cost of a $2.50 *chaman* cleansing compared to a $250 doctor's visit won Marisol over.

Because Daniel was sure to get lost, she agreed to go with him to Alegría's visit. June was left in the care of Aunt Mary.

Daniel Cana drove to the northern part of Manteca, where Marisol assured him Great-grandfather Francis lived. Passing Josefina's grocery store, Alegría was reminded of why she was being taken to see the mysterious Great-grandfather Francis. If she did not stop falling asleep in school, talking to Mateo, and otherwise "losing her marbles," her mother would return to the shell of a stranger she'd seen during the trip out of the school office and into the store. Looking out the window, she saw the roofs of the houses become flatter and the cold vacancy of the sky become clearer. No white splotch of cloud appeared in that canvas to calm the anticipation building in her stomach like a monster.

In those days, the northern part of Manteca hadn't yet been remodeled to match the other parts. The streets still twisted and twined into a convoluted mess of dead-ends and cul-de-sacs that resembled Alegría's angry intestines more than anything else. As Daniel navigated the winding road to the great charlatan's house, he questioned Marisol's sense of direction. She, in turn, rebuked his authority on roads in Manteca as a Prudent native who hadn't grown up there like she had.

Thirty-five minutes later, they parked their sedan at the edge of a crescent array of squarish concrete houses. "There," pointed Marisol to the two-story house in the middle. Like the other houses in the area, its mint-green paint job was flaked and fading. Getting out of the car, the three Canas walked up to the big, powdery white steel gate that protected the house. Loose pieces of gravel crunched under their feet. Standing next to a baby-blue trash bin, Daniel Cana shook the rusty gate open. His wife stopped his impatient hand and told him it was part of the ritual to wait. "Adds to the mystery," she said. He looked at her from the corner of his eye skeptically and crossed his arms.

Once Alegría felt her bowels were going to burst from the wait, a white-clothed man came out the front door and walked to the gate. "I see you're back," he said to Alegría as he lifted the latch. He talked with his upper lip meeting his bottom lip so it looked like he had perennially pursed lips. His cheeks were sunken, his skin weathered, but under bushy eyebrows, his eyes were clear and bright. He smelled strongly of rosemary. "The bathroom's just inside, to the left." Entering the home, the indistinguishable earthy smell of a thousand herbs and spices hit them. The fuzzy light appeared magenta and orange through the thick fog of the muddled odor. While Alegría ran to the toilet, Great-grandfather Francis seated her parents on hard wooden chairs around a table. The room was decorated with two cuckoo clocks, a 1984 poster of *Ghostbusters*, three spray bottles, and figurines of turtles, bears, frogs, and bats. Daniel Cana noted the table mantle was a woven pink yarn. "Sorry to make you wait." Francis scraped the cement floor as he sat down at the table. "Adds to the mystery." The down-turned corners of his lips were mischievous. Marisol looked at her husband with raised eyebrows but said nothing.

When Alegría came back, the *chaman* got straight to business.

Scrunching up his eyes and scratching at his close-cropped, receding hair, he asked the family what the problem was. Marisol started with Alegría's insomnia and Daniel ended at her conversation with the inanimate monkey. Great-grandfather Francis began tuning a *guitarron* he'd picked up. He asked Alegría to tell her version of the events. Immediately, she began talking about Grandma Susana and *piñata*s and the sky. Nodding as she finished, he struck the second A string, pushed in the corresponding peg, and delivered his verdict: "she needs a cleaning and a bottle of my waking concoction."

The cleansing was done by taking Alegría to a small room upstairs and laying her on a cot. The *chaman* whacked her with a bush from head to toe to get rid of any evil spirits lurking around her, then whacked her five more times for good measure. From a basket in the back of the room, he procured a black chicken. Lifting the clucking chicken, a single black egg was produced. The egg was rubbed all over the young girl's body and then cracked into a clear bowl by the foot of the cot. If black blood came out, then the imbalances in the girl's spirit had been removed. If a yolk was produced, then a far deeper form of cleaning was needed. A viscous, black liquid came out, spotted with the transparent white of a normal egg. Great-grandfather Francis grunted. Sending Alegría back downstairs to meet her parents, he skipped the hocus pocus and moved into the kitchen to prepare his waking concoction. Boiling dark maca, oregano, guarana, and beetroot, he made a brown liquid and packaged it into seven individual vials.

Downstairs, he handed the vials to Alegría's mother and instructed her to give her daughter one every morning after waking up. "And what did I say about dwindling?" The *chaman* gave her the look of a parent speaking to a child in the wrong.

Outside of his house, he spoke with Alegría again about her dreams in the night. A slight wind whistled through the flat houses around them, picking up loose gravel and clove-colored dirt. "So: you see dead people, eh?" he asked with a playful glint

in his faded eyes. "People call that a gift, where I come from."
Alegría didn't know whether it was a gift or not, but her adventures in the night were making her rainbow sweater too tight, her mother unhappy, her sister disgusted, and her father spooked. After sending the family off, Great-grandfather Francis stared at their sedan as it drove away into the looping streets under a darkening sky. He wondered what would become of them and knew that their first visit would not be their last.

It so happened that at the precise moment Great-grandfather Francis was telling Alegría to beware of talking with spirits from the other world too much, the whistling wind passed through his open house door and came out burdened with whispers of information. It traveled past the flat cement houses, the ancient street of shops, and into the parking lot of the grocery store. Josefina, who was taking out the trash three streets away, ears, sharp and pointy as a bat's beard, heard Great-grandfather Francis's words carried on the air. The words surprised her so much she dropped the trash bag on the edge of the dumpster and it split open, sending peels of bananas and plastic wrappers flying every which direction.

Josefina was the owner of the grocery shop in Western Manteca and the biggest gossip around, knowing everything about everyone and more than willing to spread her knowledge, *santo y seña*. She was a firm believer in the fantastical and visited Francis the *chaman* regularly. The only reason Francis could support his *atole* and ramen addiction solely on his earnings as a *chaman* was because her big mouth had blabbed wonders about his perceptibility of the other world. Her lips were so thick and resembled the horn of a trumpet so considerably, people called her *La Trompuda*. She carried two essentials on her person at all times: a water bottle on a chain and a 1.75 oz tub of Vaseline. The tub of Vaseline was for her ever-dry lips, which chapped and cracked whenever she got into a juicy story about the sly librarian and the unfaithful museum attendant near the street of shops. The water bottle was for her dry mouth, for she opened her mouth so wide so often, it was like a cotton ball had sucked up all the moisture inside. Her saliva congealed and became sticky, like her gossip.

Upon entering her shop, she washed her hands, tucking her water bottle inside her green attendant's vest to avoid getting it wet. Alegría, she remembered, was the daughter of Marisol Cana. That woman often shopped at her store, tense as a stick. She would turn a mighty cheek to anything Josefina said and ignore her knowing smiles. Proud Marisol was the black sheep in Grandma Susana's family. When the good woman had died, she had left a quiet hole in the community. Nobody could believe that the laughing, proud grandmother of thirteen grandkids could have gone out of the world as easily as she'd entered it. Shifting the piece of news about her granddaughter around her mouth, savoring it like bubblegum, her spit congested into a mucus-like consistency. She spit into the pot she kept by the sink for exactly that purpose.

She saw Miss Turtle come to the front of the store to check out a bag of spinach and a carton of almond milk. Josefina smiled, manning the check-out counter her most faithful employee had abandoned for a bowling tournament. Miss Turtle was always receptive to any news she could get her hands on.

"Did you hear?" Those words alerted Miss Turtle's flower-pierced ears to the beginning of a provoking rumor, and she lowered the prewashed packaged spinach she'd been about to hand Josefina to lean in closer. "You know Marisol, the one who got engaged to a weak Prudento and then eloped without telling anybody? She took her youngest daughter to go see the old *chaman*, Francis. Apparently the daughter has a weight problem—probably got it from her glutton of a father—and during the cleaning, he discovered that she's got the gift." Miss Turtle leaned closer to Josefina, until she could see the thick saliva stretching stickily like a spider web inside her mouth. "The gift of seeing the dead. Poor girl, I hear she's being haunted by her grandmother, Susana, may her soul and witch-donkey laugh rest in peace."

After such a shocking revelation, Miss Turtle felt it was only natural that she validate Josefina's rumor with what she'd seen of the girl in her class. As her spinach was scanned, she talked about Alegría's lazy lack of respect, probably gotten from her Prudento father, and her strange solitary nature, which could only be procured from her serious mother. They both concluded that the girl had brought her accursed gift upon herself, though she'd been predestined to do so by having two parents who were useless.

As Miss Turtle left the store with her spinach, neither woman noticed the small bit of mucus from Josefina's mouth that had landed on her shoulder. Taking a small detour to the first and most famous library in Manteca to return a book, she casually rubbed her shoulder against the golden oak doors as she exited.

When Jacob Ramos visited the library later that evening to check out a pulpy historical romance, his forearm accidentally touched the mucus left behind on the library doors.

Immediately, he became aware of Alegría's gift of seeing the dead. Surprised at the sudden revelation, he jumped in his car to go visit Aunt Teresa and find out what she knew that he didn't. On his way through the elite circular streets of southern Manteca, he stopped at an intersection as mandated by the law. A soft, pollen-laden breeze blew in through his open window, causing his nose to itch. He sneezed into his forearm like any sanitary citizen, and the force of his sneeze caused the mucus on his arm to travel through his open window and land on Hector Flores's cheek as he was heading home from a friend's house by the intersection. Struck with the knowledge of his crush's little's sister's gift, he hurried home to tell his parents his discovery. When Jonas Flores greeted his son with a bear hug, he knew his son's news before he even opened his mouth.

Aunt Teresa's understanding of Alegría's situation ensured that all descendants of Great-grandmother Lolita and Great-grandfather Lewis understood equally well. Coupled with the spread from Jonas Flores's chest and other infected areas, all of Manteca and some parts of Prudent became aware of Alegría's gift of seeing the dead, which had been transmitted like a plague. And so it was that at eight years old, her reputation in the two towns grew, which would one day rock their foundations when the waters came.

11.

Since the morning of the 25th, the day after her visit to Great-grandfather Francis, Alegría'd had the feeling she was being watched. It was a particularly warm day for Manteca in February. The Big Painter in the Sky had dropped a bucket of butter-scotch-yellow on his canvas and a slightly salty wind came from the south of Prudent. At precisely 6:57, Marisol woke her youngest daughter from a restless night of empty dreams. She unstoppered the vial of Great-grandfather Francis's waking concoction and the rancid smell that escaped was enough to make them both gag. Covering her nose, she handed it to her daughter to drink. The murky liquid looked and tasted bitter like dirty dishwater. Because the *chaman* had forgotten to drain the concoction, Alegría could feel the mushy pieces of half-dissolved beetroot sliding slowly down her throat. She thought it worse than Aunt Mary's macaroni casserole and Grandma Tracy's three-day-old lentils combined.

"I know it tastes bad, but it's made to make you feel better," said Marisol, "and it'll help you lose weight."

The *chaman's* waking concoction did not loosen the fit of her rainbow-striped jacket nor produce any magical change in Alegría. It did, however, wrench her so roughly from her sleep that a booming weight formed near her temples. It kept rhythm with her heartbeat and made her irritable. The weight drowned out any cravings she'd had for breakfast and her mother had enough pity to allow her mushy bowl of cereal to remain untouched before driving her to school.

Walking to her classroom, Alegría felt like a horse, like someone had put reins over her head and was yanking her up, forcing her to stay awake. The chatter she'd heard outside her classroom door died as soon as she entered the room. Time seemed to stop as Alegría walked to her desk by the window. The heads of students followed her movements like those of owls. She sat down next to Bo, who stole a glance at her before putting his head down. Slowly the world resumed spinning and the noise of the students began anew and grew louder. Though she kept her eyes glued to her scratched desk, she could hear the whispers of the students around her and feel the burden of their stares on her back.

The loudest whispers came from Paolo near the front of the class. "At the party—yes, yes, she didn't move—her dead grandmother—she's weird," he said loudly and authoritatively enough for anyone to hear above the chatter of the class. Alegría wished she had the heat vision of the Powerpuff Girls' leader, Blossom, to burn a hole through Paolo's pants so that he'd stop talking about her already. It was bad enough that when he spread rumors about her, he couldn't whisper properly and confused "weed" for "weird," but now he'd somehow involved her grandmother in his rumors. She stood up to teach him a lesson when she smelled Miss Turtle's cupcake perfume from across the room. Miss Turtle eyed Alegría with new interest and suspicion, which made her sit down and resolve to teach Paolo a lesson some other time.

With the artificial alertness of the waking concoction, Alegría managed to stay awake for the entire class. She kept feeling like people were looking at her but when she turned around to see who, all eyes were on the board where Miss Turtle was teaching new vocabulary. She turned around so many times that the teacher told her to keep her eyes glued to the front. Paolo snickered and she colored. But the watchfulness was always there.

The next two days at school were the same. The drum in her

head weighed down the rest of her body, the relative lightness made her steps seem like they were floating. When she entered and exited the pumpkin house, when she opened and closed the back doors of her elementary school, the feeling of being watched persisted. The mysterious pair of eyes appeared from all directions, but she was never able to catch the culprits.

On Thursday, Alegría, June, and their mother went shopping at Josefina's. Marisol had become worried that Alegría was losing weight too quickly, for she barely touched her food anymore. Any bites she was forced to take would make her gag. So her mother had decided to make the trip to the store to find the ingredients needed to cook Alegría's favorite recipes.

The pairs of eyes followed Alegría through the store. She entered with her mother pushing the shopping cart and with her sister glued to her phone. Any people they passed between the aisles of canned pineapple and tubs of cornstarch talked in low voices and pointed discretely to the three Cana women. Their whispers slipped out of their mouths like smoke and settled on the polymer floor. The thick fog of whispers was dense enough that four-foot-tall Alegría had a hard time seeing her feet when she walked. The hissing of the fog confused her, so that the watchful eyes seemed to come from everywhere at once, from behind the packages of anise seeds and sticks of cinnamon.

As they turned the corner into the toiletries section, Alegría turned her head abruptly to catch the perpetrator in the act. All she did was walk into a shelf rack stacked with toilet paper. Packaged rolls came tumbling down with her while Marisol and June kept walking into the fog, leaving her behind. Picking herself up and feeling for the white rolls in the obscuring fog, Alegría could see her mother and sister getting farther up ahead. From the blanketing mist, a pale brown hand emerged and tapped her on the shoulder. Alegría jumped up from the floor and spun around to face the pair of watchful eyes. They were the color of peanut butter and scrunched up so they appeared wider around the edges. The eyes belonged to a hunched older man wearing a thin orange-and-beige striped sweater. He was smiling, but the red rims of his eyes were a warning.

"You're her, aren't you? Susana's granddaughter?" he asked, his eyes growing bigger. Alegría stared back at him. She nodded her head yes but chose to remain silent. The lead in her head thudded against her skull.

He slapped his knee and wheezed out a laugh. His breath was musty. "I knew it! You can see the dead, can't you? You've been seeing your grandmother for a while, haven't you?" His watery eyes glittered in expectation. His questions reminded her that Grandma Susana hadn't visited since she'd started taking daily doses of Great-grandfather Francis's waking concoction. She didn't know if her grandmother was angry at her for telling the *chaman* about their nightly cooking lessons.

Alegría looked past the man to where her sister and mother had gone. She saw their heads above the fog as they went into an unknown aisle. She made to follow them but another woman barred the way. It was the sly librarian who joined the striped-shirt man with her shopping cart.

Her eyes were watchful, too. The thumping in Alegría's head grew louder.

"She has, heard it from Turtle herself. But that's got that nothing to do with you, George, has it?" She looked him up and down and pursed her lips. "Anyways, I was wondering if the little lady here can see people other than her grandmother." Before Alegría could reply, more shoppers from the grocery store crowded around Alegría. They were all watchers. Her head drummed faster. They asked her if she could tell them whether their dog was happy in heaven and whether a late cousin twice-removed had any messages for them and whether she could prophesy their date of death.

The different adults crowded around Alegría, pelting her with questions and making the fog on the floor rise up until Alegría couldn't see the store ceiling above her any more. Every thud in her head was another footstep her sister and mother took, getting farther away, until they'd be lost in the fog and she wouldn't be able to reach them.

While curious shoppers were asking Alegría about her "gift," Marisol was walking down the hair care aisle comparing shampoo prices. Unaware of her lost daughter, she fretted over two different types of shampoo: the purple one for the thin hair she and Alegría had and the gray one for the thick hair her husband and June had. Scanning the prices for a more affordable alternative, she found the Easy brand of gold shampoo her husband had bought her when they were first married. Such an expensive shampoo seemed a luxury now. In her youth, she'd never had to beware high prices. That had all changed when she'd met Daniel.

She had first seen him at the Manteca library. She was 17 and interested in the simplicity of numbers, gone to the library to find a book about arithmetic, what Mary called an abomination on earth. It was the biggest library in all of Manteca and Prudent, with heavy oak doors that hid shelves upon shelves of multicolored books and rows of poplar wood tables. That day, she'd fought with her mother and had wanted to lose herself in the maze of multiplication and division. Elbows rested on the yellow poplar wood table, mind all in a whirl, she snapped her head up to meet the stare of a curly-haired boy sitting two rows in front of her. Unlike the boys in her high school, the curly-haired looker, who couldn't have been older than 23, wasn't intimidated by being caught in the act. He just kept staring blindly at her. She turned her head away, her face grown hot under his unnerving blatancy. She pushed her hair forward, hoping to hide her face from his stare. Peeking behind her curtain of hair, she saw that the boy had finally returned to his book. But now she couldn't focus on her book's numbers anymore. She kept peeking up at him to check if he had returned to staring but he hadn't. Then she grew indignant. What right did that boy have to stare at her and distract her from her polynomials. She was angry with the boy, with her mother, with herself. Finally, she slammed her book shut and left the library after a mere thirty minutes of reading.

What Daniel Cana had never told her about that day was that he'd been staring at her only because she'd had makeup on one eye and not the other. The left eye seemed bigger, marked by black eyeliner, while the right eye disappeared into her brown face. He kept looking at her because he couldn't figure out that she reminded him of Popeye.

The first time they'd formally met was at the park for a Los Chayotes concert. Although Marisol did not usually like popular artists, Los Chayotes had stolen her heart, especially the lead guitar player with straight black hair. Her mother, Susana, had suggested that the three sisters attend the concert in the park together, but Marisol immediately rejected the idea. She wouldn't go at all if her sisters went along with her. The night of the concert, she'd snuck out the back door and decided to walk to the park. However without a car, she'd underestimated how long it would take to travel the distance from the pumpkin house to the park. Thus she'd arrived an hour late to the concert. Daniel Cana, who had traveled from Prudent to listen to Los Chayotes live, had got lost down one of the dead-ends of Manteca's roads. When he arrived at the park, there were wrappers and posters on the grass, leftovers from the concert ended an hour ago. He'd seen a girl sitting down on the steps of the pavilion. It was the same girl from the library, only both of her eyes looked the same now, black streaks coming down from them. The girl was crying. He walked over to her and introduced himself as Daniel Cana, the future king of bookbinding. Unlike other girls who laughed and walked away from him, Marisol stayed for his self introduction. She did so out of curiosity. No other boys had ever made it past her intense glares. He never mentioned that he was from Prudent, only that he didn't live around the park or library, and she didn't think to ask. They'd spent the rest of the night talking, watching the stars over the Mipared River, and one way or another, fallen in love, or something similar to that.

They dated all through Marisol's last year in high school,

always keeping their outings hidden from Marisol's family. When she graduated high school, she didn't know what to do with her life. She hadn't thought as far as the future. Daniel Cana, who was 24 then, had a plan for Marisol: to marry him. Because he said he loved her and because it would allow her to leave the family she hated, she agreed. She called her eldest sister, Teresa, to tell her the news of the engagement and plans for the wedding.

"When did you think about telling us? When you were pregnant with seven kids in Prudent?" she said through the line on the phone. Teresa was furious at her and at the type of hurt she was knowingly causing their mother. Marisol clicked off the call.

The wedding planned for the 15th of May never happened. Daniel Cana told Marisol he couldn't wait three more months to be married. He loved her too much and wanted the ceremony to be already past so they could all move on with their lives. He suggested they elope. The truth of the matter was that Daniel didn't have the resources saved up to pay for the wedding. Marisol let herself be led by him because by then, she had already committed herself to their life together and besides, she didn't have any plans for her future. So the day after her elopement with Daniel Cana, she called her mother to tell her the news. She was the only person she told.

"I'm married to Daniel already. We eloped." She made her voice harsh, daring her mother to say anything against their nontraditional union. The line was quiet for an eternity. Static filled the silence. She heard her mother heavily inhale.

"When will you come visit? I can prepare dinner for your husband, if you'd like." Marisol could hear the forced smile on her mother's face. She knew that her mother didn't approve, only pretended she did out of gratifying self-sacrifice. Her mother was a fake.

Marisol said she didn't know when they'd have the time. Daniel and she were both very busy with newlywed life and he was calling her right now to hang up. She gained a sort of sadistic pleasure in ending the conversation between herself and her mother, in knowing she could silence Susana with her words.

What Marisol didn't know as she hung up the phone was that Susana had been prepping to make pineapple *empanadas* that afternoon. After the phone call, she had quietly and methodically put the sugar back in the pantry and the shortening back in the fridge. She'd closed the blinds and sat on her pink and yellow flower-patterned couch. She hadn't baked again for five months. Susana never fully exhaled the heavy breath she'd taken.

Life with Daniel had been happy at first. He didn't own a house so they lived with his parents the first few weeks of their married life. Tracy and Facundo Cana were willing to accept Marisol as their daughter-in-law as long as they remained in Prudent. They helped their son rent a small house near theirs and move in with their new daughter-in-law.

Daniel entered the house on Pinnacle Street with his hands on his hips. He could see it for what it could be. He didn't have a job yet but planned to set up his own bookbinding workshop downstairs. He would usher in a new era of traditional bookbinding. Marisol and he would retire on the white leather couch in the living room. They'd be surrounded by their children and their children's children forever in bliss and comfort, living off his success as a bookbinder.

But before he could start his business, he had to save enough money to pay the monthly rent. He took a job at a bookbinding company that produced cheap paperbacks by the thousands. The owner didn't particularly like him, but hired him at the request of Tracy and Facundo Cana.

Their first month of living on Pinnacle Street, Daniel and Marisol had ten times gone shopping for new furniture. They couldn't agree on a couch. Marisol didn't have the cultured taste of her husband. She sought out the most raggedy-looking couches with the highest price tags they could afford, which wasn't much. He looked for the couches that would last into their future.

Oftentimes, Daniel would go shopping after work for some little trinket, some imported chocolates or shimmering necklaces that would show his love for Marisol. At first, she appreciated the gifts and felt comforted in his efforts. That ended when she received mail saying they were behind on their rent payments. Then she understood that Daniel had been lying to her. He'd acted like he had everything under control and splurged on what they didn't need at the moment. She'd been deceived by his gilded visions of splendor and had followed him blindly into marriage. The expensive gifts he'd brought home turned into reminders that she'd left the pumpkin house with only a high school degree. They were reminders that she'd purposefully distanced herself from her family and that she didn't have anyone but Daniel, who—when he told her to match her outfits and pin her thin brown hair a certain way—she became more and more convinced loved her for her potential more than for herself.

And then June had come along. She didn't want the baby girl she'd brought into the world stained by her mistakes. Ignoring her promise to the sister she'd drowned, Marisol named June after the month she was born in, when the tulip poplar trees blossomed with the promise of something new, of a blank-slate mother-daughter relationship. She was a good mother to June, affectionate and attentive, until she'd gotten a call from Teresa. Their mother, Susana, healthy and strong as a kangaroo, wasn't doing well. And then Marisol was plunged into the waters of remembering. Memories surged around her, seeping through her clothes and into the cracks of her skin. They wouldn't let go of her. The old guilt came back. The dormant blood of her younger sister, Alegría, cried out to her and screamed out falsity and broken promises.

In an attempt to muffle the howls and shrieks that she heard in her waking dreams, she'd had another child. Once it was in front of her, she named her Alegría and smiled knowing she could rest easy. She had done what she'd promised and her conscience was clean again.

But the child was special. Though her thin brown hair was her own and her slim shoulders were her father's, Marisol could see in Alegría's big saucer eyes that it was her sister come back to haunt her, to make her remember what she'd done. Marisol gave Alegría special preference over her husband and eldest daughter. She treated her like she'd never treated the younger sister she'd had. They went on walks, just the two of them, and she sang her songs and stroked her hair and read her bedtime stories. When she called her name, she was calling the name of the sister she'd led into the water a lifetime ago.

As Alegría grew older, Marisol sunk deeper into the river of her past. Everywhere she looked, she saw reminders of her childhood and regret paved her path. However, there was something about Alegría that kept her anchored to the present. She'd be regretting what she'd said to her mother of yesterday while she cleaned the shower stalls. Then Alegría would come in and ask her an endless string of questions about the necessity of showering that forced her back to the now of lemon-scented cleaning detergent and hard acrylic bathroom tiles. She would reach out her hand and remind Marisol redemption was possible.

When her youngest daughter turned four, Marisol did what she hadn't done since her marriage with Daniel: she attended the yearly family party at her mother's orange house. It was there that she offered Susana her youngest daughter as a sort of compensation for what she'd done. She hoped Alegría's cheery nature would help her mother recover and make up for the daughter she'd taken away from her.

Susana had seemed accepting of Alegría, as if she'd been her own daughter, which is why Marisol was surprised when she'd received the phone call from Teresa announcing her death. If her mother couldn't be saved by Alegría, then what hope was left for she who had done so much wrong? Now that Alegría was having trouble sleeping, eating, and separating the real from the make-believe, she couldn't help her mother find her way back anymore. Her cheery little Alegría had abandoned her for the strange, pudgy girl who conversed with her toy monkeys and fell asleep at school. Alegría of the past was gone.

Marisol looked all around the hair care aisle. Shampoos, conditioners, hair brushes and irons. Her youngest daughter was nowhere to be seen. Absorbed in her reminiscing, Marisol had let go of her anchor.

"Where's your sister?" She asked, retracing her steps to the entry of the store's toiletries section.

June looked up from her phone. "Don't ask me, I'm not her mother." She shrugged nonchalantly and stuck out her bottom lip. Marisol ignored her and continued walking forward, the the metallic ringing of the shopping cart's wheels accompanying her brisk walk. She squinted to see through the fog, which had filled up the whole store like a sauna. Finally she saw the biggest source of fog by the shelves of toilet paper. A crowd was gathered there, the different shopping carts arranged outside the circle of people like a fort.

"Alegría? Alegría!" she called out.

The crowd turned to look at Marisol. Most people she recognized as neighbors and residents in Manteca. They grumbled and dispersed a little to allow a bewildered Alegría through.

"Mom!" She ran to give her mother a hug. "You found me." Her smile stretched from cheek to cheek and made her eyes into moon crescents. June edged further to the back, hiding behind a cloud of smoke.

"I found you," she said.

12.

June was neither a Mantecana nor a Prudenta. Before Alegría was born, she was talkative as Josefina and candid as Aunt Mary. She would tell anyone stories, long tales about why the sun was round like an orange and about why the dirt dried hard into rocks and crumbled like gravel. When Aunt Teresa was first introduced to June, she could not believe that she was her quiet sister's daughter, for she thought, "Surely, the apple has fallen far from their family tree." If there was one personality trait that she inherited from her parents, it was her self-consciousness from her father.

The weeks after the hairless Alegría was brought home, June noticed that her mother didn't look at her the same way. Even frankly approaching her mother with the truth of her change didn't result in anything more than a tired "I'm an adult so I understand some things you don't. When you grow older, then you'll know. Go play with your piano." What her haunted mother forgot under the layers of dark circles was that it'd been a year since her pink toy piano had broken, and any pleas to fix it had been pushed aside by her parents amid crib construction and diaper storage. The older June got, the less she felt loved by her parents. The more she understood, the less she spoke with her mouth and the more she wrote with her pen.

At school, she felt still more isolated. When the history lessons in her Prudent Studies class blamed Mantecanos for being greedy and selfish, June hated her mother all the more. Her mother was the reason her classmates had missed out on the fluffy scored bread and the reason why there was an abomination of nature at the border of the two towns. Though her classmates didn't directly blame her, she still felt like she had to turn her shoulders inward so no one would detect the half of her that made her shoulders wider than the other girls.

At 11 years old, her body had started to undergo changes. The skin on her face grew angry red, her sweat turned sharp, and her hair grew faster in secret places it had not grown before. At this crucial age, a despicable boy, whose name is not important enough to be mentioned, told her that guys only like skinny girls with big bosoms and tiny waists, and that she was not pretty enough to be liked. After that, she started counting her calories and sucking in her cheeks and waist when she looked in the mirror. June wanted to become what others deemed attractive, what her parents saw as a good child. She wanted her body to change into what it had been, back when she was carefree and happy. She wanted to go back to before Alegría's questions drowned out her answers, her stories. She wanted to go back to being loved.

Moving to Manteca, she didn't feel like she was leaving much behind. The few people she talked to at school would probably forget her. They would move on with their lives. The polite words they'd exchanged would be lost in the wind. The few ingenuine laughs they'd shared would be buried in the dirt.

At her new school, she kept her head down and did her homework. This was precisely what interested Hector. June didn't laugh like other people. She was like the quiet girls on television, who had a lot to say but no one to hear them. When a popular, smart, handsome guy like himself talked to her, he was sure she would come out of her shy shell and become the cute, cheery girl who'd fixedly worship him like in the movies. June was a damsel in distress, and she needed to be saved by him.

He approached her, with his thick eyebrows and heart-shaped lips, to entrap her with his words and get out of her what he wanted. June was a challenge. She defied him with her silence. He tried other methods to make her talk and say what he wanted her to say. When he'd invited her to his family's Christmas party, she'd said she needed to ask her father first. He convinced his father to invite her entire family to the party so she'd have more reason to go. His plan had worked and she'd attended the party and even danced with him, until his little brother ruined everything by getting into a fight with her little sister.

It was after the party that he'd found out June's father was from Prudent. But the girl he made a point to sit by during lunch wasn't a thief or dishonest like other Prudentos. She was separate from them. From the way she quietly worked on her homework and paid attention to the writing teacher, he could tell she wasn't a lazy opportunist like them. He was not wrong about Prudentos in general—they'd proven him on more than one occasion. She was just the exception. To get on her good side, he'd formed a plan. Getting together with his friends one afternoon, they'd discussed forming the type of club that would impress her. He knew she liked writing. And homework. And the color green. Quick as a light bulb, it'd come to him. They'd start a writing club about peace, because it was green, and math, because it was homework. They'd call it the PM Club and meet every Friday after school. Only Mantecanos would join, except for June, of course, not because they discriminated—Hector and his friends didn't discriminate—but because the travel distance for Prudentos was too large. If there was a middle-school Prudento who could travel inconspicuously across the river to join their club, he would naturally be welcome.

On the last day of February, Hector and his friends approached June sitting at a lunch table with a clear plan of action. He sat on the table, flanked by the new members of the PM Club. After a few words of the menial small talk, he went in for the kill.

"So did you hear about what happened in Prudent?" He looked her intensely in the eyes until June felt like she had no choice but to maintain eye contact. She shook her head. Though she was curious about what had happened where she used to live, she was also cautious about anything that came out of Hector's mouth.

"I heard this Mantecano was trying to buy *churros* from this bicycle vendor in Prudent. But the guy refused to sell him any. Totally unfair, right? And then the guy started beating the Mantecano up. The police had to come and the Prudento got thrown in jail." Though he looked only at June, he spoke loudly and waved his arms around so it was clear that his friends were his audience.

Then June got up to throw her lunch away and said, "It depends."

"What?" Hector blinked. June didn't usually interrupt him. She usually listened and agreed.

"Whether it's unfair. It depends."

"Oh, right." His friends stiffened around him. People didn't turn on his questions. They answered them with blind agreement. He cleared his throat. "Anyway, we were saying how he got thrown in jail. My parents thought we should join some after school activities, to get off the streets, away from crazies like that guy, you know? Not that crazies like that exist in Manteca but…"

Slightly louder, June said, "I don't think he's a crazy." She forgot that his eye contact was intense. "If he had a reason." Hector again cleared his tightening throat. He didn't know that she'd felt guilty in Prudent for greedily keeping the scored bread away from Prudentos. Now that she was in Manteca, she saw that Prudentos were called lazy for no other reason than spending their money on scored bread, for naturally spreading across Manteca trying to make money.

And then remembering that June was half a Prudenta, he continued. "I mean, it might have to do with the thing—between Mantecanos and Prudentos, I mean. The guy probably had a thing against Mantecanos, don't you think? Or do you think the guy was right to beat the Mantecano's face up just cause he asked for a *churro*?" June wondered what the Mantecano had said to make the Prudento reject making a profit, but looking at Hector's expectant face, and that of his surrounding friends, she nodded her head yes.

He took this as a sign that she was back to agreeing with him. His throat loosened. "Right. So the guy was biased. Anyway, me and my friends are thinking of starting a club. To get us off the streets, you know? It's a writing club. You like writing, don't you? You said you did.

"We're having a meeting tomorrow, want to come?" June could feel the slow coil of his words around her, tightening ever so slowly. "You don't have to if you don't want to, I mean, I already told the guys you were coming. But you don't have to." His lips pouted and he ruffled his hair nervously. His words constricted her until she couldn't move. There was no way out. He'd already told his friends. If she didn't go, she'd have to come up with some excuse for not going. The surrounding faces were waiting.

"Okay," she said.

The next day at the club meeting, June had been bored out of her mind. Even being babysat by Aunt Mary with Alegría was preferable to sitting down on the cold grass of the middle school field, being pestered by Hector's nosy questions. Someone had brought a piece of paper with a pencil, a green peace sign, a black addition sign, and the letters "PM" drawn on it. That was where any semblance of a club ended. None of the youths talked about writing. They just played on the field and gossiped. She wished she hadn't agreed to come.

When the club meeting ended, June's mother wasn't there, though June had specifically asked her to come thirty minutes past three. Hector asked his father to drive June home. Instead of waiting for her mother to show up, she agreed. The ride to the pumpkin house was unnaturally loud, with Jonas and Hector Flores filling up the space with strangely enthusiastic small talk. They discussed the weather, the things they wanted to buy, the day at school, even the terrible club meeting after school. No topic was left untouched. They laughed and elbowed each other and winked at inner jokes. Jonas Flores kept looking back at June through the rearview mirror and jabbing his son's ribs even more. Whatever inner jokes they had, some had probably been made at her expense. She fidgeted with her thumbs. June bristled at the thought that while Hector's father clearly loved his son, her mother hadn't even noticed her absence at home. She could've just not come home at all and still, her mother wouldn't have noticed.

As soon as she knocked on the white, chipped door to the pumpkin house, it opened and Alegría smacked into her shins with a bear hug. "Where were you? You took forever. Did your boyfriend drive you home? Wait, can you drive?" Algeria tacked on the last question with confusion. Had her sister gotten a car without telling her?

June unwrapped her sister's arms from around her. The house smelled of frying oil and starch. Her mother was probably making her sister's favorite *tortitas de papa*. Apparently she hadn't forgotten about her other daughter. She was walking down the stairs when it dawned upon her that Alegría had said boyfriend. She asked for clarification.

"The tall boy with long hair, the one who asked you to dance at the party," said Alegría, wondering who else her sister's boyfriend could be and if it were possible to have two boyfriends at once. She had seen that long ago in a movie she'd watched with her mother.

"Hector?!" June sputtered and her face flushed. "What? He's—he's not my boyfriend. Ew, he's not even my friend. And there's a difference between a friend who's a boy and a boyfriend. You don't even know anything!" She thought back to his constant interruption in her life. He was definitely not anything more than an acquaintance. Her dumb little sister had definitely lost all her marbles if she thought June was dating him.

Alegría said, "Oh. Okay. Sorry, I just thought. Because you danced with him. And you never dance." She looked down at her feet on the stairs.

"You thought? Ew, gross, no." If Alegría thought she was dating Hector, then who else could have been given the same idea? Not other people at school? Is that why they expected her to come to the club meeting after school? But no, that couldn't be. June had never purposely approached Hector. And they'd only danced that one time, nothing else.

The two sisters entered the kitchen, where the mother was frying the potato cakes in a pan.

Some of the cheese escaped from the middle of the potato cake and oozed into the oil, making it and the mother jump. Turning to face her daughters, she gave them a quick nod and returned to removing the golden cake and any crisped-up cheese from the oil.

Marisol had been preoccupied with cooking dinner early for her husband, who had decided to go door-to-door in the evening offering his bookbinding services, when she received a call from Jonas Flores letting her know he was driving her daughter home. She'd breathed a sigh of relief and thanked him. She had enough on her plate with the economic burden brought on by her husband's denial and persistence in the bookbinding business. He wasn't making any money and they needed to eat. She was a thirty-two-year-old woman with only a high school degree. The jobs she could get in Manteca were limited. Besides, her husband wouldn't let her work. His pride in the home was as the provider of the family.

Marisol thought of helping her husband get his delivery job back at the Estandar cereal company. She knew that Teresa's husband was chummy with the manager of the company. Maybe she could ask her for her husband's help. But she would have to grovel in front of her high and mighty sister.

"Why do the small potatoes jump when they're in the oil but not when they're smushed together?" Marisol was startled by Alegría's sudden appearance next to her.

She gave her a small smile and placed more potato cakes in the oil. The cakes' edges crackled and popped. "Don't get too close to the oil. I don't know, your sister could probably tell you." The mother turned to look for June in the living room but she was gone. Her eldest daughter was probably feeling disappointed.

116

Though she'd received Jonas Flores's call, she hadn't had time to check in with her daughter and see if she was okay with a stranger driving her home.

She remembered all the times her daughter had accused her of bad mothering, and then she thought of all the times she had accused her own mother of bad mothering. Teresa had been right when she said children who mistreated their parents would get paid back double-fold when they had children. She was seeing herself in her daughter and there was nothing she could do about it. The past determined the present and future, until there was only the past, nothing else.

13.

Up until she was 35 years old, Aunt Teresa had never let Marisol leave her house without a chip of advice. She was the eldest daughter of Grandma Susana, and according to Josefina, the only one who hadn't ended up a disappointment. She lived in the elite circular streets below the street of shops in Manteca, where the houses were big as the paychecks that sustained them. Every time Marisol Cana drove past the hedge marking the entrance to the circular streets, she felt she was leaving behind Manteca and entering the world of money. Somehow, the air seemed fresher and the sky clearer. The main road led all the way past the concentric rings of three-to-four-story houses to the center of the elite circle, where the oldest pool in Manteca had been converted to a trendy recreational center. Teresa lived in a red brick house in the outermost ring of the elites.

Same as Marisol, she'd married straight out of high school. However, her dentist husband hadn't been a loser, like Daniel Cana. She was pretty, with thick, short, naturally-wavy hair. Her stature was not tiny, but dwarfed when she stood next to Mary. She had the mothering experience of 11 children, ages 18 through six. And despite not attending college, had learned enough about life to know a little something about everything. Her constant fountain of advice, which always seemed to be right, bothered Marisol to the point she tried to avoid it all costs.

On the Saturday Marisol came to ask Teresa for help with her husband's work, she prepared her husband's breakfast early and watched him head out the front door. She moved with efficiency, lest her husband discover how she, a woman, would interfere with his career and strip him of his pride. She brought with her her two daughters as a type of protection, hoping their presence would maintain the innocence of her visit and give her the strength she needed.

Shortly after entering the house, her daughters abandoned her on the massive gray couch in her sister's living room. As expected, June immediately went upstairs to find Stacy. Though Alegría usually stayed with her mother on such visits, she took initiative and asked her mother if she could go play with her cousin Nico. She hadn't forgotten Mateo the stuffed monkey's message and wanted to ask him about it. Reluctantly, Marisol let her daughter go, leaving her on her own in a purple room with her older sister.

Marisol sat on the sofa across from her, legs crossed, hands over her knee. "*¿Hola, que pasa?* I haven't seen you since the family party back in—oh, what was it? September! Everything's well, I hope. What can I do for you?" Teresa had the deepest voice of the three sisters. It crackled when she laughed and rasped whenever she joked. All fifteen of her boyfriends had thought she'd been sick when they'd first met her and bought her cough drops. But that was her natural way of talking, throaty and deep.

"Why do you always assume you can do something for me?" Marisol softened the end of her question and shifted on the couch. She was there to plea aid and could not be confrontational.

But the way her sister had asked the question—all calm and out of the blue—was too much of a coincidence. Did her sister already know about her husband's lack of work? Was she just waiting for Marisol to embarrass herself at her feet?

"Because every time you come to see me, it's only because you need something." Teresa's tone was blunt but her eyes twinkled with playfulness. "It's okay, just tell me. Oh, I heard you finally took Alegría to see Great-grandfather Francis. Did he help?"

Marisol didn't want to give her oldest sister any excuse to gloat by admitting that she had been right again. "Yes, the drink he gave her is helping her stay awake and lose weight... but not only is she losing weight, she's lost her entire appetite." She rushed her last words. There. That would show Teresa she hadn't been completely right about Francis.

"Oh dear! I know just the thing to help her get her appetite back. The same thing happened with my little Brisa when she was Alan's age ... But that's not why you're here."

For a second, Marisol wished that her sister would give her advice or keep talking about her kids as an excuse not to say what she needed to say. She clasped her hands. "The thing is ..." Marisol looked at the carpeted staircase at the edge of the purple living room, its polished handrails with wrought iron spindles. The two rail posts in front looked like pencils, or vials of Francis's waking concoction. She squeezed her thumb and breathed in. "Daniel's bookbinding business isn't going so great. And I was hoping ... Well your husband is such good friends with Franco. And they meet up, yes? They talk. So it wouldn't be much of a bother ... What I mean is, I was hoping your husband could to talk to Franco—put in a word, and get him to ..." Marisol's face flushed as she saw Teresa squint her eyes in mock misunderstanding. Teresa was judging her with her pretty face and all-knowing gaze. Marisol grew lightheaded with shame. No matter, the poor couldn't be prideful. She could dance with the truth no longer. "... to help Daniel get his job back." She spit the truth like a hot *chile*.

Teresa raised her eyebrows. "Franco from Estandar? You never told me he got a job there."

Marisol knew her sister was faking her surprise. Teresa always knew about everything. She probably just wanted to milk her humiliation and her marriage to a husband who couldn't hold down a job. "He did."

"Well what does he work—what *did* he work as? Is he a consultant on something? Or?" Marisol swallowed hard. She knew her sister wanted her to say "delivery truck driver," wanted to rub in her face what a lowly job it was in comparison to a dentist, wanted her to admit that she'd made the wrong choice in marrying him, a Prudento. She dug her stubby nails into her palm. The price of aid was too great. "Never mind. I think it's time I go. Girls?" Marisol got up from the oversized couch, gathered her purse and moved towards the staircase to look for her daughters.

"Whoa, slow down. You only got here a few minutes ago." Teresa held out her hands to stop her.

"You know perfectly well Daniel's a truck driver. I'm sure of it." Her eyes were as hot as her shame.

Teresa bit her lip and looked to the side. "Okay, yes. I knew. I only didn't say because I knew you wouldn't like it I knew." Her voice was croaky.

Marisol clutched her discolored purse closed. "Then why did you ask?"

"So you could tell me and we could talk about this openly. Come." Teresa wrapped her arm around her sister and led her back to the gray couch. Marisol's eyes glazed over and she let herself be led. They sat together, on the same couch. For a moment, it was as if they were children again, Teresa 15 and Marisol 13, fighting over who'd lost the lipstick. "What happened with Daniel?"

"It's just been, oh you know. The same as always. The economy. It's hard." Teresa rubbed her back and nodded. Marisol blinked and shook her head as if from a dream. "What am I saying? How could you know about the economy? Your life is perfect." She got up from the oversized gray couch, gathered her purse again, and started heading for the door. Her sister held out her hands to stop her.

"Whoa, slow down. Whoever said my life was perfect?"

"You did. You married rich and had eleven children. You had the perfect wedding. I know, I was your maid of honor."

"What do my husband and children have to do with perfection? You think raising eleven kids is easy?" Teresa put her hands on her hips.

"Well you never complain."

"Just because I don't complain doesn't mean my life is easy."

"But you never have to worry about money. You don't know what it's like."

"Oh yes I do. Berto may make more than Daniel, but I have eleven children. Eleven children! We're only in this position because we've learned to stretch what we have."

Daniel is incapable of saving or stretching what little he earns, thought Marisol. She was jealous of her sister, the perfect path her live had taken. She clasped her purse closer. "But you've never had to live like I do."

Teresa sighed and rolled her eyes. "Is this about Ría again?"

Marisol frowned. "What?"

Throwing her hands up in the air, the older sister said, "I can't anymore. You need to let it go and *move on*. You think you're the only one who carried any guilt? If I hadn't been so whiny back then about my scraped knee, mom wouldn't have been distracted enough to leave Ría with you. I carry guilt, too. We all do. So stop making yourself a victim."

Marisol squinted her eyes. "I'm not. You are the ones who forgot too quickly. I mean, look at mother. After the first days, she didn't even cry. She made everyone go on with their lives as if nothing had happened." Marisol swayed on her feet and Teresa helped her sit back down.

"Are you blind?" she said in her soft, raspy voice. "Mom cared the most." Putting an arm around her and signaling for Genesis to take away little Brisa, who had both shown up at the head of the stairs at the yelling. "Let's take this outside."

Leading her sister through a door in the kitchen to the outside patio, Teresa realized that for Marisol, nothing had changed. She was still the little girl who fought with their mother and harbored a secret poster of Los Chayotes' lead guitar player.

The air was dry and carried the light, woodsy and slightly vinegary smell of the tulip poplars planted in the backyard. The trees were bare but for a few dried tulips that rustled with the wind's breath. They wouldn't flower again until late May. The two sisters sat on gray, aluminum chairs so cold they felt wet.

After a few moments, Teresa began, "You didn't see mom cry because she didn't want you to see her cry. But she did. And she did care."

Teresa knew what Marisol didn't because she'd glimpsed what their mother had so carefully hid from them. Back when they were in elementary school, Grandma Susana lived with her four healthy daughters in the pumpkin house of Manteca. She was busy and happy, cooking dishes in the kitchen every day for those she loved. The day before Ría's death, she prepared *enchiladas*. For her youngest daughter, she knew not to boil more than five serrano peppers with the tomatillos so that little Ría wouldn't find the sauce too spicy. For her quiet Mary, who couldn't tolerate much acidity, she would make the *salsa verde* with only firm, purpling tomatillos bursting from their papery husks. When she fried the *tortillas*, she turned the heat on low so that the crisp corn edges weren't too hard for her nostalgic Marisol's soft teeth. After dipping the fried tortillas in the *salsa verde* and stuffing them with shredded chicken, she would roll them up tightly so that her oldest Teresa helping her in the kitchen wouldn't have trouble placing them inside the glass baking dish once owned by her mother, Lolita. Before placing the full baking dish in the oven, she would pour the leftover salsa and *crema* on the *enchiladas* and sprinkle grated and crumbled cheese on top, the two types of cheese her husband, George, most enjoyed.

Then the next day, she took all four of her daughters to the pool and everything changed. The day of Ría's death, the world seemed to stop. The whole of Manteca was frozen in disbelief. The naive, four-year-old girl with her hair up in pigtails and unruly eyebrows had drowned at a time of happiness, and no one had foreseen it. For a while after, people left Susana's family alone, unsure of what to say. Any comforting words seemed inadequate, hollow.

And then time rushed to catch up. Life was quickly patched

up together and the missing pieces laboriously ignored until time smoothed back to a constant tempo. Susana smiled for her children and made sure they got the care they needed. She couldn't laugh for some time after. A nausea gripped her heart and suffocated any laughter. But she still cooked and cleaned and talked her daughters through the death of their youngest sister.

Marisol saw this as her lack of care. How could her mother still smile and behave as usual? Her mother didn't care about her late sister as much as she did. She was too carefree to be weighed down with the guilt she felt at her sister's death. Her mother didn't even blame her for her part in Ría's death. Rather she stretched out her hand and sought to wrap her in a hug. But Marisol didn't need a hug. It was too late for a hug. A hug was what she needed back when the water swallowed her late sister and pulled at her so she couldn't help her. What she needed now was punishment for her crime. If Susana wasn't there for Marisol when she needed her most, she didn't have any right to be there for her now.

Eight-year-old Teresa saw something entirely different in her mother's behavior. When her mother, Susana, finally started laughing again, it didn't sound the same. The lines around her eyes seemed strained. When she caressed her head and sang to her, there was a heaviness that slipped into her voice and made it thick like molasses. Her laugh, too, changed. The witch-donkey notes changed from a G Major to a B Flat.

Susana comforted her children and sought comfort in her husband, who had none left to give. All his energies were being sapped at his work in the lumber yard. When his wife hugged him late at night, he couldn't hug her back. His arms, which would never again carry Alegría or teach her to dance, were lifeless forever. The more she sought comfort in him, the more he realized he could never be what Susana needed. When they'd first met, he'd known she was too good for him, but her braying laugh gave him hope that he could at least try. Now that her laughter had changed, he was sure he wasn't right for her. He was a failure of a father, who couldn't console her or his children, and that scared him. He, who was weak, couldn't succor the strong. So he drifted apart from her and two years later, disappeared for good. The only trace of him left in the pumpkin house was his smell of sawdust encased in the envelopes he sometimes sent with apologetic money.

Even with his cowardice, Susana still loved him. She needed him. She was tired from managing the household and her children's needs. After he ran away, the burden was even greater. No respite could be found. And still, she smiled for her daughters.

One day, about a year after Ría's death, Teresa was cutting up pictures of girls' dresses in the living room. Her sisters Mari and Mary were playing with dolls and music upstairs. Her mother was in the kitchen making tea and toasting bread as a late-night snack. The air was warm with the bright, sweet smell of the linden blossoms and honey. And then Teresa heard gasping, choking sounds coming from the kitchen. Alarmed, she got up from the flower-patterned couch and went to investigate.

She found her mother leaning against the counter, gripping the edge with one hand and gripping her mouth with the other, as if trying to hold back the inhuman sounds escaping from inside her. Her fingers on the counter's edge were white from the pressure and the marks on her face from the grip of her fingers were red. Salty water fell from her eyes and Teresa knew it was tears.

She stood there by the wall, silently watching the woman whose insides were wracking her body trying to get out, until she remembered that woman was her mother. She stiffly approached her and put her arms around her. Teresa could feel her mother's convulsions as she struggled to control the water flowing from her eyes.

Susana turned around, fell on the floor, and hugged her daughter. She cried freely for a few seconds, releasing *gritos* that scared eleven-year-old Teresa. Slow and halting, the sobs turned into gasps and the jerks turned into shudders. Her breathing stable, Susana released her daughter, held her at arms' length, and smiled at her. But her chocolate-brown eyes were turned down like bananas and the edges of her lips were wrinkly like prunes.

Mother and daughter got up from the floor and sat down at the kitchen table.

Susana looked at her daughter with eyes shiny and red. She felt guilty for letting her daughter see her cry. The faint sound coming from upstairs of Marisol and Mary's singing could be heard. She got up to turn the bubbling tea off. "Do you remember the story of the rabbit?" Teresa nodded. Susana returned to the kitchen table and let out a shuddering breath. "You are my rabbits, you and your sisters. I know I'm not always the best mother, and that I can't take care of your needs like I used to," and she looked down at her shaking hands clasped on the table, "but just know that I love you. And that I'd do anything for you."

It was at that moment Teresa knew her mother needed her. She grew up faster to help her mother cope with one less family member. She would help Mary get dressed for school and Mari resolve her math homework. When her father finally did leave, she made sure no one mentioned him. His name became a bad word in the family household, and in time, her sisters sufficiently forgot him. As time ran its course, four plates at the dinner table became normal.

But every so often, and without fail every June 16th, Mary would be woken by the sound of the pumpkin house shifting, the running of water from a faucet, the opening of the fridge, and the muffled swish of the front door sliding shut. She would tiptoe out of bed, run up the stairs, and climb up unto the sill of the cyclops window. Through the blinds, she could see her mother walking down the street where the sun was barely stretching and the ruby-throated hummingbirds still sleeping. Before she could see where her mother was headed, she would feel the tap on her shoulder of Teresa, who'd followed her out of bed and was calling her back to sleep.

Helping her sister down the window sill, she escorted her back to bed, tucked her into her padded covers, brushed the hair off her face, and returned to her own bed. Teresa knew she needed to watch out for her sisters while her mother left the orange house. She knew her mother left the orange house because she hadn't forgotten the day she took her four daughters out to the new pool in Manteca.

While his mother talked with Aunt Mari downstairs, Cousin Nico showed Alegría his action figure collection.

"So you can see dead people?" he asked.

"I guess," she replied, raising her voice at the end, "but only Grandma Susana."

"No way! And you went to visit Great-grandfather Francis? Mom talks about him sometimes."

"Yeah," said Alegría. She didn't come see Nico to tell him about her visit to the *chaman* but to ask him a question. She wanted to know what her monkey, Mateo, had meant when he talked about the sky on Three Kings' Day. Her first choice to ask had been Grandma Susana, but she hadn't visited the whole week, since she'd started taking the *chaman's* waking concoction. So she'd settled for Cousin Nico. He was eleven, mature for his age, and like his mother, had something to say about everything. Before she could get a word in, Cousin Nico was asking questions he didn't need answered.

"Is he old? Mom says he's old. He gave you some type of drink, right? Like medicine? And it's supposed to help you stay awake and lose weight? Say, you are a little bigger than the last time I saw you. Is it working? Everything should be fine now that you have the drink."

"Kind of... I can keep awake better. But my head hurts and my stomach doesn't feel good when I eat."

"Yeah, but you won't fall asleep anymore." Cousin Nico looked at Alegría with his head cocked to one side and scrunched up eyes. He couldn't understand why Alegría wasn't happy now that she had Great-grandfather Francis's help. He thought the medicinal-like drink was supposed to make everything better. He didn't understand that the drink came with side-effects, bitter drops in the sweet cure.

"Anyway, I wanted to ask you something."

"Yeah?" He perked his head up in expectation. Like his mother, he was always ready to give out advice.

"Do you know who the sky is?"

Cousin Nico scrunched up his almond eyes even more in confusion. Her face showed she was serious. He pointed to the window. "You mean the one outside?"

"No, I mean..." Alegría looked down and played with her feet on the carpet. She didn't know what she meant.

Nico opened his eyes and uncocked his head. "Hey, I saw Jacob Ramos at the library yesterday. He was flirting with the librarian. I saw it with my own two eyeballs. He was leaning on the front desk and had his thumb on his belt. You know the one with the big star buckle? And he was talking about books like he knew something. Then she laughed. That weird laugh she does when she covers her mouth with her mouth. The one that sounds like turkeys gobbling."

Alegría nodded and sighed internally. She remembered that creepy laugh. But Nico needed to get to the point soon.

"Well after she laughed, he got closer and called her *mi cielo*. My sky. I think it was supposed to be cute because she laughed some more. You mean that kind of sky?"

The eight-year-old girl's eyes got bigger. "What does that kind of sky mean?"

Nico scratched his head and Alegría saw little white flakes come out of his hair. "I think it's just something you call girls you like." He shrugged his shoulders and let his arms fall flailing. "Like *guapa*. Or hey bootylicious."

Alegría nodded solemnly. So that's what Mateo meant when he said the sky was a who, not a what. The sky was a person.

Probably a girl. Maybe not. She smiled at Nico. Her visit hadn't been in vain.

When she reunited with her mother and older sister at the front of the house, Alegría noticed that Aunt Teresa was quieter than usual. She took her mother's hand. It was cold. Her mom was also quiet, but Alegría didn't know if it was the car-ride-to-the-store-after-being-called-to-the-office-type of quiet or regular quiet. By the time they were leaving, her aunt had regained her usual self.

"Aren't you going to give me your goodbye kisses?" said Aunt Teresa, laughing with her crackling voice and stretching out her arms. June hugged her aunt awkwardly, barely making the kissing sound women did when they touched each others' cheeks. Then it was Alegría's turn. She wrapped her arms around her aunt, who crouched down to meet her. She rested her head on her aunt's shoulder. Instead of giving her sister her usual chip of advice, Aunt Teresa whispered in Alegría's ear, "Take care of your *mami,* for me, will ya?"

The Story of the Rabbit

A long time ago, when the world was still cold, and the land wasn't yet sold, there lived a family of rabbits.

There was a mother, a daughter, a son, and a father, and they jumped and they danced and they were happy.

But time is both fiend and a friend, it breaks and it mends, it gave change to the daughter, her heart grew disquieted.

She wanted to jump in the neighboring fields, eat a crisper grass. From all these the mother couldn't shield, nor prevent their coming to pass, so she let her daughter go freely, though she loved her dearly, and said to her these words:

"Wherever you may be, whatever you may see, remember me. I'll be here. Remember who you are, when you look up at the stars. You are my daughter."

So the small rabbit left, and started on her way. She hopped on the highest plains and skipped up to the the smoothest lakes.

One day as she chased a water lily, she moved from the edge to the end far too deep for her to keep her head above water.

The mother from far away, heard her voice cry in dismay, and made to set out that very same day.

But the son's words stopped his mother: "Why all this bother? While your daughter is out, frolicking someplace new, I'm in here doing my best for you, and father is, too.

Neglect us not."

So his mother responded:

"Dear son, who's been tried and is true, let me speak to you, a few words of comfort.

I have not forgotten you nor your father, but because my love is the same, I cannot forget your sister, my daughter.

If you felt abandoned, neglected, it was all unintended. Sometimes a child needs more help, some special attention, but that is not to say the others are without mention.

I must go and see what I can do. Just know that were it you stuck in the water, I'd do the same for you."

Past the plains and the lakes, the mother traversed. Though her fur had grown mangled, and her speed was inconstant, she kept moving forward, fearing the worst.

When she arrived at the scene, she saw from the water's rippling sheen, where her daughter had been.

She dived in that spot, though it took a lot, and pulled her daughter out, who revived with a spout.

"Mother you found me," she said with a sputter.

The mother smiled and simply said, "You are my daughter."

With those words, they both made off, to head for home, where the son and father were waiting, two souls all alone.

When they made their entrance, the welcome was great. All the rabbits hugged and embraced. Except for the son, who held a strange look on his face.

He saw in his mother's eyes that she was tired. In her journey she'd grown old and wearied. And Indeed she retired, to a bed of finality, as her body required.

Before she passed, she spoke words to her children, she knew'd be her last.

"You're both my world, my earth and my sky. I must now say goodbye, but don't cry for too long.

"Remember you're strong, and I'll be with you all along. Look down at the water, see the reflected sky. It's as big and blue as my love for you. Because you are my rabbits."

14.

On the way home from Aunt Teresa's house, Alegría kept hearing the whisperings of sleep in her ear. When she leaned her ear forward to better hear what they were saying, her entire head followed until the only thing holding her back from the two year-old stain on the abrasive gray car mat was her seat belt. It was her first day without having drunk a full dose of Great-grandfather Francis's waking concoction. Earlier that day, her mother in agitation over her impending visit to Teresa's house, had unstoppered the vial with superfluous force, causing the vial to jerk upward and three-sevenths of its contents to spill out. Alegría had still been made to drink the remaining concoction, but she definitely hadn't cried over the spilled murky liquid on her bed. The effects of an incomplete dose were now making themselves known to her.

As the jean-blue sedan lurched to a stop, Alegría woke up to find she, her sister, and mother had already arrived at the pumpkin house. Getting out of the car with half-closed lids, she dragged herself across the cement driveway, up the front door steps next to the late Grandma Susana's dead flowers, and in through the open door of the orange house. Her sister took her shoes off and walked down the steps with them in hand all dignified, like Cousin Stacy had taught her.

Alegría followed her as their mother locked the door, the bronze keys with the plastic princess crown keychain her two daughters had gotten her for her birthday jingling in her hand.

Walking down the steps, Alegría again heard the whisperings of sleep and her heartbeat pounding in her ears. The sound grew louder and faster until it was like the runnings of a river. Moving her foot forward, she missed a step and fell forward with her arms stretched out like a starfish, trying to catch hold of anything that would stop her.

Marisol dropped the keys and yelled at June with a voice to calm earthquakes and stop birds in mid-flight, "Catch her!" It was these words, which resonated in June's hardened mind when she watched her sister sink into the overflowing Mipared River the pluvial night she snuck out of the pumpkin house to meet Hector and the rest of the PM Club.

June's shoes flew in the direction of the dimly-lit hallway as she reached her arms out to catch Alegría by the foot of the stairs. Her little sister's body was limp, her head slumping between her shoulders like the stuffed head of Señorita Monkey when she'd cut the neck stitching and pulled out the stuffing in a fit of anger after her mother had given her sister her favorite outgrown rainbow-colored sweater. Red marks covered her little sister's bare arms where she'd hit them on the walls and carpeted stairs trying to stop herself from falling.

Marisol ran down the stairs and ripped Alegría from June's arms. "Why didn't you catch your sister?" she said. Cradling her youngest daughter in her arms, she inspected her red-marked arms, pushed past her oldest daughter, and entered the doorless doorway to the living room. Her youngest daughter's sleepiness and surprise fall were forcing out a memory of when she was seven and lived in her mother Susana's house with her three sisters.

Behind her in the dark, mustard-lit hallway, June mumbled, "I did catch her."

The whisperings of sleep got louder in Alegría's ear, echoing all around her and inside her. The blood rushed in her ears. And there was the sound of water running by, bubbling, lapping, overtaking itself. Somewhere overhead, the hovering hummingbirds' thrumming wings vibrated through the air like tiny, pulsating jackhammers. The black-masked laughing falcon stole a flight through the air, perched on a tall tree branch, and let out its high, monotone cawing, turning its head to look at the numerous birds flying through the sky.

There was the teal Mipared River. Except there were no bridges or roads in sight. And everywhere there were people in light, wooden boats shaped like coffins, riding across the river from one side to the other and back. Smooth rocks paved the edge of the river, where boats would knock against them when they docked. Scrawny dark gray trees with no more than twenty leaves each were placed eight feet apart all around the river. The Big Painter in the Sky had drizzled honey on his canvas and splashed it with shades of butter, but those colors had all melted away unto the sky above the right side of the river. In their absence, the sky above the river had turned the color of persimmons and become successively darker until on the left, there were only the blue, purple, and licorice hues of plums and elderberries.

Alegría stood on the left side of the river, where the ground was green, soft, and fertile. The air smelled like grass and Aunt Mary's bar soap. Bushes and trees sprouted from the ground sporadically. Among them wound a line of people tall and short, young and old. In their hands, they held glass jars and clay jugs filled with a glossy, amber-colored liquid. The line stretched farther than she could see, fading into the purple and blacks where the trees in shadow met the sky in clouds of fog. It led to the edge of the lapping water, where boats were docked and awaiting new passengers.

On the other side of the river, the ground was drier, spotted with occasional green, bare of trees and bushes. Similar to the left side, numberless people lined up for their boat rides, waiting with the same looks on their faces as the customers waiting in line to pay for groceries at Josefina's: bored and impatient. Behind the people stood a large, metal five-story building shaped like a rectangular prism and obscured by clouds. Standing on the crumbly brown ground was her family looking around as if lost.

Alegría walked toward them, but the deep and wide river stood between them. She searched for a quick way to get across to her family. The line to the boats was too long, and she couldn't just butt people to the front. That wouldn't be nice. As she neared the river, she saw a capsized boat and a pear-shaped man touching the trees, leaning down to handle the smooth rocks by the river, and pulling out a small book from the back pocket of his navy-blue trousers. He was wearing a loose cream-colored shirt and a coarse navy-blue jacket to match his pants. His head was egg-shaped and what little hair it had once held had migrated above his upper lip, forming a bushy down-turned caterpillar that emphasized his round cheeks and turned his face into a permanent scowl. Alegría approached him and tugged on his sleeve. "Hello," she said, "My name's Alegría."

Without turning around, the man pointed to himself and said in a gruff voice, "Dominique. What do you want?" He wrote on his pocketbook furiously, making his whole body jiggle like congealed chicken stock.

She pointed to her family on the other side of the river. "To get across." She could see that her mother had broken off from her family, hiked up her jeans, crouched down by the riverside, and submerged her hands in the babbling water, running her fingers through it. "Sir," she added, in hopes it would make him pay attention faster. Adults always paid more attention when called nicely.

The pear-shaped man put away his pen and pocketbook, got closer to one of the young, twenty-foot tall trees by the river, crouched down, muttered an insult, and said in a tired voice, "You see those people lined up to ride a boat across? Go line up with them. Do you have your *hipocretina*?"

Alegría scrunched her eyebrows. Peeking beneath his jacket, she could see a slimy, little nub of a frog tail. "My what?" He turned to look at her, the left side of his face in shadow. The soft ground underneath him shifted like brown sugar. His eyes moved down to her empty hands at her sides, then back up at her face with half-closed lids. They were framed by teardrop-shaped bruises, the same as the Uncle Dominique in Cousin Nico's story. "Are you the Uncle Dominique who sold his wife for a plate of hot *tamales?*"

He rubbed his bald head in frustration and sprang up to his full height suddenly. "It was five pounds of *tamales verdes, rojos, y de elote*, and a bowl of *menudo*. Next time, get your facts straight before you speak, Adoncia." He mistook her name with confidence as the aerial birds in the sky cawed in support of his words.

"Sorry." Alegría shrugged. The waters kept rushing and the line of people kept moving.

She stayed quiet for two seconds before she thought up a question. "Is it true you were cursed with a terrible sleepiness and a frog tail?"

He said that most frogs outgrew their tails and that the amphibian part on his behind was more tadpole than frog. Other than the hassle in the bathroom, the terrible sleepiness was worse than the tadpole tail for it was only a side effect of the real curse, the removal of his *hipocretina*.

It had all started when he'd moved with his wife to the street of shops Thomas Delgado had founded. He'd had a dream of claiming land as his and renting it out to people to make a profit. Spending his and his begrudging wife's savings, he'd built fences around square acres of land and stuck in signs reading "Uncle Dominique's." But in those days, people didn't yet scribble on paper, sign it with their name, and call it a land title. Mostly, people took the land they saw was unoccupied and used it as they liked. They took him as crazy and lazy, and established their homes and shops on the free land outside his simple wooden fences.

Unwilling to give up on the idea of land as commodity, he'd refused to get a different job, much to the annoyance of his simple-minded wife. She'd pestered and nagged him all day and all night about the absence of oil in the oil jug and flour in the flour jar. Before long, the constant yelling and the pangs in his stomach had proved unbearable.

He'd spent as much time as possible outside his house, walking the pe-rimeters of his land to get away from the harassment of his wife.

It was on one of these walks he'd seen his neighbor lean on his fence, rest his chin on his palm, and stare lustily at his wife hanging the sheets on the clotheslines. Dominique thought he'd approach his neighbor and ask whatever he saw in his wife. His neighbor couldn't understand how any man could fail to appreciate his wife's striking figure. He offered Dominique a deal, anything in return for his wife. At that point in his marriage, Dominique was willing to pay his neighbor to take his wife away, bodacious figure and all, but he thought he'd make the most of the situation and satisfy his current craving of tamales *and* menudo. *His neighbor was surprised but complied the very next day, coming with a bowl of* menudo *and a plate of green, red, and corn* tamales.

Dominique had called his wife out to the open door of the fence and without her having the chance to object, exchanged her hand for the plate piled high with steaming tamales. *Once in his neighbor's arms, his wife had spit on him and cursed his days with a tadpole tail and the removal of his* hipocretina.

The tadpole tail had come quickly and taken some adjusting to, but he could live with it. As long as he wore a long jacket, no one would notice the growth in his behind. No sooner had he grown ac-customed to his modified method of using the toilet than he found he could not sleep at night. Something in her curse had disturbed his sleep cycles. He stayed awake staring at the ceiling, growing tired and unable to do anything about it. Over time, he'd grown so tired, he'd fallen asleep making himself dinner, almost burning his house down, and while walking his land's parameter, almost falling into a pot-hole. Even with his drooping eyelids, he experienced nights of inter-rupted sleep, waking up more than twenty times a night. Then he'd developed a strange slackness in his muscles whenever he felt sur-prised. The strange spell of slackness lasted anywhere from five to thirty-five minutes. When he did dream, the sounds and images were so vivid he couldn't tell what was dream and what was reality. In time, the figures in his dream invaded his life, so he could see the river in his bedroom and his ex-wife in the living room yelling at him to get a job.

Life while awake grew boring and tired, so he stayed in his dreams to explore the life within them. After a while, he'd almost completely forgotten his fenced-in parcels of land and the nagging of his wife. He was in an important dream now, one in which people used jars of hipocretina to cross the river, so real it might as well be reality.

Alegría looked back at her family on the other side of the river. Her mom was now sitting with the water up to her waist, splashing the wetness around her, cupping her hands to pick up the teal-colored liquid and throwing it in the air like sprinkles. Her father was looking behind him to the five-story building. She had to hurry up. "What is *hipocretina?*" and she pronounced the foreign word like Paolo pronounced all of his, sounding out each syllable slowly.

Moving his whiskered chin towards the line of people, he said, "It's that thing they have in their jars and jugs." His eyes traveled to the people at the river's edge getting into their boats. "See how they pour their *hipocretina* into the little compartment at the back of the boat? That's for the rudders below water. Keeps the time-bound things moving."

Alegría could hear the water shift under the added weight of a person on the closest boat, which was a little over ten yards away. On the boat floor, there were two movie reel-shaped wheels connected to each other by a wooden handle. After the amber-colored liquid was poured on the strange mechanism near the bottom of the boat, the person turned a handle connected to the mechanism, making a clicking noise like the wind-up toy monkey Cousin Nico had once flaunted in front of Alegría. Then the handle was released and the boat's rudders came to life, cutting through the gurgling river slowly, making the slow ticking sound of a clock. "What happens if you don't have the *hipocretina?*"

The man with the pocketbook laughed once loudly like the jean-blue sedan's car honk. "Oh, Adelina. Then the handle will remain stiff, and you can't spin it enough times for the mechanism to make the rudders work and take you across the river. You can end up capsized by the river," he looked at the overturned boat beside him, "or worse, abandoned to the whims of the river and led into the darkest abysses, where the river leads."

"Okay," said Alegría, "what are you doing to get across?" Her eyes flickered to the other side of the river, where her mother was now up to her chest in the water and her father had left June, walking towards the tall, rectangular building. June was shifting on her feet, walking a little towards her mother by the river's edge and then back towards the building with her father.

"Me?" The bald, mustached man scoffed. "I'm not like those dimwits going from one side to the other. My problems are far more important and too complicated for these folk." And he went into a lengthy, conspiratorial explanation about his one purpose in life: predicting the secret future event that would one day take place at the Mipared River. He beckoned Alegría towards the young tree and showed her the bark. He guided her hand to the roots of the tree. It was rough and cold and wet. Running her hand up the veins of the tree, she realized the whole bottom part of the trunk was wet higher than she could reach. It was like the tree was partly submerged in water. He told her that the wetness was drowning the tree, scorching some leaves yellow, forming water-soaked blisters on others. He showed her the soil at the bottom, its sour smell indicating that the soil couldn't breathe. Small gradient ginger mushrooms and rust-colored algae covered the trunk near the roots.

The pear-shaped man explained his careful documentation of the height of the tree and the point where its wetness reached. Using his long hands as a ruler, he had measured the height of the wetness and found it to be exactly eight feet and eleven inches. He couldn't be wrong, for he had measured it multiple times for precision. He was sure the trees spaced out eight feet apart around the river were a sign of something. Some future event no one but he was aware of or cared about. He knew that despite being cleverer than all the ignorant fools who went about crossing the river, he would end up just like them, dead without witnessing the forthcoming event. Before it was his time, he planned to seal his pocketbook with all his data and observations inside a clay jug, and hide it near the edge of the river, for future generations to find and realize that he'd been right all along. It was this same clay jug Alegría would later find on a family trip to the Mipared River.

"Now leave me be, Amaranta" said Uncle Dominique, "I've got more important things to do than to chat all day with a bug-eyed little girl." He turned back to the tree, took out his pocketbook and pen from his pants pocket, and continued furiously scrawling. The overhead whistling, chirping, and cawing of birds grew louder. Alegría looked up to see birds of all colors and sizes, with tufted crowns, striped underbellies, and beaks no bigger than her pinky nail—all kinds, swirling above her and settling on the dry branches of the dark gray trees. Their strong wings rustled Dominique's beard and her thin hair. Behind her, the line of people advanced quickly and imperceptibly. People fresh off the docked boats would walk up the green grass and line up to take a ride back to the other side, where her mother was neck-deep in the water, dipping her chin in and jerking it out. Her father, having reached the five-story building, was nowhere to be seen.

June had sat down and was clawing fists of dirt around her, throwing them on top her legs as if to bury them.

Alegría knew she couldn't wait and that Dominique wasn't going to help her. She moved to the river's edge and stepped into the water. It was cold. The wetness got into her sneakers and into her clothes. She kept pushing forward and the river kept pushing her rightward. She waved at her mother and sister but they didn't see her. The river was wide and deep. The ground dropped off and she struggled to find her footing, flapping her arms in the water.

That's when Alegría realized she couldn't swim very well. Her mother didn't like the pool and her father had only taken her once. And that hadn't been enough practice.

The building with her father had disappeared from her line of vision, and her sister and mother were getting hard to see with the water sloshing in her face. She gasped and the water got into her mouth and eyes. Both burned with saltiness. The persimmon-colored sky above her disappeared into the teal of the water. Her ears were plugged with underwater currents and she felt them ringing. As she was falling, falling, the darkness rose up to meet her, and all was still.

Beneath her, springs groaned as she shifted. A clock tick-tocked nearby. The ringing turned into blurred voices. They were her mother and sister standing over her. Alegría was on the green couch with the broken springs in her living room.

"She's awake! See? There was nothing to worry about. *Grilla* here will never not wake up." June tucked her hair behind her ears, crossed her arms, and gave her mother a pointed look.

The only response her mother gave her was "*Callate,*" and then she turned her full attention to her youngest daughter. "How do you feel? You scared us when you fell." She was stroking Alegría's hair. Her mouth was turned down at its corners and her eyebrows had pulled together, pinching the skin between them.

June sat on the arm of the couch by Alegría's feet. She rolled her eyes. "She didn't scare me," she said.

Alegría puffed out her cheeks and scrunched up her eyebrows. "I fell?" All she remembered was being tired walking down the stairs. There were fragments of a river and Uncle Dominique and trees and scary pretty birds, but those fragments were melting away. The couch springs creaked underneath her.

"Yes, you fell asleep on the stairs. You really need to lay off the *frijoles*. I was barely able to catch you." June picked at the fabric of the couch arm. It ripped a little. Her eyes widened and she smoothed out the fabric to hide the fresh tear before her mother noticed.

Marisol remained worried and pensive. Seeing Alegría fall a second time, she had remembered who her daughter's first fall on Christmas Eve had reminded her of: her late youngest sister. She continued stroking her daughter's hair, tucking the little wispy hairs behind her ears, hoping against hope that her daughter was normal.

15.

Aunt Mary was armed for war. With her 14-count pack of paper towel rolls, 9.7 oz fresh citrus multi-surface spray, 40 oz bottle of bleach, and gallon bottle of lavender-scented all-purpose cleaner homemade with half a cup of white vinegar and two tablespoons of baking soda, she was doing something she had put off for seven months and three days: deep-cleaning the kitchen.

Though she was a fairly neat person and proud of her organizational skills, even more so than Teresa, the kitchen was a sacred place. It was the last place to retain the corn-flour smell of her mother. Alas, her husband had gotten a new woman and she needed something to distract her. Aunt Mary hadn't inherited the power to make others pay attention like Teresa or silence them like Marisol, but she had inherited Susana's resiliency. Cleaning was a way to keep order in her messy life, and so the heavier the burden, the cleaner the kitchen.

Mary turned the trumpet-shaped light fixture in the center of the room on. From a distance, the pink and yellow tiled place seemed clean. Marisol would've taken one look at the shiny, uncluttered L-shaped set of counter tops and deemed the place spotless. But with her watchful eye, Mary could tell the blackened burner bowls on the stove top needed to be replaced. Looking under the white nose-shaped range hood, she knew that the sticky grease-spotted air vent needed to be taken out and cleaned.

The condiments on the shelves on either side of the range hood were jumbled, their labels facing every which way, and the containers of cinnamon and sugar were stained with tiny, eight-year-old fingerprints. Without Susana's care, the pots below the left wall shelf hung out of order. Below the right wall shelf, the rarely touched microwave had collected dust from disuse.

Mary didn't even want to think about what the top of the white fridge looked like. Just from the little sliver of space between the fridge and the pantry, she could tell it would be grimy with filth dating back before Susana's death. She started with the sink, emptying it out of glasses, dishes, and utensils, and filing them into the dishwasher, which like the microwave, had not been used for more than decoration by her mother. Once the dishes were done, she started on the pots and pans.

Washing the deep steel pot used for boiling corn, she felt like Susana, who would wash the same pot after dinner, singing, her face warmed by evening sun. Except unlike her mother, who at her age was giving birth to her fourth daughter, Mary was infertile. And now she was without a husband. All because he preferred fertile women. And though she taught ten-year-old children, she would never have one of her own. Never a sweet daughter with hair to braid. Nor a son to tuck into bed. Because she was infertile. And her husband's thirteenth woman wasn't. And her two sisters weren't either. Especially Teresa with her eleven children. She brushed the bottom of the pot rougher, trying to get the stain out, clanking the plastic of her scrubber against the walls of the pot and watching the froth from the soap form on the water. While she couldn't wage war on her issues, she could wage war on the stains in the pots.

She looked up through the four-pane casement window above the sink and saw the sky open. The sun's gentle rays peeked out as they do on early March afternoons in Manteca, as signs of the upcoming Spring. Their warmth felt like a comforting hug from her mother and her heart was still again. Looking out to the backyard, she saw the dying grass and resolved to make it live again another day, after she'd left the kitchen sparkling.

Not two hours later, Mary had sprayed and scrubbed the

entire stove with her homemade all-purpose cleaner. She wiped down all the cabinets, including the open faced one beside the sink displaying Susana's prized china set, which was missing a cup since the annual family party when the children had broken into the house and dropped it. She moved on to the microwave, opening its crusty door to inspect the inside. No beep sounded, indicating it wasn't plugged in.

Inside were the normal white walls of a microwave. But underneath the glass plate, Mary found a picture distorted by the glass. Lifting the plate, she pulled out a photograph of her mother holding a baby in front of a white background. The baby had the same eye bags as Susana in her later years and a mouth open wide as a newborn songbird. She was wrapped in a pink blanket, which in those days signified the baby was a girl. Susana was smiling brightly, showing her sparkling array of horse teeth, though the lack of color in her lips and the slight gloss in her eyes betrayed her exhaustion. The photo was most likely taken after she had given birth. Flipping the photograph over, Mary read the date of the photo along with the words, "For my future Alegría, I hope you have happiness *todos tus días*."

It was strange that the photograph was below the glass plate in the microwave. There was no clear reason why Susana would place it there. Mary didn't get the chance to muse any further, as she heard a knock on the downstairs wall meaning her sister was trying to get her attention. Her sister, Marisol, who'd walked around like a dead woman since the passing of their youngest sister. Her sister who'd done everything she could to annoy their mother. Her sister who had married a Prudento to separate herself from her family. Such a sister couldn't see a picture with both late mother and sister. "Yes?" called Mary while she shoved the photo back in the microwave and closed it in haste, a decision she would later regret when the rains came and the air turned foggy.

"I need you to watch June while I take Alegría somewhere. Is that okay?" said Marisol. She was climbing up the stairs and entering the living room. Even with her late mother's ugly flower-patterned couch taking up too much space, the room was still bigger than the living room and dining room area downstairs.

"It's fine. Where are you going again?" Mary positioned her ample figure in front of the microwave, hiding it from the view of Marisol, who took no notice of anything strange other than the suffocating smell of disinfectant and lavender.

"Somewhere. You're cleaning?" Marisol didn't want her sister to know that she was taking Alegría to see Great-grandfather Francis for no reason other than it was her own business and no one else's. Mary's forehead was slightly sweaty, probably from the exertion of such meticulous cleaning. The kitchen looked spotless. "And why do you have the light turned on? There's light outside." To have both on was a waste of energy. And money.

Mary smiled thinly and her cheeks colored faintly. "Sorry. It wasn't so bright when I turned the light on." She wanted to move from her station in front of the microwave to turn the light off, but then feared Marisol would see the picture through the microwave door. She watched helplessly as her older sister walked closer to turn the light off and stared her down into silence.

There was a question Marisol wanted to ask Mary as the sister closest to the late Ría. Then the dishwasher stopped and the room suddenly seemed too quiet. Why was Mary standing there still as a statue, not saying anything? Maybe the time wasn't right to ask. But she needed to know, for her youngest daughter's sake, what their late sister had been like. She cleared her throat. "Do you remember how Ría used to laugh?"

The question caught Mary off-guard. From the higher pitch of her sister's voice, she knew Marisol was talking about their late sister. For a moment, she thought her sister had somehow seen the photo hidden inside the microwave she was covering, but then she brushed the paranoid thought away. "Yes," she said trying to make her voice as impassive as possible.

Marisol simply stared at her for a moment before her eyes turned distant. "Okay." She walked back the way she came, by the poplar wood kitchen table, across the large living room, and down the cold stairs. When she was by the front door, she turned around and said, "I'll drop June off around three and then I won't be gone for more than an hour and a half." Mary nodded stiffly in response. It wasn't until she heard the creak of the last step that she released the breath she'd been holding. Turning away from the microwave, she moved to the cupboard by the fridge, took out a cup, took out the *sangria* she had stored in the fridge, served herself all the way to the top of the cup, and downed the whole amount in a mouthful.

At the foot of the stairs, Marisol thought once more of the late Ría. She was the type of girl who felt everything strongly. When she was sad, she cried rivers of tears. When she was angry, she threw tantrums and promised never to speak again as long as she lived. When she was happy, she laughed with her whole body. She was clumsy, and like her mother, careless. She would fall asleep wherever she wanted, regardless of whose company she was in. She was young and couldn't yet count up by fives. She liked snuggling up to people and playing catch with Mary, who was one year older than her. Often while trying to catch the ball, she would laugh and miss the ball, falling down from joy.

It was her falling laughter that plagued Marisol. She remembered being out in the backyard of the pumpkin house, with her three sisters and mother. It was summer and the air was humid and the grass was green. Back then, the wooden fence hadn't sprouted growths and was still the color of desert oak. Teresa and she were jumping rope by the farthest right corner of the yard. This was before Teresa grew bossy. Like usual, Mary and Ría were throwing a big, blue rubber ball back and forth. Susana was cooking *tacos de chorizo* inside, glancing at her daughters every few moments from the window above the sink. The spicy scent of the *chorizo* wafted outside from the open dining room door her mother had forgotten to close and mingled with the sweet smell of dewy grass.

While she jumped, Marisol looked at Alegría's unsteady

motions. She seemed drunk. When Mary would throw her the ball, her arms would constrict before they'd stretched out the sufficient distance to catch it. Her whole body would fold over on itself and she'd lay on the grass laughing and gasping. When she would try to throw the ball at Mary, she'd get a loopy smile on her face, then in the middle of throwing the ball, she would lose her grip on it and fall down in laughter again. At first, Mary laughed along with her, thinking she was teasing her. But after ten or so failed attempts at playing catch, she'd grown sober and suggested they play a different game. Ría had become frustrated with her clumsiness. She wanted to keep playing the game. However, her failed attempts had convinced her she was no good at it or at anything and never would be for her entire life. She'd started cursing the ground for being so slippery, the ball for being so round, and herself for falling down. Susana had heard Ría's angry curses, wondered where she'd picked up such obscenities, and run outside to see what was the matter. Instead of acting like a good, strict parent, she'd hugged her daughter, picked up the ball, and consoled her with simple throws and catches. Mother babied the younger sisters too much, or so Marisol had said to Teresa.

As a result of Susana's irresponsible trip outside, some of the *tortillas* on the stove had burned and hardened too much for Marisol's soft teeth to bear. Not waiting for their father, who wouldn't get home until later, they'd all gathered for dinner inside and eaten the *chorizo* with a squeeze of lime on *tortillas* that looked more like *tostadas*.

The memory plagued Marisol because her late sister's fall reminded her of her daughter's fall on the stairs and on Christmas Eve night. The night she got back from Teresa's, she tossed and turned in bed, making her husband pull the pillows over his head and ultimately sleep on the living room sofa. The memory plagued her all the Sunday after, while she cooked and cleaned, making her burn her own *tortillas,* causing her daughters to burst in the room yelling "the house is on fire!" and leaving the stench of the skillet for weeks after. It made her absent-minded.

On Monday morning, her husband told her about a miraculous call he'd received from the delivery manager at the Estandar cereal company offering him his job back. He said how in the space of six long months, the man had finally come to his senses about senselessly firing him and might even give him a delivery schedule more suitable for a working family man. She nodded her head with glassy eyes and said, "She fell just like my daughter." After that, he ceased his excited chatter about the possibility of more money to plug into his bookbinding dream. Seeing her eyes swimming in memories, he knew it was useless to talk to with her. She wasn't paying attention one bit. He turned over on his side, got up from bed, and curtly told her, "Don't forget to take Alegría to see Great-grandfather Francis today. It's been a week and his concoction has run out."

She'd gone the rest of the day in the same daze, only snapped enough out of it to ask Mary to babysit her oldest daughter in the afternoon. She'd wanted to ask her if she'd seen the same thing in the late Ría that she saw in her daughter. Over and over in her mind, she kept thinking about the strangeness of her daughter and whether her sister had been the same. If her sister'd had the same sleeping and falling problem as her daughter, had she done something horrible when she named her daughter after her? Had she cursed her daughter to get rid of the guilt at the back of her mind? She closed her eyes. If her late sister had been the same, had their mother noticed anything strange in her? Had she done anything about it? With the passing of her mother, there were only types of people she could ask and get answers from: her family and a very honest witch-doctor.

When she opened her eyes, she was in the jean-blue sedan with June outside of Alegría's school waiting for her to come home.

16.

Thirteen minutes before Marisol Cana arrived at his iron gate with her eight-year-old daughter in hand, Great-grandfather Francis had the premonition that someone was coming to visit. He was in the kitchen, on the top floor of his two-story concrete house, sitting at a small, two-person blue plastic table flush against the wall under the window. He liked to lean forward on his chair more suitable for a patio than a kitchen and look through the button-sized hole in his translucent red curtains at the changing world and the unchanging people. It was 3:36 on a gray March afternoon, simultaneously too late and too early for a cup of *atole*. But feeling peckish and knowing someone would soon come swinging his white gate, he sprung up with a litheness that at twenty-seven, Aunt Mary would've said was past her years, and made to sauté minced garlic and onions in a saucepan in preparation for a bowl of instant ramen.

There were three likely candidates for the visit. The first was always Josefina, who was known to leave her grocery store in the middle of the day for a consultation and a cleaning and who had become convinced that the recent disappearance of her spitting pot was caused by a *brujo's* curse, probably solicited by Salome, whom she hadn't allowed to double-bag her ounce of *chiles de arbol*. The second candidate was the lovestruck Jacob Ramos, who kept pestering the *chaman* for a love potion, despite all his warnings that love was not a trifle, and who had given up his traditional solitude in ardent pursuit of the loose librarian. The third likely visitor was Alegría, accompanied by her mother for a follow-up to her hallucination, sleep, and weight problems. The father wouldn't come. He had resumed his hours as a delivery truck driver for the Estandar cereal company and would be working at this hour.

Great-grandfather Francis added to the saucepan water, black beans, corn, chicken, and a secret mixture of spices known only to him and Josefina, *La Trompuda*, which meant the mixture recipe had already circulated all of Manteca and part of Prudent. He brought the mixture to a boil. It had been precisely one week since Alegría and her parents' last visit. Assuming she had followed his instructions and drunk a vial of waking concoction every morning following his last meeting with her, then she should've drunk her last vial today. If she and her mother waited until tomorrow or the next day to visit, then he had misjudged the connection between her symptoms and ancestry; his simple waking concoction had worked for the little girl and her life would regain balance. A follow-up visit would just be eagerness on her and her mother's part to get another week's vials of his waking concoction, or gratitude for another successful cleaning. But in his experience, people seldom remembered a *chaman* once they were healthy, in-balance. Please and thank-you's were reserved for occasions when there was something left to gain. A follow-up visit today could mean the little girl had not yet regained balance, that he had not misjudged the link between her family and her symptoms, and that time had anew proved itself an indestructible loop.

The *chaman* moved from his gas stove to a pantry no more than five feet away beside the fridge, where he kept his secret herbs and ancient spices, as well as his prized collection of every kind of instant ramen available at Josefina's. Feeling adventurous, he picked out a packet of lime chili shrimp flavor instead of his usual chicken or beef flavored ramen. Opening his cupboards, he looked for scissors to open the packet, but found only those used for the sacred cutting cleansing ritual. The broth on the stove was boiling. The scissors were sacred. He used them anyway while uttering a silent apologetic prayer to the cleansing spirits. He was weak for ramen.

Breaking his ramen in two, he placed it inside the saucepan, dumped in the contents of the lime chili shrimp flavor packet, gave the soup a stir, letting the crispy noodles meld into the flavors of the broth for three minutes.

By this time, it was 3:49. He heard two car doors close in the still outside. Moving to the window, he peeked out the hole of the translucent red curtains he'd received as a gift from a seamstress he'd helped cure of cancer. An old blue sedan parked by his curb. It was the third candidate, Alegría and her mother.

Great-grandfather Francis went to his fridge and pulled out cilantro leaves, *chiles en vinagre,* and a lime. He washed the lime and cilantro, cut the lime in half on a yellow plastic cutting board and shredded the cilantro. From outside, the gate jangled violently with two quick yanks. Ignoring the impatient sound, he turned the heat off, moved the saucepan to his blue plastic table, grabbed the halved-limes, squeezed them into his ramen, and garnished his masterpiece with the shredded cilantro. Taking the hard *tostadas* left over from his breakfast from the cast iron griddle on the stovetop, he crushed them with his fingers and sprinkled the shards of hardened tortilla over his ramen.

Using a fork, he brought the steaming noodles into his mouth. The chicken and lime chili shrimp was not a bad flavor combination. He raised the saucepan to his lips and drank from the broth. The burning heat was pleasant, his mouth accustomed to drinking boiling *atole* from his youth, when he lived with his mother and had had to drink an entire cup of the *masa*-based beverage in two sips to avoid missing the *camión* to pick up fresh *tortillas* from the *tortilleria* on winter mornings.

The front gate jangled again. Marisol, the beautiful Susana's second daughter, was spoiling his ramen with her ruckus. But her jangling was no use. The crocodile did not catch the gazelle by slapping its tail against the water and alerting every animal within a ten-mile radius. Likewise, he would not be moved by her even if she tore the gate down and brought all of Manteca to throw rocks at his window. It was custom for his visitors and any ailing souls to wait a minimum of fifteen minutes before they'd be allowed entry into his house. The wait was a test of his visitors' patience and a sign of respect for his status as a *chaman* and the spirits he conversed with. Also, it added to the mystery and authenticity of his business. He thought she would've learned to wait by now, seeing as it was her third visit.

Great-grandfather Francis took his time eating, opening the jar of *chiles en vinagre* and munching on the pickled *jalapeños* in between slurps of noodles and broth. Finishing his afternoon snack, he scrubbed the saucepan in the sink and put away his jar of canned chilis. He was a clean person.

Checking the window one last time, he exited the upstairs kitchen through the orange curtained doorway into the small dark-lit room with the cot reserved for cleanings and strolled downstairs to the main floor, where consultations were held. He opened the door into the flint-colored sky, which even in its dull grayness seemed bright after the smoky darkness of the house. From the looks of the somber clouds, a storm was coming. According to some *chamanes*, when the people of Manteca grew dark, their bad overtaking their good, their spirits would seek to regain balance and be rid of the dark, and it seeped out of them like smoke and rose up in the sky. The darkness in the flint-colored sky would grow into heavy clouds, pregnant with vice, until the sky couldn't hold it anymore. And that was when the rains came, when the people of Manteca needed a good cleansing.

Great-grandfather Francis walked across the cement driveway, gravel crunching under his feet, and opened the white gate, which had aged along with him and left rusty white paint residue on his visitors' hands when they gripped its vine-like rails waiting for him to open the door and let their tattered souls in. Without a word, he led Marisol and her daughter up the cement steps and through his curtained screen door into his mint-green cement house.

One week's time had not changed the house. The air was still muddled with the sharp and sweet smells of herbs and spices so strong an hour in the room was insufficient for visitors' noses to adapt themselves to the odor. The light which passed through the front window turned shades of oranges and purples from the curtains. Somehow the air in the room seemed fuzzy, like that of a faded photograph. On the right, a hard wooden table with its four chairs and pink woven mantle was immediately visible, where consultations took place. To the left was another table, but this one decorated in a mystical style, with animal figurines, candles, herbs, oils, flowers, and three spray bottles of water that were used in the quick water cleaning. On either side of the mystical table was a cuckoo clock. The walls were decorated with auspiciously-patterned fabrics and a single poster of the *Ghostbusters*.

The one witch-doctor and his two visitors sat down at the pink-mantled table. The little girl's eyes were rimmed with red and watered easily in the smoky room. She moved the chair lazily and plopped down on it haphazardly. Her rainbow-striped sweater was noticeably looser than a week ago. The mother sat down mindful not to scrape the legs of the chair on the cement floor, which seemed to suck the warmth from her exposed ankles. She played with the yarn at the edge of the pink mantle. Now that she was face-to-face with the *chaman*, she didn't know how to put into words her worries about Alegría and her resemblance to her late sister.

"Speak," said the witch-doctor, picking up his *guitarrón* where it rested against the leg of the table and strumming the strings softly. Marisol managed to unclasp her jaws an inch before he stopped her with a wave of his hand; he may or may not have been trying to teach the mother a lesson in patience as retribution for interrupting his ramen meal. "First the girl." Motioning to Alegría with a slight jerk of his chin, he prodded her quietly, "Go on, my child. My waking concoction has been effective, I see you've lost weight. But something is troubling you. How is your condition?"

"Worse," interrupted Marisol, "she fainted on the stairs."

The *chaman* gave her a look that made her feel small again. She pursed her lips and turned to look at her daughter, who was slouching on the chair. Alegría's manners were getting worse, too.

"The same," she said, "Except I can stay awake. But I don't like it."

"Why?" prodded the *chaman*. He continued strumming the same five combinations of notes absentmindedly.

"Because. My head hurts."

The *chaman* nodded, as if expecting her answer. "How have your meals been?"

Alegría's voice was hollow. "Bad. I like food. My mom made me *tortitas de papa*. I like them a lot. But when I smelled them, I felt bad. like throwing up. But I know that I like them and I need to eat so *mi mamá* is happy and so I don't feel as tired. So I plugged my nose and put some potato in my mouth. I had to spit it out. I felt like throw up." She slouched further down on the hard chair to reach the cement floor with her foot and give it a kick. Marisol's tan skin colored faintly at her daughter's impropriety. Her husband would've pulled Alegría forcefully up by the arm. But he wasn't there, so she did nothing to stop her daughter.

Abrupt as a hiccup, Alegría began shaking in tearless silence. The *chaman* stayed quiet, observing. The mother, who had begun remembering every time her husband had thought something improper was stirred to action, brushing her hand listlessly across her daughter's back. "Why? I like food," said the young girl, whimpering. Her emotions were getting harder to control, and the devastation of being unable to enjoy something that had seemed so natural before was too much for her. The pain was that of having the fried cheese-stuffed potato cakes before her, after days of hunger, and desiring them so much, but having them turn into a poison that would make her stomach turn. That which she loved seemed taken away forever, and her resolve to enjoy it as she had once done was not enough to overcome her body's rejection of it.

"It's the waking concoction," said Great-grandfather Francis. "No cure is without side effects. And your case is special. I could not give you a cure without a full diagnosis. I do not do what I do not know."

Marisol turned to him and blinked her eyes as if seeing him clearer would also aid her understanding of his words. "You mean you don't understand what Alegría has? How are you supposed to fix her then?" Her voice rose in strength as her fears about Alegría came back, and the guilt of her youngest sister made itself known again like a rekindled spark. Her daughter, for her part, lowered her head and hunched her shoulders, growing smaller at her mother's words.

"She is not broken," said the mysterious *chaman*, calm but with a firmness that resounded against the concrete walls and made the water in the spray bottles quiver. Taking a deep breath, he repeated, "She is not broken, and therefore needs no fix. This is what I know.

"One should not sleep too much or too little, else the body will be imbalanced. Our bodies are like a pot of water on a stove. The knob on the stove turns on the flame under the pot and the water inside starts to heat up. Bubbles start popping up, going to the surface, and the water is boiling. What happens when you turn the knob back? The flame under the pot disappears, the water inside loses its heat. The bubbles disappear and the water calms. The knob controls the water, going from one stage to another, from colder to hotter.

"We have something like a knob inside of us, too, controlling what we do. That power inside us works according to time, to hours and seasons. It is the reason we sleep at night and wake in the day. People like I suspect you are, have this knob taken away from them. So the water boils and cools without control. You fall asleep and wake up at times irregular. On your body, that takes a toll."

"Oh. Okay," said Alegría. She squinted her eyes in confusion. She understood something about a pot and water. Plus a knob. Like a doorknob. Sitting back up in her chair, she looked to her mother, hoping to get clarification. Her mother was looking elsewhere.

Great-grandfather Francis sighed the deep sigh of one who has traveled the desert and back for nothing. A different method of explanation was necessary. He held his *guitarrón* by the neck with his left hand and with his right began drumming his fingers on its soundboard so it sounded like rhythmic sea waves slapping the shore. In a voice that came from deep within his stomach, he began singing, and it was low and monotone and reminded Alegría of a chant.

"Each and every being has two sides. There is the hot and the cold, the young and the old, the dark and the light, the wrong and the right. When in us one side matures, to its overbearing (we've) inured, then comes the need of a cure. Each and every being has two sides. I am the chaman. *When the imbalanced come, I must do what I can."*

His eyes lost their focus, became distant, as if he were looking through the thick swirls of magenta and orange smoke into the beginning of time, the beginning of life.

"Before the eldest son of Anthony Delgado leaned on his shovel, looked to the west and proclaimed it as novel, a place where a bakery might be, where a people might grow old and happy, people like you (Alegría) existed. They slept in the day and woke in the night, their parts were imbalanced, their souls were in plight.

"The first seen of your kind in our beautiful Manteca was a man not meek. When his wife caused him stress, urging him over what they did not possess, he did not turn his cheek, but sold her for a bowl of menudo *and a plate of* tamales. *His name was Dominique. When he had what you have, people thought him mad. They thought him cursed for his misdeeds, fated to suffer, fated to grieve. To the people, his soul was imbalanced, his spirit crying out to be freed from the dark within him. So his spirit escaped, whether it be noon or midnight, to the land of dreams.*

"But his woman, short after leaving him, she had a daughter, who turned out like her father. And the people, they thought, that his fate was hereditary. The sins of the father must be answered by those he has fathered."

Alegría raised her hand to be called on as she was programmed to do at her elementary school. For fear of interrupting Great-grandfather Francis in his song, she had resisted the excited impulse to raise her hand and tell him she'd met Uncle Dominique once, in a dream, maybe, and the hesitant itch to ask her mother what the words "plight" and "hereditary" meant, but she understood that Uncle Dominique's daughter had what she had, what made her tired and grumpy all the time, what was the cause of having to drink the vomitrocious waking concoction in the mornings, and the reason why she couldn't enjoy her food anymore, and that somehow, it was the father's fault, so she could not keep from shooting her hand up to quench her need for answers.

The singing grandfather stopped his drumming and in the sudden quiet nodded once towards her, solemnl y giving her permission to speak. He still had the reverberating aura of a *chaman* in song.

"That's not fair. His daughter didn't do that—sell her wife," said Alegría, "why did she have to get the same thing as her father?"

In the enunciated fashion of his song, punching every word on beat, the *chaman* said, "A turtle cannot bury its shell. It must carry the shell it's been born with for life," and then breaking into a low conspiratorial voice that made Alegría feel as if they were the only two in the room, "I don't think it's all that fair either. But in this world, every action has a consequence. That father should've considered his future daughter before acting, eh?" Great-grandfather Francis winked at Alegría, who smiled back, and then turned his indiscernible eyes to Marisol, who'd grown stiller than the creased 1984 poster of *Ghostbusters* on the wall.

Clearing his throat, he said, "Shall we continue?" His fingers began their rhythmic drumming once more.

Marisol interrupted a third time. "We have to leave and I have to ask. When my mother came to visit you all those years ago, what did she come for?"

"You already know. You've dwelt in the rivers of the past long enough to remember."

Marisol's eye twitched. "Did my sister, my youngest sister, did she have the imbalance that my daughter has?"

The *chaman* gave his *guitarrón* a last longing look and put it back down by the wooden table leg. He would not finish his song today. "She was too young. I could not precisely tell. But I suspected she did. She's the reason I gave your daughter the waking concoction so quickly."

"What she has, can it be cured?"

Great-grandfather Francis looked towards the *Ghostbusters* poster. He did not meet the mother's eyes. "Yes. But to be cured does not mean to be rid of all physical symptoms. To be cured means to be in harmony with this world, with yourself and others. To be cured means to find peace, to gain balance."

While the adults were talking about her and her late aunt, Alegría was struggling trying to remember more about the dream on the stairs, the one about Uncle Dominique. "Excuse me, grandfather, what happened to the man? The one who's like me?"

"He died, terribly."

17.

June was a perilous, pit-pat-pattering pipe bomb. She was left in the care of Aunt Mary, dropped off on the front doorstep of the pumpkin house, given six whole seconds to knock on the door and be received by her aunt and babysitter for the next hour, before her mother felt sufficiently reassured that she would cause no trouble, moved the stick to 'drive,' and stepped on the pedal in the direction of Great-grandfather Francis's house, leaving nothing but the afterimage of her sister's half-raised wave in the backseat and the annoying sedan screech like a dying dolphin in her wake.

"Good afternoon, come on in," said Aunt Mary, leaning in for the customary hug and kiss on cheek. June accepted the hug from her mammoth-like aunt half-heartedly, wrapping her noodle arms around that sturdy frame limply and ducking her head to the right to avoid the dry kiss. Her aunt's usual bar soap smell was masked by the stronger smell of disinfectant and all-purpose cleaner, which she carried from the upstairs kitchen. Mary separated herself politely from June as if they were strangers, mere acquaintances at a party and not blood-related. She closed the door, locking it with a click, and asked her niece how her life was going.

"Fine," June said. But her life was not going fine.

Ever since a week ago, when Alegría had visited the *chaman*, there had been whisperings going on around the school, talk about the strange elementary schooler who could see into the world of the dead. June knew this news was false. (The only spirit lurking in her sister's and her shared bedroom was the peevish Spirit of Wakefulness and Loud Noises, which appeared at unsightly times no human being should be awake, prompting the irritating creaks in the bed behind the deck of cards curtain, where Alegría would toss and turn from slumber to sleeplessness.) But she bent her head behind her books and said nothing, contradicted no one. As long as the talk was concentrated on the younger sister, no one paid any attention to the older sister, and she was able to escape the confining claws of gossip.

In a time when news was running dry and even a trip to Josefina's after school would only gain the same-old gossip, the middle school students drunk in any tittle-tattle that could distract them from their studies and the end-of-year tests they were inching towards. The strange Alegría's unusual gift was a well. Students constantly mentioned her name in conversation, the hard gree's in 'Alegría' so often said that, in truth, were a stranger to visit their middle school during lunch time, he would've thought the school overrun by a chorus of chirping crickets. So often was she mentioned.

Absorbed in preparations for the conquest of June and the start-up of the PM Club, Hector and his friends, the only other people who knew her identity as the ghost-seer's sister, neglected making her status known. For this, June was grateful. Though the cricket chorus of her sister's name grated on her ears, she felt that was long as her anonymity was preserved, this storm, too, would pass. After three days of persistent chirping, a *churro*-selling Prudento had attacked a Mantecano, and Alegría was temporarily forgotten by the students of Enrique Delgado Middle School as the new scandal circulated the faded classrooms and hallways. It seemed that by Friday, life would be back to normal.

But Alegría's interruption in June's life was not something simply confined to home or school life. No, her interrupting presence had reached even to the three Cana women's trip to Josefina's grocery store. On Thursday, June's drooling little sister had been dopey enough to get lost in the between the aisles of toilet paper and tissues. She'd purposely gotten herself in trouble, somehow earning the interest of their fellow-shoppers and neighbors, and more importantly, the full attention of their absent-minded mother.

For the rest of the grocery trip, her mother had brought down her arm firmly around her once-lost Alegría, like a protective bar warding off all danger and—excluding June to the outside. The eldest daughter pretended to text on her phone, to the outside world feigning teenage nonchalance with perfection, but for the solitary glances every now and then at the bar leaving no entry behind her sister's back. Not once did the mother look back as she exited the store with her most important daughter, not even to see if her trailing eldest daughter was still following behind in the tar-stained parking lot. Probably, while crossing the lot, June could've been hit by a car, her body found splattered and strewn among the vast sea of cold, gray cars and her mother wouldn't have winked an eye.

That was not the only interruption in her life either. After the club meeting with Hector on Friday, June's mother had failed to pick her up, all because she was busy making her sister's favorite potato cakes. They'd sat down for dinner at their little round, toast-colored table, with the yellow-checkered mantle put away in their father's absence, between the kitchen and living room. The slight smoke from the oil in the air reeked of her mother's love for Alegría. The nice white dishes with the blue rims were set with a fork at three o'clock and a full water glass at one o'clock.

Sitting facing the kitchen, Marisol had picked up the paper towel-lined tray with the stacked potato cakes from the center of the table and served her youngest daughter two, in rose-colored hope that she'd partake of them and joyfully break her picky fast as of late. June, on her left, was expected to serve herself. The joke was on the mother, though, because no sooner had her youngest daughter picked up her fork and taken a whiff of the potato cakes than she'd started gagging.

Steeling herself against the odor, Alegría had plugged her nose with one hand, and with the other raised her fork to her mouth, all while her mother watched in a mixture of hope and horror.

The potatoes had made it as far as her lips before she'd started gagging again. There was dismay splashed on her face. She'd taken a hard drink of water, wiped her mouth with the back of her hand, sharpened her brown eyes to steel, huffed out a determined breath and, as if she were downing a vial of the *chaman*'s waking concoction, taken the fork and shoved the potato into her mouth. Her eyes widened. Her jaw flexed. She slapped her hand over her mouth.

June could almost hear her chirpy sister's voice strain out "I must like this. I will like this," foolishly determined to do what she couldn't. She saw her sister's throat move in a dry swallow.

And then Alegría's shoulders jerked forward and she spit out the unswallowed potato on the blue-rimmed plate in front of her. And she gagged and gagged and gagged. And there was the clatter of dishes on the table beside June as her mother ran like a duck to her sister's aid. Alegría's body convulsed as a fish would do without water, and she made awful retching noises, heaving over the blue plate over and over again, her body trying to rid itself of an empty stomach. Tears streamed from her eyes and her nose ran with the effort.

Her mother rubbed her back furiously and reached across the table to get napkins for her precious daughter. In distress, she grasped at her hair and kept rubbing her daughter's back, incapable of doing anything more to help. She looked at her youngest daughter the way one looks at a raging house fire, small and helpless, flailing to stop to a disaster she knew she'd caused.

And watching the circus that was her open-mouthed mother desperately trying to console her shaking, whimpering, treasured daughter, June sat still in her blue-cushioned chair and felt a smile tug at her bottom lip. A sort of malevolent happiness.

But the satisfaction lasted only a moment. Then Marisol called out, "June! Get a bowl!" and she was up from her chair and into the kitchen, getting out the big, green bowl from the poplar wood cupboard and closing it with a clatter. June stood next to her sister holding out the green bowl below her for the vomit that wouldn't come, feeling sick at the glossy spit-up potatoes on her sister's blue-rimmed plate and nauseous at her own smile from a minute before.

Qué asco. She felt disgusting for enjoying her little sister's pain. Awful. Horrible. Callous. Ugly. June was ugly inside. There was dark inside her Frankensteinian body, black, viscous bile. She hated herself for having cruel thoughts, for wishing her family harm, for staying stationary while seeing her sister suffer. She hated herself for hating her sister.

From that day on, June developed the taste of carrion in the back of her throat, caused by her self-loathing, which gave her extremely bad breath in the mornings. Before brushing her teeth after waking up, the odors emanating from her lemon-shaped mouth were sharp enough to bring down five horses, forty well-equipped Prudento farm workers, and twenty-three gliding birds of a feather. Her bad breath would bother her during her life's most poignant and embarrassing events, including her first kiss with Hector, her first job interview as a reporter, and her first morning with her husband after their wedding night. It also ensured her habit of carrying spearmint-flavored gum and orange-flavored breath mints in her purse and pockets whenever she left the house.

On Saturday, the three Cana women had gone to see Aunt Teresa, and June had been comforted by Cousin Stacy and a recipe for bad breath acquired from her mom, Teresa, and left feeling better about herself while distracted by the visit.

Alegría, however, hadn't let her forget her self-loathing for long. The three Cana women had been home all of two minutes when the youngest flung herself down the stairs in a deep sleep. Somehow, June felt responsible for her sister's fall, as if her earlier ill will towards her had been answered by the universe in the form of the fall. Unlike her previous passivity at the Flores

Christmas party, she actively stretched out her arms to catch the sailing Alegría and stopped her complete obliteration at the bottom of the carpeted stairs.

The only thanks June had received for her efforts was a reprimand from her mother. Her heart stiffened a little and the rotten taste came back in the back of her throat. Nevertheless, seeing Alegría lying bruised and still on the tough green couch, reassuring Marisol that her precious daughter was, indeed, breathing and would soon awake, June felt perturbed and responsible. She had been just as relieved as Marisol when Alegría awoke.

Come Marisol and Alegría's follow-up meeting with the *chaman* on Monday, June didn't complain. She sat in the sputtering sedan outside her old elementary school shaped like a sheet-cake, waiting for her sister to push open the heavy, metallic doors by the bare flagpole, to which children paid ode every morning by reciting classical Manteca poems meant to inspire hard work and cooperation, such as "Break Bread, Make Peace," "The River's Rising," and "Courage, Industry, the Little Boy Said."

Earlier that day, while walking the through the dull tan hallway ready for lunch, June heard César from the seat across her in history, tell his best backstabbing friend, Brutilda, how he'd heard elementary schooler Alegría, whom he'd never laid eyes on before, was five feet and two inches tall, never, ever drooled on her pillow (as part of an oath she'd sworn with Great-grandfather Francis and the spirit of an elk to maintain her eternal youth), and wore a shrunken head the size of an acorn around her neck at all times, in hopes that it would strengthen her connection with the dead; indeed, the shrunken head was the reason she could fall into a trance, closing her eyes and laying down immobile (but never drooling) at any time, even while shopping at Josefina's, while she contacted the spirits of her neighbor's ancestors.

Hearing such an astonishing description of her sister, she could not help but mutter to herself, "That's ridiculous—Alegría drools sometimes," in the anonymity of the crowded, chatty tan hallway.

However, the people of Manteca, adults and children alike,

tend to perk up their ears while gossiping, so as to never miss a crucial detail. Thus it was that even the crowded hallway could not keep June's forty-five decibel muttering out of César from history class's ear shot. He turned around rapidly, his chewed up bangs, which looked to be the work of a lawnmower, shaking all out of disorder like dead aspen leaves in fall. "Who said that?" His eyes searched behind him.

Dachshund-faced Brutilda turned to search also, knotting her eyebrows.

They were almost to the cafeteria, the blonde light visible at the left end of the hallway. June stared holes into the ground, believing that she could disappear if she just remained silent. She could not know that the ever-hovering Hector was walking behind her, having heard her little remark and watching César and Brutilda in the act of blind searching.

Maybe he was tired of June's anonymity. Maybe he had grown frustrated with her inadequate responses to his hard-working efforts at conversation, the silence deafening. Maybe he had found her performance at the first PM Club meeting less than satisfactory, her enthusiasm lacking for something that was only done with her happiness in purpose. Maybe he really didn't understand that June valued her anonymity at school, that she kept quiet on purpose. Whatever the reason, he spoke up behind her to their two peers in front of her "She did," putting his arm around her shoulder. And with those two clipped words, let the entire four-hundred student body of Enrique Delgado Middle School know she was the older sister of Alegría, the ghost-seer.

"Who's that?" asked Brutilda, giving June the once-over and knotting her knotted eyebrows until her dachshund forehead looked like the gnarled face of a tulip poplar tree. She knew June briefly as "that one girl Hector and his gang hung around."

"June," said Hector. "And you should listen to her."

Once students discovered her identity as the older sister to a ghost-seer, June was naturally taken as the authority on all things supernatural. Weeks after that Monday afternoon, peers unknown still came to ask for her solemn witness on the fantastical happenings inside her grandmother's house, where the ghost-seer resided, and where legend by word-of-Josefina's-mouth was where the great Susana had died.

They came like flesh flies to carrion in summer. "Hey you," buzzed a long-faced boy with hair gelled up sharper and pointer than the hills southwest of Manteca in her ear. He had ears the shape of butterfly wings, was wearing a black and yellow track suit, and was a complete stranger to June. "Does your sister have a specific time limit for how long she can view the dead? Does she eat anything special to see them, like honey?" Peers came asking questions while she took notes in her science class, while she blew her nose discreetly in the corner of the classroom by the trashcan, even while she made a much-needed trip to the bathroom. "If the dead sneeze, can your sister catch a cold?" asked a girl with a wide nose and a short neck as June came out of a bathroom stall.

More often than asking odd questions, students wanted to know if they could come over to the pumpkin house for a seance with Alegría. They wanted to meet with late teachers who'd taught at their middle school in the past to discuss the answers to the upcoming math test. They wanted to communicate with the all-seeing dead to know once-and-for-all, what boys most liked in girls, and whether handsome Johnny in second year liked Juanita of the long tresses or Yoana of the pretty dresses. They wanted to discover from those most knowledgeable who had gone into the other world what the *taquera* who sold in the park on school days really put inside her eighty cent *tacos de papa* to make them so addictively good, even when everybody knew the green sauce she drizzled them with was watered down to economize.

They asked her, prodded her, badgered her for answers, dragging her reticent self from the caliginous cave of isolation she'd retreated to into the blinding light of middle school popularity, all bleary eyed and hunchbacked.

But standing just inside the entrance to the pumpkin house,

answering Aunt Mary's question through her teeth, June could not know that her life would not return to a normal "fine," and that the voice she gained as the ghost-seer's older sister would be used for more than answering curious questions; it would be used for a revolution.

The air prickled June's nostrils with the scent of disinfectant and homemade lavender-scented all-purpose cleaner as she sat waiting for her aunt to come back with the tea. Tired as she was from fending off her classmates' questions about her ghost-seeing sister, she wanted to put her feet up on the dinged low coffee table, which was poplar painted to look like maple. But Aunt Mary wouldn't approve. On the walls were hung pink and orange floral decorative plates. Centered on the right wall that kept the kitchen out of sight was an array of family portraits and collages.

All four of Susana's daughters were there, captured at various ages, along with all thirteen of her grandkids. There was a picture of Teresa and Uncle Berto on their extravagant wedding day and a posed family picture with their eleven children in front of Uncle Berto's dental office.

Framed in official black was Mary in black robes with bachelor degree in hand. Her usual thin smile was pasted on. In another photo were Marisol and Daniel Cana, standing by a willow tree near the Mipared River. Daniel had one stiff arm around Marisol; her hands were straight down her sides. Other photos of Susana's daughters at various ages were hard to place. There was a faded, fuzzy picture of a flushed girl doubled over, laughing; June assumed it was her mother, who was prettier when she was younger. The one photo that most captured her attention was one of herself and Alegría in front of their old house on Pinnacle Street. Her little sister, as always, looked effortlessly flawless while she looked like a chubby-cheeked alien, with red eyes, a rectangular body, and a too small head.

Mary's footsteps thundered behind June. After handing her niece the *tecito* with a spoon to stir it, she reached for the television remote on the coffee table and sat down on the camel back couch. Marisol had promised she'd be back in an hour and half; she was counting, awkward under her niece's sour stares.

June could not help looking at the way her aunt's stomach jiggled and grew new folds as she sat down. Those folds were part of the reason her face soured whenever she interacted with her aunt. To June, the disgusting folds and their accompanying arm flab meant her aunt had given up. Mary had lost self-restraint to the *pancitos* and *gorditas* and *taquitos*. She did not love herself anymore and had resolved to grow heavier and fatter until one could no longer tell the difference between her and a rhinoceros, between her and a gluttonous pig. Aunt Mary was what June feared: she feared losing control of her life to food.

"What do you want to watch?" said Aunt Mary. The knee injury she'd gotten falling from the window sill of the pumpkin house's top floor window was acting up, itching and sending tingles up her thigh, as it often did when a storm was coming. As she switched the channels, her arm fat moved. Each roll and quake was a reminder to June that she needed to watch her diet.

"Whatever is fine with me." She tensed her stomach, sucking in and out to see where the folds formed. Her changed body was a greedy beggar, hungry often and clutching to whatever she fed it, making it impossible for her to lose weight.

Mary settled on a crime mystery show, in which a woman uncovered a secret family photograph in the attic of her long-lost twin sister. For a while, the only sounds that were heard were the distant hum of the refrigerator in the kitchen, the screams of the woman on the television as she was chased down the attic stairs by the ghost of her long-lost twin sister, and Mary's sporadic slurps and spoon clinks against her tall cup as she stirred her sugary tea and drank it, too.

"Aren't you going to drink your tea?" asked Mary.

June looked down at the amber liquid, which had grown cold and still in her hands. Drinking sugary tea was just like eating liquid food. It would make her gain weight in all the wrong places. "Yeah, it just got cold. I'll heat it up." She got up, walked to the kitchen, and had her hand in front of the microwave door when she heard a firm "No!" from the living room.

Aunt Mary came into the pink and yellow tiled kitchen like a raging bull. June froze with her hand on the handle. One push and the microwave would open. "Tea doesn't taste as good if you heat it in the microwave. It's better if we heat it in a saucepan."

Her niece looked at the used saucepan in the sink. If they heated one cup full of tea in a new saucepan, her aunt would have to wash two saucepans instead of one. Already, she could see there were beads of sweat on her forehead. "That's okay, this is faster." She pushed open the microwave door but her aunt quickly slammed it shut again.

"Food cooked in the microwave doesn't taste as good as at a stove or in the oven." Mary reached for the tea.

June pulled it closer to her chest, out of reach. "Tea isn't food." Somewhere outside a bird twittered. The refrigerator stopped and restarted humming with renewed vigor. The floor of the house shifted with a creak. The microwave door opened with a click and pop of its own accord. Mary closed it.

She raised her voice slightly. "Listen, you don't really have to drink the tea if you don't want to."

June really didn't want to. But Aunt Mary's strange demeanor, her taut face with the eyes that watched the microwave, piqued her interest. She raised the white, smooth ceramic cup to her mouth with both hands and took a sip. Cold and sweet with a bitter aftertaste. Carbs. But non-special carbs that didn't deserve all the attention Mary was giving them. Her aunt must be nervous for a different reason. Her eyes kept wandering to the microwave. Maybe it wasn't the tea but the microwave that was the cause of her aunt's distress.

"Okay. I'll drink water."

Mary took the white cup from her niece's hands and putting one hand on her back, corralled the lost little lamb back to the living room. "Okay. I'll get it for you." That was even stranger. Mary should've made June drink the tea. She shouldn't have facilitated her niece's pickiness. Then she wouldn't have raised June's suspicion. Then June wouldn't have found the picture under the glass plate. Her strict no-nonsense aunt was hiding something.

Time passed unheard between them. June sipped on her water while Mary played with the hem of her shirt. They sat on the firm, overstuffed cushions of the pink and yellow flower-patterned couch looking at the same TV, the same crime mystery show about a woman and her lost ghost twin sister, listening to the same fuzzy screams and running footsteps from the *tele*, in the same room with a window on the left and an array of family photos on the right and the dark hallway and dining room behind. But they were strangers in different rooms in different houses, one raising suspicion and the other being suspicious, both incapable of going back to their previous familiar relationship, for the them of that day was not the them of yesterday. They were changed people.

When Alegría and Marisol got home, they brought with them a chance for June to escape to her room downstairs and news of the *chaman*'s visit. Everything with Alegría seemed in order. She'd been smacked with a bush and been sprayed with sacred water from a hot pink spray bottle, and her smell had not been unnatural so she was obviously fine. Great-grandfather Francis had given her seven new vials of his improved waking concoction. He'd adjusted the potion as per Alegría's symptoms, reducing the dark maca and adding more beetroot, and would keep adjusting the waking concoction every week (for a small fee) until he found the right ratio of ingredients personal to the little girl; only then would her balance be restored and her nausea go away. To the mother, he gave a homemade emergency kit complete with smelling salts and a rain jacket, grimly reminded her not to dwindle so much in the waters of yesterday, and advised her to stay in high and dry places.

After a quick greeting and thank you from Marisol, Aunt

Mary sat back down on the couch and tried to think up a better hiding place than the microwave for her late mother and sister's picture. The three Cana women headed down the two flights of stairs. At the open entrance to the living and dining area, Marisol turned to give Alegría a small hug and a gossamer kiss on the forehead, as if she were afraid her youngest daughter would break, and walked to the kitchen to work on dinner, which she was late in starting. June looked at the loving mother-daughter scene with clenched heart and teeth, and then she and Alegría retreated to their bedroom further down the dim-lit hall and to the left to do homework and rest.

For a moment in the pumpkin house, all was at calm, all was at peace.

18.

Plays were just the type of thing to put one's name on the map, at least according to Miss Turtle, who'd been brainstorming, plot-planning, drafting, writing, analyzing, rewriting, evaluating, and grammar-checking a play titled "One Woven Thread: The Tragedy of Verónica Socorro and Raúl Banderas." Finally, five-eighths of the school year over, the play was ready to be brought to life by her second grade class at Crecimiento Elementary. She'd spent too long perfecting her beautiful tragedy, for she'd submitted her play proposal and gotten it approved by the school principal since before the beginning of the school year.

It had been three years since a theater production was held at Crecimiento Elementary. Most extracurricular elementary school events occurred in the richer schools further east in Manteca, rarely in the west, so it took the principal no small effort to convince the district board a chunk of the budget needed to be put aside solely for the production, which in return for their generosity, was sure not to disappoint. All of Manteca was already expecting Miss Turtle's great show, the show that would be the culmination of her extensive theatre career: the five acting classes she'd taken in college. Despite her screenwriting difficulties, the show must go on. Now in the beginning of March, two months of preparation would have to be enough. Two months *must* be enough to bring her masterpiece to life. With her indisputable leadership and impressive direction, anything was possible.

The play was announced on a Tuesday and auditions were on Thursday. Each student who auditioned had to prepare a small song lasting no more than one minute and read well a section of either Raúl Banderas's aside in the second act if a boy, or Verónica Socorro's ailing soliloquy in the third act if a girl. Any and all interested students had to get a copy of their assigned audition readings from Miss Turtle by the latest Wednesday, so they could at least have a whole day of preparation.

Slouching over her desk, Alegría asked Bo what kind of role he wanted and if he was going to audition for a main role. He said, "I don't know" once, to answer both questions and turned away from her, fingering the air around his nostrils pensively. No doubt he wanted to stick his fingers through the dark wells and go digging for gold. But his mother, in an exasperated effort to break him of his nose-picking habit, had rubbed chile all over his fingers and into his fingernails so that were he to attempt one small little peek into those unfathomed caverns, the burning pain would be unbearable.

For her part, Alegría had decided to give her all into getting one of the main roles, preferably that of the villain, Pantaleon the Prudento, over that of Verónica Socorro, the main female protagonist, who in her mind, was whiny and useless. At the end of class, she stayed in her seat while the majority of students picked up their backpacks from the back of their chairs and exited the classroom. Four or five classmates walked up to the left side of the whiteboard, where Miss Turtle was sitting at her desk arranging the audition papers. Seeing the oppressor of Prudentos and tyrant of the second-grade, Paolo, waving goodbye to his gang of 48-inch-ers, from whom he had unwavering support, at the classroom door and joining the other auditioners, Alegría's resolve wilted like a flower under too much water, but regaining her earlier confidence, she perked up, stood up, and placing one foot after the other on the carpeted floor as sure and strong as a soldier, made her way to Miss Turtle's desk.

The teacher, uptight after a long day with querulous students, still smelled strongly of cupcakes, sweet and artificial. When she handed Alegría the half sheet of cream-colored paper with Verónica Socorro's soliloquy printed on it, the young alleged ghost-seer made the mistake of returning the soliloquy and asking for Raúl Banderas's aside instead. "Verónica's too dumb," she said, "I'd rather do Raúl's part."

Miss Turtle did not respond but with the grace of a scorned screenwriter, shoved the female protagonist's soliloquy back into Alegría's hands and moved on to the next student, handing out soliloquies and asides with ears hardened by wax. The eight-year-old girl shrugged and stuffed the soliloquy in her sparkle-spotted backpack. On the way to the jean-blue sedan, she dodged Paolo's jeers that she couldn't tell the difference between boy and girl roles.

Though tired and grumpy, Alegría prepared diligently for the audition, striving with twice as much effort as she had ever given solving math problems or reading. For her one-minute song, she chose "Una Flor de Mil Colores," which Grandma Susana had sang as she cleaned the dishes on their weekly cooking lessons and taught her to sing.

Before dinner, she did not take her usual nap but joined her mother, Marisol Cana, who was sweeping the floor of the common living and dining room area. She asked for her help with the song, which she was sure her mother knew. Looking into her daughter's big saucer eyes, the mother could not help opening her mouth, from which no musical note had escaped since the previous Christmas Eve, and singing the tune for her to hear.

"A flower of a million colors," sang smooth-toned Marisol with a voice rusty from disuse, "Through rain or thunder, ne'er grows duller. But blooms in crimson glory, in emerald splendor, in shades of gold and ember." The air still smelled of the sweet mucilaginous *nopales* she'd grilled for dinner. She beat the cement-finished floor with the broom, running the rough brush bristles against the raised border where the unfinished dining and living room floor met the terracotta-tiled floor of the kitchen, and where she had often tripped in a daze bringing food to the white dining table and empty plates to the sink. Marisol noted with shame and regret how her voice, once like warm milk, had cracked on the word "ember" from disuse and took it as a sign of her age.

Her daughter, however, did not notice the crack. Or if she did, she paid it no heed. Instead, she danced around her mother and the sashaying broom, jumping to avoid the piles of dirt her mother had left like a breadcrumb trail all along the cement floor. Alegría sang along with her mother and tried to raise and lower her pitch at the beginning and end of each verse, the way she remembered Grandma Susana doing it, the way that made her sound like she was on an oarless boat in the soft, undulating sea.

In that moment, she was happy. But after two rounds of song, the little girl sat down on the couch, for she had felt her knees weakening while dancing and had the sensation she was falling forward, like seasickness, though when she looked down, her legs and knees were perfectly in order.

Next, Alegría practiced reading Verónica Socorro's soliloquy, which expressed a lot of hooey phooey about being unable to tell Raúl her true hardships for fear that he'd turn worried and head home from the war, and her anguish at the plight of her uncle, and her woe at her inability to do much else than subject herself to Pantaleon the Prudento's ruthless cruelties as she faithfully waited for Raúl to leave the war and come home. Alegría read the difficult words with the help of her mother. Ignoring dull pain in her head, she squinted her eyes, pushing through the lines until they flowed from her mouth and performed the piece as an over-the-top drama, enunciating each consonant and drawing out all the vowels. She even got down on her knees when Verónica professed her undying love for Raúl for special effect. Finishing the piece, she laughed at herself and her melodramatic performance, which caused the invisible ripples in her knees to start again.

At the after-school play auditions on Thursday, Alegría performed her song and soliloquy with head held high to a classroom empty but for the judge and playwright, Miss Turtle. She felt joyful, like she was floating higher than the whiteboard in the classroom, higher than the curly brown tendrils of Miss Turtle's hair as she sat evaluating at her desk to her left. For a moment, she could see Grandma Susana sitting at her desk by the window, cheerful audience to her small show, singing along to the familiar song of their cooking lessons. And then her performance was over and she was told she could go home.

Grabbing her backpack from where Susana had been sitting a minute ago, exiting through the *tortilla*-colored door with the shuttered window, and passing the three anxious students who were waiting their turn outside the classroom door, she met Paolo, who had already auditioned but had waited long enough to tell her that with her small shoulders and lack of star quality, she would never be chosen. Alegría ignored him and focused on the slap of her shoes against the floor. She felt content in what she felt was her best effort.

The next day, the teacher clapped her hands for attention at the beginning of class and announced the result of the auditions for the main roles. The part of Verónica Socorro was won by a pretty girl who always wore a bow in her hair named Violeta. Milo, football aficionado and wearer of the bright red baggy sweat shorts, received the role of Raúl Banderas. Paolo, who had also auditioned for Raúl, earned the role of Pantaleon the Prudento instead. Initially, he refused to play on stage a Prudento, insisting he would not portray a person so lazy and hateful. It took some coaxing from Miss Turtle to convince him only a model student like he could do the role justice.

With the main roles decided, the teacher called out the names of the rest of the characters, auctioning them off to the first student who raised his or her hand. If more than one student raised his hand for a role, either one student withdrew his claim or they played rock-paper-scissors for it. If no students raised their hands, then the role was assigned by Miss Turtle to whomever she saw fit. In this way, Bo was assigned the part of the war general,

Mario, and Alegría that of Verónica Socorro's confidante, the *tortilla* maker Martha.

That day, as her mother drove her home, Alegría looked out the car window at the disappointing sky, empty of birds and colors. On the bland, vanilla white canvas, the Big Painter in the Sky had sluggishly slathered the dirty water he cleaned his used brushes with, not bothering to open up a jar of egg yolk yellow or cornflower blue. She tried to summon up the same happiness she'd felt earlier in the week, when she'd been full of hope and spirit, by humming her audition song quietly. She did not make it past the first verse before June, sitting in the passenger seat having skipped the PM Club meeting, whined she was too loud and shushed her. Marisol, who before had been preoccupied with past memories, looked at Alegría in the rearview mirror and knew the audition had not gone well; she started the song where her daughter had left off and they both finished it and started it all over again in an endless cycle until they arrived home. By then, Alegría had brightened considerably and June had fallen into sullen muteness, moving her tongue across her teeth and the roof of her mouth, tasting the rotten, foul odor inside her.

From the top floor of the pumpkin house, Aunt Mary heard their sedan squeal to a stop and got up to look out the cyclops window. She had gone home early from the high school she substitute-taught at, as the knee she'd broken falling off the window sill when she was seven, had started itching and hurting. Raising the blinds twisted and scratched from constantly peeking through them, Aunt Mary noticed the flies clinging to the closed windows, as if trying to get into an invite-only soiree, like those held in the elite circle of Manteca. Somewhere by the Mipared River, the weeping willow trees turned their leaves upward and the frogs could be heard to croak. The air in Manteca grew clearer and its smell reminded Mary of inching her face, eyes closed, towards a boiling pot of her late mother's mint tea. Leaning closer to see the sky better, the wooden window sill creaked under her palms. From the sky, a fat drop descended. And there was rain.

19.

Uncle Tim was the older, better-looking brother of Daniel Cana. Tall. Long, sturdy, legs with calves thick as elephants. Shoulders broad as a Mantecano's. In high school, he'd been a prodigy of everything from basketball to boxing, although he loved soccer the most. Unmarried by choice, he'd been the source of many a girl's breakup in his prime, a light under whose shadow the self-conscious Daniel Cana had comfortably hid. With his natural abilities, exceptionally good athletic build, and high praises from his coaches that he'd be good enough to play with the Oregano Heroes FC, he'd earned a golden-bordered fast pass to colleges in both Manteca and Prudent. Choosing familiarity over fame, he'd enrolled near home and quickly gained acclaim as the curse-breaker of DelaSal University Threshers' five-year losing streak.

During the soccer championships of his junior year at college, he'd scored the winning goal but after the match, been attacked by gamblers who'd supported the other team. He'd suffered a fractured tibia and fibula that cost him his athletic career. As he healed from his injuries, he felt thrust down from cloud nine, carrying nothing on his back but past glory. Within a year, he'd dropped out of college, unable to keep up with the curriculum too advanced for his ninth-grade reading level.

He now spent his mornings and evenings lying on his most prized possession, a two-position leather recliner, with a cup holder and built-in massager, watching sports matches on his second most prized possession, a thin, black LED television he'd named Telesita.

Left with a love of chips and salsa and an athlete's appetite but not the metabolism, his belly had grown rotund while his limbs remained strong as ever. Clothes from his prime years still fit him, but his belt and jeans nipped at his waist. To avoid the pinched pink pressure lines around his girth, he often went pantless and open-chested at home, saying man should roam freely naked as he was born.

Four years back, Uncle Tim had been instructed by his mother, who'd been instructed by a sister, who'd been instructed by a daughter, to give his fifteen-year-old, trouble-making cousin, Vernon, driving lessons. Despite the twenty-two-year age gap, the two struck up a natural relationship, for they had the same personalities and interests. They watched college soccer games, formed their own dream teams, looked at calendars of girls, cars, and girls with cars, and crashed every party with good food in southern Prudent. As often together as they were, Grandma Tracy liked to joke that Vernon was Tim's twin without a potbelly.

Vernon looked up to Tim. He loved hearing stories of Tim's past glories and mischief, of his days spent on the soccer field feeling the wind in his face and the sweat run down his back, and of his time spent taped on the binder covers of the swooning female species. At the end of each story, Vernon would ask Tim how he'd reached superstar-status with nothing more than a soccer ball. In turn, Tim advised Vernon to spend less time with hooded friends on the streets and more time on the field wearing cleats. Despite taking each word out of Uncle Tim's mouth as holy, spending less time with his friends was the one advice Vernon could not follow. Everything else Tim did, Cousin Vernon emulated. He would've even adopted Tim's pantless habit, had his mother not threatened him with the loss of his signed soccer ball and driving license. Instead, Vernon had settled for wearing a big, flashy belt with an oval-shaped buckle, just the kind Tim wore when he played the part of a party-crasher.

Around the time Aunt Mary was looking out the cyclops window of the pumpkin house, watching fat drops of rain fall down the sky, roll down the window, and kill the mosquitoes clinging on the glass pane for life, an incident was reported further east in Manteca. An old, bald, broken-nosed man had been found unconscious on the muddy park grounds near the main road and the circle of elites, surrounded by a gang of young, jobless, disruptive Prudentos; near his head was a park bench shifted eighty-five degrees clockwise and a shiny belt with an oval-shaped buckle; the old man's sweatpants pockets were turned inside-out. The red-handed proximity of the gang was proof enough for the stick-wielding policemen to forcefully handcuff them and throw them in jail, just until the prosecution could dig up enough evidence to hold them in prison. The unconscious man was packed up into the whining ambulance, forms were filled out, and the Prudentos' parents were called.

Vernon's mother called her mother, who called her sister, Tracy. Knowing the relationship between Tim and Vernon, Grandma Tracy called Tim to inform him what had happened. He hung up on her.

When the news of Vernon's arrest crackled from his phone's speaker in the distorted high-pitched voice of his mother, Uncle Tim felt a pain he had not felt since his tibia and fibula had been fractured by the soccer championship gamblers. He knew Vernon like his own son, had mentored him, earned his respect, watched him lose his senior soccer game and struggle with college applications, and was thus convinced he would never do anything so vile as beat up an old man for a reason simple as a grudge or pleasure. Tim trusted him.

But the joined courts of Manteca and Prudento were not in his favor. He was considered part of a gang. And those who had come before him had tainted history so that the present was prejudiced against him.

Around the time of the civil war, gangs of Prudentos and Mantecanos had formed in the darkest and poorest neighborhoods.

Amidst the sweet, musty, metallic scent of mixed blood, cement, and urine, they fought each other for territory, especially that near the Mipared River. As the situation grew rougher, even the wealthy weren't left unscathed. Families locked their doors, boarded their windows, afraid to leave their houses after sundown for less than a life-and-death emergency.

From early morning to late afternoon, wives and children peeked between the blade-thin slivers of the window boards and saw sharp flashes of knives, glimpsed sangria-colored blood splattered on the men's faces as they waited, apprehensive, for husbands and fathers to come home.

In the smoky, auburn evening, mothers sang muffled lullabies in feeble attempts to comfort their children. But when the soft patters of footsteps and loud gunshots were heard from the ceiling above, their whispered croons fell silent, for that was when they knew the violent ruffians had moved the fight onto their roofs. In those days, mothers and children crept into bed with their shoes laced on, ready to flee should a gang member gain entrance into their safe houses; from this civil war habit originated one of Aunt Teresa's favorite sayings: (*El que listo este, no teme el anochecer.*) /(*El que tiene sus zapatos no le teme a los disparos.*) When the chilling howls of the injured and the spiteful whoops of the looters grew too much for the children, they hid under their rough, threadbare covers, pressing their hands tightly against their ears to block out the vicious, tormented, animalistic screeches of the night, until the air grew stale trapped under their cramped covers and their burning lungs forced them back up.

Then the gangs offered common families an easy proposition: a small, monthly fee in return for their protection. In the economic crisis exacerbated by the civil war, fathers' incomes were already stretched paper-thin. But whether they could afford it or not, Prudento and Mantecano gangs forced paid protection on them. Gang leg-breakers knocked on the doors of houses in their territory, selling their services *por las buenas o por las malas*. If a family was unwilling or unable to pay, then the ruffians would, like a respectable bank, take the liberty of seizing their home and belongings—if they were one of the few lucky. More often than not, the leg-breakers would punish those unable to pay, punching, bashing, and striking hot cuts and bruises on their skin as a warning to those under their protection. Once a home was under gang members' protection, they treated it as their own, coming indoors with foul mud-encrusted boots and the ripe, sour stench of sweat, taking whatever they wanted (and whoever they wanted). Early on, the Prudentos and Mantecanos learned it was better to give willingly than to be ruthlessly robbed of everything. For them, passivity ensured survival.

The modern derivative of the civil war era's despicable gangs was relatively harmless. Modern gangs often consisted of young men, aged fourteen to thirty-five, who would lounge around their neighborhoods, shoot twelve bullets on New Year's, and at most steal a pack of gum from a local gas station. Children like Vernon, who patrolled the park with his friends where the neighbors could see him and talked up future plans that would never bear fruit, were considered full-time gang members.

Nevertheless, the people of Manteca and Prudent never forgot. They could not forget. Their children and their children's children remembered the unspeakable horrors of the civil war era, the sickening feeling of powerlessness and confinement; and their inherited memories clouded their judgment and painted all and any innocuous gang activities and affiliations in suspicious shades of midnight blue.

When Grandma Tracy didn't hear back from Tim, she immediately called Daniel Cana, who was returning to the pumpkin house after an Estandar delivery trip, and demanded he come home to Prudent and show support for the family.

"What's happened?" He asked, sniffing the air, one hand on the wheel, the other shifting his phone from the left to the right shoulder.

With impatience at her son's indifference, Tracy said, "Your cousin Vernon is in jail. They think he and a gang almost killed somebody, a rich Mantecano."

Daniel Cana pulled up in his white Estandar delivery truck, opened the front door of the pumpkin house and pounded down the stairs, booming out his wife and daughters' names. In their peace and obliviousness, Marisol had not bothered to leave her *orejas de elefante* in the hot pan to burn; June had not inconvenienced herself to drop her pencil on her desk in the midst of a math problem; Alegría hadn't disturbed her after-school nap to throw off her butterfly bed covers and greet her father, the sole provider of their family, at the door. They were all ungrateful. Daniel called out their names, giving his beneficiaries a chance at redemption. While unlacing his work boots, he heard them scrambling out of their activities to greet him at the foot of the stairs. Good.

Once the three Cana women were in front of him—Marisol with a steaming spatula, June with a pencil, and Alegría with drool on her face—Daniel announced in a voice that left no room for questions: "We're leaving in thirty minutes. Get ready."

Marisol understood she was to turn off the stove, pack up what dinner she had made, and make herself presentable. June whined to the ever-attentive air around her about how now that she'd been interrupted, she might not have time to finish her homework by Monday. Alegría wiped her face, rubbed her droopy eyes, put on her rainbow-striped jacket and shoes, and laid down on the couch to nap while she waited for someone to tap her on the shoulder and tell her to get inside the car.

Being the Canas that they were, the family didn't crowd into their jean-blue sedan until forty-one minutes later. They headed down the main road that ran the whole southern perimeter of Manteca and across the Mipared River into Prudent. It was a four-lane road with a seventy-mile-per-hour speed limit that anyone who wanted to travel anywhere quickly took, for it connected not only Manteca and Prudent, but also all the neighboring vicinities. Estandar Cereal Company drivers, such as Daniel Cana, often took this road when transporting hard red spring wheat from Prudent into Manteca, and when transporting processed flour from Manteca to elsewhere.

Still on the main road, the Canas crossed the renitent anchor-gray bridge over the Mipared River, built after the short civil war as a conciliatory sign between Mantecanos and Prudentos that bygones were bygones, that both sides had matured past their petty hatred for each other, and that the future held excellent economic opportunity for collaboration. Unlike the hasty wood and stone bridges built elsewhere across the river by Prudentos in defiance of their rejection and deprivation of scored bread by Mantecanos, the main bridge was reinforced underneath by a linear layer of steel triangles that from a distance, looked like Great-grandma Lolita's neat zigzag stitches; it stood on countless, thick concrete pillars that during construction, seemed a great source of strength but when the rains came, would prove a weakness against pressing trees and vehicles.

Daniel Cana turned on his left turn signal and exited the main road into the familiar sepia streets that like tattered photographs held his solitary childhood memories in a breath of almond and damp vanilla grass. He held the thin rim of the steering wheel as he navigated the wide streets of southern Prudent, passing the corner where eight days ago, a cycling *churro* vendor had attacked a visiting Mantecano. He looked for his parents' house with two front doors and one window amid the flat, beige houses. His pocket vibrated with an incoming call. His mother, Grandma Tracy, was calling for the second time that day. Lifting the phone with one hand to his ear, he greeted his mother.

Marisol looked over at him, forever nervous of his habit of talking on the phone while driving. She saw her husband's hand on the wheel tighten, heard the quiet garble of her mother-in-law, then the click as the line went dead. Daniel turned the sedan into the nearest driveway, then reversed the car so they were heading back the way they came.

"Where are we going?" Alegría asked, stealing the words from Marisol's mouth.

"To the river. We're going to meet your uncle."

Long before the Canas reached the Mipared River, a slightly salty smell like moldy limes assailed their noses. It stretched teal-blue farther on each side than anyone could see. The rushing sound of the waters soothed and calmed against the dark stormy sky, which was receding into the west, the opposite side of the river, and leaving utter darkness in its wake.

Uncle Tim sat by the rocks at the edge of the river, oddly under the willow tree's shade in the cold, early evening. His big, round leather belt pinched his girth so tightly, the skin and fabric visible from underneath it reddened and puckered. He had on light blue jeans and a checkered shirt, which he left open to reveal the few golden wisps on his chest. A brown, straw hat bent low cast his face in shadow and hid his dark, glistening eyes.

Daniel Cana parked the car at a nearby little area cleared of all flora for visitors, popped the car door open, and got out. The area looked too picturesque. One could count the spacing between the trees as eight feet apart. The river was beauty planned. Before snapping the door shut, Daniel instructed his wife and two daughters to stay inside while he talked to Uncle Tim for a few moments.

Alegría watched as her father went up to her uncle and said something she could not discern. Her uncle was like a statue, unresponsive and cold. The trees shivered in a slight wind that passed by, shaking the rain from a few hours before on her father and uncle. The air took on the ethereal clarity that comes with the setting sun and the end of a day. Bullfrogs and thrumming insects chorused to fill in the cold vacuum left by the air.

After nearly two hours of waiting, June threw herself back

against her seat and growled. "How much longer? I have homework. I don't even understand why we came. We're not doing anything."

"We came because we're a family. And you're too young to stay at home by yourselves."

Alegría had been observing her uncle, who she noticed had not stood up since they'd arrived, not even to give her father his customary bear hug. Curious, she acquired a pink plastic flashlight from her mother and got permission to get out of the car and remind her father they still had an hour to get home. June reminded her she was disobeying their father. In the damp air, Alegría clicked the flashlight on and off. The yellow light from the pink tube was sure to attract every moth near a fifteen meter radius. Half walking and half running on the muddy clove-colored ground, Alegría skidded to a stop before her uncle and father, who had both heard the car door close and the squelching sound of her shoes on the soft dirt.

"What are you doing here?" asked Daniel, "I told you to stay in the car."

"I wanted to see Uncle," she said. From below, two crickets joined in the after-rain song. "Hey. How's my third-favorite person?"

"Third-favorite? Who's your first-favorite?"

"You know it's *Telesita*."

"Your second-favorite?"

His face froze. Instead of giving his customary answer, "Vernon," he replied, "Daniel, my old brother," with a trembling smile.

"Uncle, what happened?" Uncle Tim didn't look right. His face didn't move as much when he talked.

"Your uncle's tired. He requires sufficient rest and peace." Daniel grabbed Alegría's shoulders to forcibly guide her back to the car, silently promising himself he would punish her for her disobedience when he and his family were alone in the privacy of their car. But Alegría squirmed out of his pressing fingers and ran to hug her uncle.

"Oh, Alegría. Some things in this world are really unjust," he said, sounding hollow. "Some things aren't meant for young children's ears," mumbled Daniel.

"And then it's hard to find the light at the end of the tunnel."

"Why's it light at the end of the tunnel?"

"Cause that there's where hope is. Hope and happiness."

Alegría looked down at the plastic pink flashlight in her hands. She clicked it on and off. "Well here." And she offered Uncle Tim the pink light source. "In the meantime, you can have my flashlight. While you look for hope."

Uncle Tim accepted her flashlight and her niece smiled at him with the northeastern moonlight glinting in her big maple-syrup eyes and the wind blowing her thin baby hairs in her face. She patted his thick arm with a hand the size of his palm.

"Okay, it's time for Alegría to return back to her mother," Daniel said, giving his daughter a practiced, widened-eye look he hoped was significant. He was mortified at the insensitivity she had shown his soccer-legend of an older brother. His daughter was still a child and oversimplified adult affairs.

Alegría got the message, gulped, scrunched her eyes and lowered her head, knowing she had done wrong in disobeying her father. She got up, shook herself off, and waved. "Bye Uncle!"

"Goodbye my *Alegrita*," said Tim, "Thanks for the gift! Careful on the way back, don't go falling into the river," he joked. Daniel nodded in the direction of the car.

She waved one last time, to her father and uncle, then made her way back to their old sedan, following the worn, chiffon-white rocks lining the river by way of the moonlight. Her father and uncle's voices faded to a murmur behind her; the last thing she could make out was a constrained voice saying, "I apologize, she doesn't know about Vernon." She could see the outline of the car up ahead in the distance, but the sky had quickly darkened and without her flashlight, it was hard to make out her squelching sneakers in front of her. The sound was like playing with sticky, too-wet *masa*, like watching the dough cling to the skin on her palm and then fall off slowly; it made Alegría remember her cooking lessons with her grandmother, how she had taught her the trick to fixing too-wet dough was to add more flour.

While thinking about her grandmother, Alegría heard a voice coming from the waters of the river. She stopped with the family car still over twenty feet away and listened closely. A soft burble. A whispered gurgle. A light hiss as the water brushed against the rocks at its edge. The sounds seemed to spray an urgent message. Curious, Alegría stepped nearer the river to investigate. The nearer she stepped, the gruffer, the more insistent the voice became. She bent down by the wet, glowing rocks, trying to discern consonants and vowels in the voice. The water swirled in dark whorls of salty black ink, alluring and hypnotic. Alegría stretched her hand out to feel the water when a small wave reached out, slapping the rocks and spraying her. She let out a yelp, recoiled back in surprise, slipped on a flat, glistening white rock, lost her balance, and in falling backward, knocked the rock out of place.

A car door slammed shut.

Where the rock had been glinted a wet, clay jug colored like dark chocolate. Alegría picked herself up, brushed off her gritty hands, and pushed the wet rock further out to retrieve the primitive clay jug. The voice in the river hushed. Squelching footsteps grew louder.

"Alegría!"

"Mom," said the eight-year-old girl, wheeling around to face her mother, still holding the jug in her hands. It was small, about the size of a mango, with a short handle on the side and a brown stopper stuffed in the curved top. "I was…" Alegría knew she was in trouble with both her father and mother. She thought up a distraction. "Here!" Holding out the clay jug, she said, "I found this!"

"What is that? Where's your flashlight? Never mind, let's go back to the car first."

The mother and daughter held hands as they walked slowly the way the mother had come, trying not to trip on a rock or an invisible tree root. In her haste to find her daughter when she screamed, Marisol had forgone finding a flashlight. Instead, they used the light inside the car like a lighthouse, which June had turned on in her mother's absence.

The car doors popped open, filling the old sedan anew with the smell of the river.

"I told you to keep the car light off. It'll kill the battery, and then we won't be able to get out of here." Marisol reached between and above the front seats to click off the yellowed interior light. Inside the car was plunged in darkness while the three Cana women's eyes adjusted to the moonlight.

"Sorry," mocked June, "when's dad getting back? He's been talking forever!"

"I forgot to ask," said Alegría sheepishly. "But I got a jug!" and she brandished the chocolate-colored clay jug in front of June, who snatched it from her hands.

"What's this? It's old."

Marisol forgot her daughter's scream for the moment and took the jug from June. "It's a drinking jug."

"Cool." Alegría stretched her hands out and squeezed them twice, indicating she wanted to look at it. "What's the squishy thing on top?"

"A stopper," said Marisol. "You can open it," and she took hold of the brown cover soft from the absorption of water.

"Wait don't open it!" June stopped her mother's hand. Alegría frowned. "It's not ours. We should take it to a museum or something."

"Let's open it," said the youngest daughter.

Marisol pulled the stopper out, and turned the jug upside down. Nothing came out. She reached her fingers in and felt the rustle of thick paper, miraculously dry. She tried to clasp a rough sheet between her fingers but couldn't pull it out.

"Is it stuck?" asked Alegría.

"Ha!" said June, "See? I told you we weren't supposed to open it. It's a sign." Alegría frowned. "Can I try?"

"We'll take it to Great-grandfather Francis. I'm sure he has some idea what to do with it."

"Museum! Take it to a museum!" The darkness hid June's disrespectful eye-roll at her mother. "What does that old witch-doctor know?"

"He's nice," defended the young girl.

Marisol hushed her daughters. "Your father's coming back."

From the dirty windshield with the crusty white marks of the earlier rain, the three Cana women watched as the outlines of Daniel and Uncle Tim walked together as far as the nearest willow tree, stood for a moment with their thumbs in their pants pockets, then went their separate ways: Daniel to the family car, Tim back the way they'd come, in the direction of his parked car. Daniel had wanted to drive his brother home personally, but his brother didn't want to leave his car stranded by the river.

Once inside, the father dialed his mother's phone, the beeps sounding strange in the quiet car. The phone rang once before Grandma Tracy answered it.

"Yes, he's fine. He's on his way home." Daniel started the car and backed out of the small parking area, looking over his shoulder between the headrests.

Marisol placed the clay jug between her feet, out of the way. The sound of seat belts clicking into place echoed across seats.

"We will visit some other time. It's too late for the children." The car tires sunk into the wet clove-colored ground.

As he pulled into the highway that led into Manteca and the pumpkin house, he said, "Me too. They won't get away this time."

20.

All Prudentos' problems stemmed from the meddling of Mantecanos. At least that's what June overheard from her father. Standing by her usual eavesdropping spot behind the doorway, she saw her mother in the kitchen and her father sitting at the table with the yellow-checkered mantle, eating late-night peanut butter toast with a glass of milk. Both were in conversation. Apparently, they'd gone to visit disconsolate Uncle Tim at the river because some pig-headed Mantecanos had falsely accused a guiltless cousin of attacking an incompetent old man, emphasis on pig-headed and incompetent.

"Careful," said the mother, cleaning the containers from their packed dinner at the yellow synthetic kitchen sink that matched the one upstairs. Water drummed on the plastic surface. "You know who you're talking to." Her voice had a sharp edge to it.

"Oh, now you identify as one of them? I remember hearing something very different from you when I took you to live in Prudent." Daniel took a big bite of his toast. Annoyed. He ran his tongue over his teeth, swirled his cup, and chugged the last of the milk.

Marisol sniffed. "I was young then. And stop changing the topic. You're just shifting the blame for your family's problems onto someone else." She shut off the faucet and put the cleaned container to dry on the metal dish rack. "Of course, it's just like a Prudento to do that."

The chair scrapped on the tiled floor. Daniel Cana stood up and stomped to the kitchen, empty cup and dish in hand. "Like a Prudento? Me? Don't talk to me like that. You knew who I was when you married me."

Marisol filled a red pot with steaming water. In her hurry to follow her husband out the door, she hadn't had time to wash the pots and pans she'd used to make dinner. Now the *frijoles puercos* were stuck to the pot and it needed to be soaked. The pitch of the ringing water grew lower as the pot grew fuller. "No. I didn't know you were like this," and she turned to look at her husband full in the face. "Otherwise ..."

"Otherwise what? You wouldn't have married me? Is that it?" He walked closer to her. "That's not what I said ..."

But he cut her off. "It's what you were thinking. Why would a high and mighty Mantecano marry a lowly Prudento like me?" Spittle flew from his lips. "Poor. *Ocioso. Useless.* A dreamer. Why couldn't I be more like Teresa's husband?" He threw the cup and dish in the right side of the sink, where they clanged precariously.

She could've silenced him. She hated that he thought that way. She hated that he brought up her sister. She hated that he was partly right. Marisol could've uttered the words that would've sliced at his soul and pierced through his manhood. But she didn't. Because she was afraid. Instead, she let him scream and complain like a baby, let him stomp to the couch, fists clenched, sulking and licking his wounds, so that in a few days, the wounds would be numb and scarred over and they could go back to being a family, pretending nothing had ever happened. Marisol let the water run until the red pot was overflowing and then some. Then she picked up the rough green scrubber and set to work on her husband's plate and dish. He would be sleeping on the couch that night.

June shuffled back to her room, heavy with the knowledge of what she'd heard. She regretted coming to the hall to eavesdrop.

Little moonlight came from the small, walled, too-high basement window near the ceiling, casting everything in shadows. She pulled aside the room-dividing red-and-black curtain and stepped into her side of the grainy-walled room. A small voice, squeaky like a mouse, sounded.

"What happened?"

"Nothing." June pulled back on the curtain. "I thought you were sleeping?"

Alegría sat up in her bed, clutching at the butterfly covers. "I was. But now I can't anymore." Typical of her little sister.

"Go back to sleep," said June, releasing the curtain and trudging into her bed on top of her cousin's used mattress. She turned on her side against the little moonlight. The room was quiet but for the sound of water and dishes coming from the kitchen. A minute passed.

"Are you asleep?" The squeaky voice was muffled behind the curtain. June huffed. "Not yet because of you."

"Are you sad?"

"No. Why?" She felt cornered. Attacked. She went back over her actions to see where she'd been exposed.

"You just ... look sad."

The kitchen faucet turned off in the distance. "Well I'm not. Stop bothering me."

"Okay." Alegría shifted on her bed, making the springs creak.

June looked at the curtain, the red squares trapped within the white squares, separated from other white squares by bold, black lines that ran in a grid pattern between them. If she stared at the squares long enough, they blurred at the edges and swam into each other, swirling into a big, dark, unrecognizable, turbid mess. June blinked. She realized she wanted somebody to listen.

"Mom and Dad were fighting."

No response. The silence stretched an eternity, twirling around the dusty wings of the motionless fan in the ceiling, between the rigid, scuffed legs of the desk against the wall, into the pinky-nail-sized holes in the baseboard where summer ants sometimes wound up, and wrapping around time itself. Then a squeak cut through silence's spell. "What about?"

June relaxed the stomach muscles she had clenched unaware. "Prudentos and Mantecanos." Which was partly the truth. "I'm so tired of them fighting."

"Mom and Dad?"

"Prudentos and Mantecanos."

"Oh. What are you going to do about it?"

June turned so she was facing the ceiling and crossed her arms behind her head. "Nothing. There's nothing I *can* do."

After a moment, Alegría said, "At school, for the play, Miss Turtle taught us about the civil war. Stuff was bad. People got stabbed. Then a bunch of people said they didn't like it. Then Prudentos and Mantecanos were friends again and ate a big feast together with scored bread for everybody."

"So?" Her sister was talking too much. She was losing interest.

"You can be like the people, say something."

"It's not that simple. People don't change that easily, your teacher taught you wrong. Plus, that only worked because other people actually listened to them." And didn't ignore them like they do me, she thought.

"I would listen to you. If you talked about it."

"Why?"

"Because. You're my sister. And I love you."

June turned on her side again. The words were unexpected, uncomfortable. She wanted to accept them or return them but they lodged in her throat like sticky, black lies. Instead, she said quickly, "Go to sleep," and threw the covers above her head, hiding under them, clenching her stomach and forcing her breaths to become deep and even. She simulated sleep until it came.

Though June could not comprehend her sister's simple words that night, the message, the idea to speak and act, stayed with her. It floated through her brain and over the weekend, marinated in her stream of ideas, picking up strength and flavor until by Monday, it had developed into a formidable plan.

As she entered school on Monday, June casually strolled through the dull tan hallways, making time until the usually unwanted Hector appeared beside her. Sure enough, a familiar arm linked around her shoulder. His eyes flickered over her face, up and down. "Hey, why weren't you at the PM meeting last Friday? We all waited up. We didn't go home until nearly four!" Immediately, she imagined his whole group leaning on one leg, tapping one glinting shoe, with crossed arms and an impatient expression on their faces. She felt a twinge of guilt. His string of words slithered around her.

"Sorry," she started, the words tightening their hold.

"It's fine. Everything's fine. Just—you're going to the next one, right?" He cocked his head coyly and winked, then ran his left hand through his glossy, long black hair.

"Um, yes." The word string pressed her arms against her sides so she couldn't get out of his arm around her, which was becoming increasingly incommodious. She was nearly where he wanted her. Only then, her formidable plan came back to her in her sister's voice. She stopped walking. "Um, no." He stopped walking. His arm grew unnervingly chill. "I don't actually like going to the meetings." She spoke stilted, as if someone with a whack-a-mole hammer was beating each word out of her.

"Why not? I made the club just for you." His tone was light and controlled. He kept his eyes looking straight ahead, at the thick, pristine, locked door of the janitor's closet at the end of the hallway. Students walked around them, a few gave them weird looks for standing in the middle of the hallway.

"I mean I do like it. I just think it could be changed, you know? Into something meaningful?" She stuttered through the words, feeling as if she was saying too much and too little. Devastatingly self-conscious.

"Like what?" He smiled and looked at her, though the smile

didn't reach his eyes. "What about starting an activist club?" Her formidable plan sparked into action.

A long curl on his head flopped forward. "Activist? What problems do you want to change?" He smoothed his hair with his left fingers.

She walked over to the left side of the tan hallway, taking Hector along with her. "Those between Mantecanos and Prudentos."

"We and Prudentos have problems?" He scratched his forehead. June nodded slowly. "Like the incident with the *churromaker*."

Hector snapped, his right arm still around her. He regained his friendly character, the one other girls went crazy for. "Right! Like what happened last weekend, when the gang attacked the old Mantecano."

"Yes. Like that," she said, a bitter taste rising in her mouth.

Then he took over, planning out their new PM Club. By a stroke of movie-like luck, they didn't have to change the name of the club on registration forms, just what the letters stood for. In fact, they didn't even have to throw out the old posters; they could keep the peace sign, cross out the math book with a red marker, and draw a symbol of unity, like scored bread, in the blank space below the 'M'.

In less time than it takes a cock to crow, June would be directing the first meeting of the Prudentos and Mantecanos Club. She would start with a throat parched and a nervous tick below her right eye. But determined, she would look down at her neatly printed notes, then back up at the pairs of expectant eyes and speak. Standing on top of the middle school field, she would tell them to forget history, to forget what they thought they knew about Prudentos. Everyone deserved to be treated as free and equal, to partake of the scored bread. The eyes would blink back up at her and she'd reach for the bottled water she didn't have. Rubbing her throat, she'd propose a demonstration of Prudento and Mantecano solidarity at the nearest community event. Her legs would tremble in the ensuing silence, until Jonah from science publicly supported her, invoking her credibility as the ghost-seer's sister. Others sitting cross-legged on the field would suggest events for the demonstration. In the end, they'd settle on the first week of May, the date of Crecimiento Elementary school's theatre production. Though she relied heavily on Hector those first few meetings to fill the gaps in her message, she would grow stronger, more confident and self-assured. In time, she would grow to be known as the woman with eyes of steel and mouth like fire.

On Monday, June went home believing herself to have won a small victory in speaking, excited with the romantic idea that she could make Prudentos and Mantecanos like each other, unaware that too much oregano on meat makes it bitter. She was reluctantly left alone in the house while her mother, Alegría, and the clay jug went to see the *chaman*. Aunt Mary would be at work for a few more minutes before coming to babysit.

At the house entrance, locking the door by the shoe closet, she heard the blinds of the kitchen window shudder. Aunt Mary would surely close the window when she got back, so June made her way downstairs. She walked with a pep in her step to the kitchen, opened up a cupboard to get a glass and the fridge to get a drink. She had to force the stubborn cupboard door open with one hand while getting the glass with the other. While the sly fridge easily opened, it closed in on her behind as soon as she reached in for some *Jamaica*. Then the bottle wouldn't open, try as she might, and some way or another, ended up injuring her right index finger. Frustrated, she left the glass and bottle on the kitchen counter and went to her room for a band-aid. However, the bedroom door seemed made of steel. It resisted her movements and whined loud as a horse whenever she twisted and pulled the handle.

From the upstairs, the smell of wet corn flour wafted, like someone was making fresh tortillas. It was too soon for Mary or her mother to be home. Her father was on a trip. The smell shouldn't have been there. Although June did not consider herself the type of girl who went into someone's private kitchen uninvited, the smell urged her.

Entering the upstairs, she felt the air conditioning was on, countering the sudden drop in temperature. From the yellow kitchen sink faucet, drops dripped down faster and faster the closer she got to the kitchen. The microwave cord fell off the counter top seemingly of its own accord.

The movement reminded June of the strange behavior of her aunt the previous week, how she was unwilling to heat her cup of tea of up in the microwave. She inspected the black box, where her aunt's greasy fingerprints could be seen on the handle; no other buttons had the trace of a touch. It was a normal twenty-two by thirteen-and-a-half microwave, black all around with a filmy, square screen in the center; it was the only black thing in Susana's kitchen. She plugged in the microwave cord in the spotless outlet. Obviously, meticulous Aunt Mary had cleaned there, too, which is why the thumbprint on the handle was so strange. The buttons lighted up, along with the inside of the microwave.

She pressed on the handle, popping the door open. Inside, four white walls stood the same, as if untouched by time. A circular glass microwave plate was placed on the bottom, but instead of being upheld by the usual screws in bottom of microwaves, it was placed on top of a faded matte paper. She lifted the plate, almost dropping it in the process, and lifted the sheet of matte paper underneath. There was a message on the back. "For my future Alegría, I hope you have happiness *todos tus días.*" The picture on the front showed a younger version of Grandma Susana, when her light brown hair reached past her shoulders and held no strands of gray. Her eye bags were not as pronounced and she was without her usual full face of makeup. In her arms, she held a small newborn girl, who resembled a small baby bird in the act of asking her mother for food.

June was confused. Susana had been older, with gray strands of hair and more pronounced eye bags, when Alegría, her sister, was born. The photograph-Susana holding her baby sister was too young. By her position in bed and the hospital gown she wore, it looked like Susana had given birth to Alegría. Which was completely not possible. There was no way her father had ever been in a romantic relationship with her grandmother. Then the truth crept up on her like mice on the railway. Photograph-Susana had given birth to an Alegría, but it was not the Alegría that was her sister.

June was in disbelief. She needed further evidence to confirm her suspicion. She ran to the living room, photograph in hand, microwave left wide open, and looked at the photographs on the wall. There. The faded, fuzzy photo of the laughing girl doubled over. She held the photograph from the microwave up beside it. Though the girl had changed with age, she had the same eye crinkles, the same lift of the cheeks, the same button nose. June had another aunt, a secret aunt, who possibly had the same name as her sister, and no one at the yearly family dinners or parties had ever mentioned a word of her. The situation was flabbergasting.

A car door sounded outside. Someone was home. From the left window of the living room, June checked that it was Aunt Mary. She sat on the camel-backed couch waiting for the door to open and close, for the thunderous footsteps to make their way upstairs into the living room, for the knowing stare on the photograph in her hand and for the grimacing, thin smile to make its way onto her aunt's face.

"Who is she? What happened to her?" June demanded answers from the one person she was sure had them.

"She's dead." Aunt Mary spoke as if she were explaining the rotation of the earth to her students.

"How?"

Aunt Mary scratched the mole near her nose. She remembered the June of old, the one who made up fantastical stories and needed help reading. She knew her niece could be trusted, that she wouldn't hurt anybody, that she could tell her with confidence. "Drowned. Don't tell your mother."

"Why? What's she got to do with my mother?"

Aunt Mary hesitated. She sat down on the couch next to her niece, laced and unlaced her fingers together. "Marisol was there when our sister drowned."

June looked at the photograph in her hands, trying to imagine the baby girl as a breathing human being. "Oh. Is that why no one ever talks about her?"

"Yes.—Your mother feels guilty about it, her death."

"Why?"

Aunt Mary took the photograph from June and fingered the bent edges. "She thinks it was her fault."

"Was it?"

She scratched at the mole left of her nose until the skin around it turned red. "No. Not entirely."

The screech of the blue sedan came from outside. Aunt Mary jumped. June hurried, asking the one question that bothered her the most, knowing she didn't have much time. "Why is my sister named the same?"

Aunt Mary touched her thin lips. Keys with a plastic princess charm jingled outside the door. The reedy doorbell rang. Exasperated, June snatched the photograph back from her aunt's hands and quickly ran down the stairs, leaving her aunt to receive her mother and sister alone. She yanked open her bedroom door, and slammed it shut. With trembling fingers, she hid the photograph under her cousin's mattress, right next to her private poem praised by her teacher, which she'd had since the fourth grade. The door squeaked open upstairs, the door seal rubbing against the floor. There were muted voices, indistinguishable chatter. June controlled her breathing. One, two, three, four. One two, three, four. Holding her heart, she sat at her desk and pretended to read a random book on her shelf, *Five Hundred and One Home Remedies for Halitosis*, borrowed from Aunt Teresa.

Footsteps bounded down the stairs, sounding like cymbals in June's ears. The door banged open. "Hi!" chirped her annoying younger sister.

June's spirit jumped out of her skin five meters. "How rude! Don't barge into my room without knocking!" She went through the process of calming her breathing down all over again.

"It's my room, too." Alegría shrugged and then plopped down on her bed like a starfish, face-first. Muffled, she said, "Great-grandfather Francis found a secret message inside the jug. He said he's going to decipher it."

"Whatever. Where's mom?"

"She's in her bedroom."

"What about dinner?"

Alegría lifted her face from the mattress. "I don't know." She flopped back down.

Two cocks of a crow later, with a slight snoring sound from Alegría, she was fast asleep. June pulled the curtain divider closed and slipped the photograph from underneath the mattress. She looked at the photograph, trying to imagine what her late aunt had been like, every day for the next two weeks before she finally mustered up the courage to confront her mother.

It was the first Saturday in Spring. The days had grown longer, and nights had grown warmer. Marisol was cleaning the bathroom in her bedroom. June stood leaning in the doorway, watching her mother scrubbing at the stains of toothpaste from her husband on the speckled brown counter top. Her mother never acknowledged her presence, though she had stood in the doorway for a full five minutes. June wanted her mother to acknowledge her. "Why did you give Alegría that name?" Marisol continued scrubbing at the counter top, in the sink and around it, pretending she hadn't heard her daughter. "Is it because you drowned your dead sister?"

The red rag on the counter top halted, then resumed its scrubbing, albeit more slowly. She swallowed hard to clear her throat imperceptibly and in her best casual voice said, "What are you talking about? Who told you that?" Marisol wrapped the red rag around her gloved index finger and used it like a brush, scratching gingerly at the thin, crusty layer of scum around the rim of the bathroom sink faucet. From years of neglected hard water stains and mineral buildup, the scum had gained an irrefutable black, green, and yellow permanence. Since her return to the pumpkin house, she had tried lemon juice and vinegar, baking soda and steel wool, but nothing had worked. Marisol would not be defeated, though. She would not crack.

"Aunt Mary. She said you killed your younger sister."

"That's absurd. We don't have a younger sister." She made her voice incredulous, almost haughty, to raise doubt in her daughter and hide her rising panic. Marisol swallowed the knot in her throat. Beads of perspiration formed on her forehead, curling the hair near her temples. She fixed her eyes on the flaky scum, willing herself to focus on it only.

"*Mentirosa.* I saw the picture." There was an edge to June's voice.

"You must be mistaken. There's only three of us. You only have two aunts." Marisol attempted a shrill laugh. Her lower back ached from bending over the sink. Her hands inside the latex gloves felt constrained, hot and sweaty; they emitted a smell like burnt rubber and garlic.

"I have three aunts. I saw the picture, I read her name on the back. I know she exists." June raised her volume. From the bathroom mirror, she could see her mother scrubbing intently around the faucet rim. She wanted to scream at her, *look at me, I'm talking to you. Does the sink matter more to you than me?*

"She doesn't. You saw wrong." Marisol's teeth clenched. She would not crack.

"I didn't, I saw right. I saw!" June whined and stomped one foot on the tiled floor. "She exists!"

From June's change in tone, Marisol knew she had gained the upper hand and turned to face her cracking daughter. Confident in her lie, she said, "She doesn't."

"She does, she does! Alegría. I saw her name. I saw it. I know! Aunt Mary said. I saw it. I have the picture. I'll show you!" She was near hysterics, her face contorted. Through swimming eyes, all she could see was her mother's plain, apathetic face staring back at her as if she didn't know her, as if she was unimpressed, looking at a circus monster on display. June made to run to her room and get the proof from under her mattress, but her mother grasped her arm roughly with one black-gloved hand.

"June." With that one word in her firm parental tone, Marisol established herself as the sane one, in control, and her daughter as the crazy one, delusional. She silenced June, who stopped moving under her mother's grasp. On Marisol's face appeared a small smile of relief as her throat loosened and her teeth unclenched. She saw her daughter under the white, rectangular outline of the doorway, in front of the bed she shared with her husband (he facing the bathroom on the left, she facing the window on the right), the same bed with the flower design her youngest daughter thought looked like the face of a bug. From the basement window, the midday sun bounced off the body-length mirror to the right of the open bedroom door, and for two-thirds of a second, in the reflected blue light, Marisol saw the bloated face of her drowned sister, gray froth filling her nose and mouth.

"Mom?" Alegría appeared from the bedroom door. She had come hearing yelling from June. "What happened?"

Marisol frowned and quickly released June. "Nothing." She wrung her gloved fingers.

June stepped out of her mother's reach and into the bedroom, by the nightstand. From a safe distance, she saw crinkles form under her mother's eyes and on her forehead as her face tensed. With Alegría as a distraction, June gained power. "We have a dead aunt." She pointed a shaking accusatory finger at her mother. "And mother drowned her."

Alegría looked questioningly at Marisol. "Mom?"

"It's not what you think."

"It's true," said June, raising her eyebrows smugly. "I have picture proof. And guess what? She has the same name as you." She looked at her mother, gauging her reaction. Marisol had twisted the black gloves off, set them on the bathroom counter, then reached her hands out to Alegría's and pulled her to sit on the edge of the bed together. Her tug on the eight-year-old's hands was much gentler than the wrench on June's arm, where five wet fingerprints marked the numb spot.

"What you have to understand is I made a promise."

Alegría scratched her head and scrunched her face, confused. The *chaman* had never mentioned anything about her mother or her birth name.

June rolled her eyes, crossed her arms, and snorted. "To who? Your drowned sister?" Marisol shot her a look.

"What promise?" asked Alegría.

Taking a deep breath, Marisol said, "I promised to name my first child after my late sister."

"But I'm your first child," said June. She pointed to herself, frowning, and shifted her weight to one leg.

"Why?" asked Alegría.

"Because. She wanted me to."

June plopped down on the bed where her father's head usually lay, making the mattress jiggle. "But she's dead. How could she even want that? That's crazy."

Marisol took a shuddering breath and squeezed her daughter's hands with her own clammy ones. "I fear. I fear I caused you to be sick." She whimpered, her shaking noticeable. "The things I see wrong with you, I saw them with my sister, too. I'm sorry. I had to name you. I promised. I had to. There was no escaping it."

Alegría didn't really understand what her mother was saying. But she saw that her mother was sad, so she stretched her arms over Marisol and patted her back.

June was conflicted. On the one hand, she was glad she wasn't sick like Alegría, and glad that ugly name wasn't hers if it would've caused her sickness. But on the other hand, she felt that even from birth, she'd been excluded by her mother, who apparently hadn't thought of her enough as a first daughter to fulfill her promise with her. She saw Alegría's peculiar namesake and sickness as the source of the special bond between her mother and sister, one which she wasn't a part of. In a way, she felt robbed of the opportunity to be sick, to be especially cared for by her mother. June remembered Marisol's sneer from earlier, how she'd been more willing to make her into a liar than to tell the truth, and how that had all changed once Alegría came into the bedroom. Marisol was willing to change for Alegría but not for June.

In that moment, the older sister remembered being forgotten at Josefina's, left unpicked up at school, ignored at the kitchen table, excluded from the tender hugs and kisses on Christmas Eve. She remembered her words, her stories, her entrance to middle school, her broken pink toy piano, her praised, fourth-grade acrostic poem—every meaningful detail in her life disregarded by her family, her mother in particular. She felt a foul, carrion taste in the back of her throat. Her face flushed and she stood up from the bed. June wanted to hurt Marisol, to scorch black burns on her skin, to make her feel the acute misery she'd inflicted on her, and the surest way of doing that was to hurt her most prized daughter, Alegría. So she used her capacity for speech, her ingenuity of thought, her inherited power to hold force behind her words and make them believable to torment them both.

"You selfish mother. You only kept your so-called promise because you felt bad about killing your sister. If *Grilla* over there is sick, it's all your fault. You did it to stop feeling bad but did you even think of what would happen to your daughter? You *used* her to help yourself."

Alegría froze with her arms still around her mother. She felt cold.

"And *you*, you're so stupid. Can't you see mother's just using you? The only reason she pretended to care was because she felt bad about what she'd done to you. Nobody really likes you." The pumpkin house creaked and shuddered, making the plug in the light fixture clink against the glass dome with the light bulbs. The bathroom door whined shut. The body-length mirror wobbled against the wall. June took inspiration from the shifting house. "And Grandmother Susana? She probably only liked you because you reminded her of her dead daughter."

Alegría backed away from her mother slowly, shaking her head and covering her ears.

"No."

"Yes. You were just a replacement for her daughter. Those stupid cooking lessons? They were supposed to be with her daughter." June crossed her arms. "In fact, Grandmother probably died because you were such a big disappointment as a replacement."

"That's enough." Marisol stood up, reclaiming her status as a mother. "June, go to your room. Now."

Alegría ran out of the room.

June stormed off with a stance like her father's. Once her fiery red anger dissipated, the satisfaction of inflicting pain and using her power evaporated. The weight of what she'd said hit her, leaving her feeling empty and gross. Now her sister was hiding under her butterfly bed covers and her mother wouldn't come out of her room. Sitting on the green couch in the living room, she stared at the blank television screen in the living room, hating herself. Then she got up and made herself a peanut butter sandwich to try and rid her mouth of its rotten, rancid taste.

21.

Before Alegría knew about her late aunt, she had a dream she was up in the third story of the pumpkin house, next to Aunt Mary. Inside the cool room, shaped like a trapezoid where the walls of the roof joined, a shaft of caramel sunlight fell from the cyclops window, illuminating silver particles of dust as they floated through the air like tiny fairies. There was Great-grandma Lolita's rocking chair nested on the circular crocheted rug in the back of the room, raspberry-colored, behind the stairs that led to the main floor hallway. Aunt Mary's television from when she moved in stood on a poplar stand in front of the chair, and rows upon rows of bookcases and crates had crawled unto the walls, so one could only see hints of the wallpaper in between shelves; it was an old-fashioned amber wallpaper, with pink carnations sprouting from woody vines painted in organic patterns and perched purple yellow-billed finches. Photo albums and pocketbooks lined the shelves, while important documents, choir programs, first-grade artwork, Mother's Day cards, letters to *Los Reyes Magos*, and student excellence awards lay neatly packed inside the teal crates.

The air smelled yellow, like dry wood. Alegría saw her Aunt Mary dressed in plain gray pajamas leaning over the white window sill with hands and face pressed to the glass, peering at a fuzzy figure walking down the street. As the figure walked further down the street to the right of the pumpkin house, Aunt Mary moved to the left, bumping Alegría with her prominent behind trying to keep the figure in sight. Though she was big, strong, and sturdy, with iron flesh, she held onto the sides of the window and tried to climb unto the sill, eyes glued on the disappearing figure.

Avoiding Mary's scrambling knees, Alegría stood on tiptoes and held unto the sill, looking for the figure that had so captured her aunt's attention. The sky was a bright blue, with scattered cotton balls colored coral by the rising sun, which fell on the terracotta-tiled sloped roofs.

Identical two- and three-story houses in different shades of the earth lined the paved street close together, so from the perspective of the pumpkin house, they conglomerated into a huge castle. Beside the green yards, paved driveways, and thriving trees, Alegría caught a glimpse of the fuzzy figure before it went out of view. Ducking below the straining arm of Aunt Mary, she leaned forward on the sill only to find it was not there.

The pumpkin house had dissipated in a cloud of dust particles, leaving Alegría alone on the sidewalk with the fuzzy figure a classroom's length in front of her. She ran after the figure, though for all her efforts, the gap between them only seemed to lengthen.

The dream recurred, multiple times a night, several days a week, and only once did she reach the figure.

On that night, Alegría chased the figure, calling out to it with no response, eyes firmly on its back until it came into focus. It was a woman, with a high-collared, broderie anglaise-trimme violet dress, black tights, matching pumps, eyelet earrings, and a jam-red shawl. Alegría followed her noiseless shuffling steps until she was close enough to tug her shawl. The woman turned around. It was Grandma Susana. The little girl smiled at the familiar face and asked her why she hadn't turned around. "Where is *mi cielo*?" Alegría turned to point and look at the sky but it had melted with the houses like crayons on a hot day, leaving a black void where only the sidewalk stretching forwards and backwards existed. She looked at her grandmother, no longer smiling. Grandma Susana took her by the arms and shook her, "Where is *mi cielo*?" she repeated over and over again. Alegría wanted to say she didn't know but couldn't. The look in Susana's eyes scared her; it was wild and desperate and unanswerable. Her head hurt and her vision spun as Susana shook her fiercer than ever, her nails digging painfully into her arms. Then Susana started crying rivers from her eyes, filling the black void up with water, and then her eyes didn't exist but for the rivers. Susana dissolved into a salty pool of tears and Alegría was left alone with a ringing in her head and a throbbing soreness in her arms.

She woke up feeling icky, like she'd done something wrong, like she'd failed her grandmother.

During her next meeting with Great-grandfather Francis, Alegría resolved to tell him of her dream and garner his interpretation. He had become her confidante of sorts, a person she felt comfortable around, and though she may not have understood his words entirely, he was always patient with his explanations.

Her trip inside the *chaman*'s house was made alone. Her mother had told her to wait by the powdery-white fence while she watched from the car. Alegría stood there, chilly under the shadow of the storm clouds, exposed in the barrenness of the gravel, feeling small without her mother's presence beside her. After ten minutes, she looked to Marisol for guidance, who nodded her head and flicked her wrist in the direction of the mint-green cement house, signaling for her daughter to stay where she was. When Great-grandfather Francis finally opened the fence, his lightweight cream-colored canvas shirt and pants were stained with sawdust.

"There you are. You were to be here earlier. Your mother's staying in the car, yes? Come in, let's talk about your progress." He opened the the screen door. Inside, it looked like a packing store had exploded. Concentrated at the foot of his mystical table, where animal figurines were located, was a mountain of boxes overflowing with instant ramen, water bottles, *atole* mix packets, grains, hot packs, emergency kits, rain gear, candles, and spray bottles. They spilled unto the rest of the main floor, covering the entrance to the stairs and half of the orange and purple-curtained window. Planks of wood lay stacked near the entrance of the bathroom. Great-grandfather Francis kicked cardboard boxes left and right, clearing a pathway to the pink-mantled consultation table.

"Okay," said Alegría, sitting down at the table comfortably. "I still feel yucky and like ... tired."

"Hmm." The *chaman* rubbed his chin, where a few, short, stiff gray hairs had sprouted like cut stalks on a wheat field after harvest. "I suspect change is in order. Apart from my waking concoction, there exists still another option: my slumbering brew, I believe, would work wonders for you. For ten extra dollars, just ten measly dollars, I'll yet throw in raw herbs." Seeing Alegría's eyes wandering over the patterns in the cement popcorn ceiling, he smacked his lips twice. "But I'll discuss that with your mother later. Any questions?"

"Yeah." Alegría shifted in her seat, leaning her head backwards and forwards. "Did you get the paper out of the brown thing—the jug?"

Great-grandfather Francis's eyes lit up like when his favorite chicken-flavored ramen was on sale at Josefina's. "*Por supuesto.*" He explained how he'd removed the scroll inside using a pair of chopsticks, a pumpkin seed, and two rubber bands. He then stood up, and retrieved the scroll from within a cardboard box by the window. "This is from an old pocketbook, from before your Great-grandmother ever learned to cook. Look."

It was a thicker paper, with threads hanging loosely from the serrated edge, where it had been ripped from the pocketbook. Small ovals with four vertical lines drawn inside littered the page; they looked like loaves of bread to Alegría. One, two, three, four dots lay in a row, sometimes alone, sometimes on top of lines. Circled on the bottom were a symbol that looked like a basketball, three dots over a dark line, and a dot over two lines. He pointed to the dots. "*Uj. Wuxpä. Buluchpé. Kin. Ha-al.*"

"What's that mean?" Alegría reached out her hand to touch the coarse paper.

"Numbers. They mean the expected is coming sooner than expected." Great-grandfather Francis paced in a zig-zag around the room, avoiding the boxes, mumbling to himself something about the imbalance in the people of Manteca and their need of a proper cleansing. Touching his left thumb with his right index finger, and then his right thumb with his left index finger in a never-ending pattern, he said, "The earth always provides what one needs, even when one does not know he needs it." He stopped abruptly. "Your mother, how is she?" The *chaman* searched for Alegría at the consultation table only to find her missing.

"Okay, I guess," said a voice behind him. She stood by the bathroom, fingering the planks of wood Great-grandfather Francis had been about to sand when he saw her waiting outside through the window. "What are these?"

"My Plan B. When the houses in this area were built, they were advised by the *chaman* Emanuel to build them out of cement, in this barren area away from the rivers and sea. The people thought that in comparison to adobe houses, these cement houses would be longer-lasting and unyielding against big waters. What didn't cross their minds was that these flat cement roofs would catch all the water. So now I'm building a boat."

"That's nice," said Alegría. "I have a question." Great-grandfather Francis stared at the little girl with lips pressed together before sighing and nodding for her to continue. "I had a dream and I kept dreaming it. Grandma Susana was there and I was running and I couldn't catch her. And then I did. But she was looking for '*mi cielo*' and it wasn't there anymore. So grandma cried." Alegría paused, unwilling to share how Susana had shaken her and pinched her arms. "Then her eyes melted into water. What does... who does... '*mi cielo*', what does that mean?"

Great-grandfather Francis narrowed his eyes and sat back down at the consultation table. "Strange. Very strange." He told her about Grandma Susana's youngest daughter, who had died tragically right before her fourth birthday. He had known her when Susana took her to visit him, for the youngest daughter had suffered from unanticipated falls and the momentary inability to move, much like Alegría herself. Susana nicknamed her youngest daughter *mi cielo* as a sign that her love for her stretched as big as the sky. That Susana would be looking for her youngest daughter was very strange, indeed, considering everybody knew everybody in the other world.

"I didn't know her. No one said anything." Alegría joined him at the table, rocking back and forth on her chair. "How do I find her daughter?" She was earnest, wanting to rid herself of the feeling she'd disappointed her grandmother.

Great-grandfather Francis whistled the high, clear whistle of the *mariachis* and laid back in his chair with his hands crossed. "You can't. Theirs is another world. Trying to mess with it is like trying to play with hot rocks and not get burned. Besides, your dreams must be in error. Might be the change in weather, but your dream-version of Susana's out of character."

Alegría left the *chaman*'s house with a few sprays from the medicinal bottle and ten whacks from the cleansing bush. She got in the backseat while he talked with her mother about the price of the slumbering brew and its effect on her. "Instead of keeping her awake during daylight, we'll ensure her dreams at night, so come afternoon, she isn't sprawled out on the floor snoring." Great-grandfather Francis winked at her from the window. Marisol hastily agreed to the new medicine, feeling her privacy invaded when he'd come out with her daughter to talk to her. She'd stayed in the family jean-blue sedan simply to avoid him but he'd made it impossible without running his foot over. He asked a quick question about her balance and if she still had his gifted emergency kit before allowing them to escape the maze of winding streets on their way home.

At school, Alegría enjoyed practicing the songs of Miss Turtle's play with the rest of the class. As Martha the tortilla maker, and

Verónica Socorro's confidante, she had a solo in the first act illuminating Verónica on the faults and virtues of men, and on the necessities of a good marriage. Practicing that solo became her favorite part of the day, for singing reminded her of Grandma Susana and of her mother. "You need a good man, a smart man; a handsome, tall, dark, fierce man. With boots to shine, a heart that's kind, and fortune with which to dine."

Alegría would smile brightly, bob her head to the music, and dance with her imaginary skirt. However, recently, her knees had started to feel weird whenever she sang her part. They gave away so she felt she was floating, and her voice would go out of tune as she stretched out her hands to catch herself. She asked Bo if he could see her falling, but he said the only weird thing he saw was her arms sticking out part-way through the song. Alegría had felt her knees buckle before, while snatching candy and taking names at the Flores Christmas party and while singing and dancing with her mother. After thoughtful analysis and three test trials, she discovered it was in her happiest moments her knees gave away.

Miss Turtle had also noticed the fault in the eight-year-old girl's voice and the flailing of her arms. She urged her to practice at home, or risk losing the role of Martha to another student. Thus, to preserve her solo, Alegría resolved to abstain from happiness while singing. For the most part, it worked. As long as she distanced herself from the song and thought of sad monkeys, she could remain stoic and her knees held. But it was hard to stay blank-faced when she wanted to laugh at the lyrics and when she felt in harmony with her class.

That all changed when June told her the truth of her mother and Grandma Susana. Alegría didn't want to believe it. She didn't want to be a burden for her mother and a disappointment to her grandmother. Alas, silence had been a confirmation of June's words.

That night, Grandma Susana had come to cheer her up, to give her another midnight cooking lesson. She'd arrived in her usual splendor, with the frilly white cooking apron of the other world and the smell of wet corn flour. "Hello, *mi Grillita*. Let's go to the kitchen and bake some *empanadas*." She stretched out her hand for Alegría to take.

Instead, her granddaughter stayed upright in her bed and said, "Is it true you don't like me and I'm just a replacement for your real daughter?" Her eyes were watery and her mouth quivered.

Grandma Susana stayed silent. Then she smiled, displaying her white horse teeth, and repeated herself good-naturedly. "Let's go to the kitchen and bake some *empanadas*. Come on." She lifted her eyebrows in the direction of the door and once more stretched out her hand.

"No." The corners of Alegría's mouth turned downward and the blood throbbed in her head. She squeezed fistfalls of bed covers.

"Come on. You can knead the dough." Susana was as smiling as ever.

"No. Do you really not like me? Am I really a... a disappointment?" Alegría felt someone was digging a knife through her heart, making it difficult to breathe. She bit down on her lip.

Susana gave no response. Her horse teeth were in plain sight. She looked like a robot, or a wax figure. She didn't look real.

"Why did you shake me and hurt my arms? Is it cause I couldn't find your *cielo*?" Alegría couldn't hold back the tears and ran crying to hug Grandma Susana. "I'm sorry. I'll promise to do better." But Grandma Susana slipped from her grasp and floated up the stairs, leaving her granddaughter with nothing but the gossamer feel of her apron. "I'll knead the dough," said Alegría running after her. "I'm sorry." And just like that, Grandma Susana was gone with the receding moonlight and stars behind gray clouds in the navy-blue sky.

In the morning, Alegría woke up to a wet pillow, puffy eyes, a headache, and the need to blow her nose. She didn't want to take Great-grandfather Francis's waking concoction or slumbering brew. She had only taken it to stay awake in school and make her mother happy. During play practice, she didn't need to restrain her joy and she didn't have problems with buckling knees. She stayed quiet in class, looking outside the window for slivers of sunlight. There were none.

22.

On the day of the play, Daniel Cana had come home early, to be seen at seven o'clock sharp with his well-fed family at Crecimiento Elementary's community event. He brought expensive *enchiladas* from the street of shops. As Marisol heated them up in the microwave, she wondered how they could afford them when her husband couldn't give her more than twenty dollars to spend at Josefina's. While her husband washed his hands in the yellow kitchen sink, she called her daughters to set the plates for dinner, and around four thirty, all four Canas were sitting down around their yellow-mantled table to eat.

"Are you ready for your performance?" asked Daniel.

"Mm." Alegría nodded. She looked at her mother on her right. Marisol hadn't said anything since calling them all for dinner; looking down at her red sauce-covered rolls of tortillas, she cut them into perfect bites and chewed slowly and noiselessly. She didn't look up. Alegría felt she'd done something wrong, but didn't know what. She squished the tortillas into the red sauce, mashing out the chicken filling. Great-grandfather Francis's slumbering brew helped her stay awake without feeling queasy, but her appetite hadn't come back.

"Don't play with your food. That's not what I bought it for."

"Sorry Dad."

"That goes for you, too, June. And keep your elbows off the table."

June rolled her eyes and put her fork down. She'd been

resting on one hand, twirling a strip of chicken on her fork in the air, trying to keep the red sauce from dripping down. The big PM Club event was that day, and she'd have to speak in front of her entire community.

"Why is everyone so quiet? I don't come home early every day." He slammed his glass on the table. The water inside quivered. "All I ask for is a nice, happy dinner when I do. I'm exhausted from work. I know I don't matter to you, but I work like a mule to keep you all fed happy ..."

At this, the three Cana women jumped in with their exclamations of "you do matter" and "thank you Dad" and grumblings of "we are happy."

"That's more like it." Daniel cleared his throat and the rest of the dinner was acceptable.

As the clock in the living room ticked closer to six, Alegría's nerves heightened. The morning of her kindergarten school pictures, the afternoon of the first grade Christmas concert, and the days of all other big events, her mother had always gotten involved, helping her dress prettily, curling her hair and applying light makeup. She'd talked to her mother about the play before, reminded her in the car ride how Miss Turtle expected everyone in their costumes at school no later than six thirty. But that afternoon, her mother didn't come into her room to pick out accessories matching the Adelita skirt. She didn't iron the white, puffy-sleeved shirt of her costume. She didn't even yell at her to get ready. Instead, Marisol sat on the green living room couch, looking through an old photo album she had buried amongst the boxes of rent receipts and credit card statements in her closet.

Unused to such calmness on the day of a special event, Alegría reluctantly got up out of bed and asked June for her rose-patterned skirt shaped like an upside-down primrose. Putting it on over her jeans, she lifted it by the two strips of red fabric around her waist and shuffled to the living room. "Mom," she said, unsure of the stranger who kept her eyes glued to the album in her lap. "Can you tie the skirt please?" Marisol didn't move, didn't lift her head to look at her daughter. Nothing had been the same between the mother and daughter since the afternoon back in March, when June had spoken those cruel words and let Alegría know she was nothing more than a *trapo* for her mother and a disappointment to her grandmother. Initially she'd been sad, then angry, though now, Alegría felt simply tired. Her attempts to treat her mother with the same warmth she used to were shut down or ignored.

Finally, when Alegría had just about lost all hope, Marisol deeply sighed, closed her book with a thump, and made purposeful eye contact with her daughter for the first time since the fields in Prudent were cleared for the hard red spring wheat. "Lift your arms for me," she said, placing her book out of the way and leaning forward on the couch. Alegría shuffled forward, trying not to trip with the skirt getting caught between her legs. She did as she was told, letting the skirt pool around her ankles. Marisol picked up the red strips of fabric and tied them in a bow slightly higher than her daughter's waist so that the skirt wouldn't drag.

With her mother's simple act, the ember of hope in Alegría's chest kindled again that her mother and she would go back to how they'd been. She wanted a hug, now that she was in close proximity to her mother. If she just turned around, she could wrap her arms around Marisol and everything would be alright, they could sing and talk like they used to. But then June walked in, took one look at Alegría and snorted. "You look like a short cupcake. You're drowning in my skirt."

"I am not. I look like how Martha is supposed to look." Alegría crossed her arms and gave her sister the stink eye.

"Is Martha supposed to look like a stack of *tortillas*? Cause that's how you look. No, no—you look shorter."

"Do not." Alegría bunched up her fists.

"Do too. Bet you can't even dance like you're supposed to in my skirt, *Grilla*."

"Can too. We practiced at school." Marisol let out a small gasp and June's eyes widened as Alegría took off at a skip around the coffee table, folding the skirt in circle eights like Miss Turtle had taught her. She stepped on the rose-patterned skirt and half-tumbled, half-fell forward. A loud rip sounded as the block of red fabric around the hem tore. "Ow," she said, picking herself up.

"Alegría Cana." A voice sharp as knives sliced through the air. "How careless can you be? Now, look. Look what you've done. You've ruined your poor sister's skirt." "It wasn't that bad," said June, jerking her head back, eyes still wide.

"*Descuidada*. Why didn't you think before acting? Why don't you ever think before acting? Or consider others for a change?" Marisol's eyes seemed the color of dark chili powder. "That wasn't your skirt to ruin. It'll have to be mended. You'll be late to the play. Thank you for making life so much harder for the rest of us."

"I'm sorry." She was incapable of saying more. Tears brimmed in Alegría's eyes as she stood with a whimpering mouth looking at her mother, who had transformed into a fire-breathing dragon, putting out the small flame of hope in heart with a single soul-crushing breath. She gathered the torn skirt in her hands.

"Leave it."

Hands shaking, Alegría undid the bow at her back and stepped out of the skirt. "Careless. Absolutely careless and inconsiderate."

Alegría ran past the open-mouthed June to her room and slammed the door behind her. She crawled under her bed covers and cried from the shock of being yelled at by her mother. She felt bad. Dancing in her sister's skirt was bad. Her mother was right, she'd been careless. But she didn't mean to ruin it. And she'd gotten yelled at so bad. Even though she didn't mean it. Her mother had yelled. Alegría was blue and red. She wanted to defend herself. But she couldn't. Her mother was right in yelling at her. But she'd yelled too loud, like a dragon. An unpredictable, unfamiliar dragon. Alegría didn't deserve to be yelled at. At least not so loudly. Her mother was acting mean. She was always acting mean now, even when Alegría didn't do anything. Maybe she didn't really love her. Maybe June was right. Mom was only playing pretend. And now that the truth was out, she didn't need to pretend anymore.

Alegría covered her mouth with her pillow. Her eyes smarted with tears but she didn't want her sobs to be heard. She felt wronged by her mother. She would not give her mother the satisfaction of hearing her cry. Alegría wouldn't try to get near her mother again. She wouldn't ever ask her to tie her a bow or to put on the special makeup or to give her a hug. Alegría would learn to do things by herself, just like how she'd learned to make *cajeta* sandwiches on her own when she was four.

She hurt. Her heart hurt worse than the deepest paper cut. Just when Alegría thought her heart would burst from holding it in with her pillow, the feeling passed and an immense drowsiness overtook her.

After what felt like days later, June nudged her sister awake. "*Grilla. Grilla* wake up. You're going to be late. Aren't you supposed to play Martha or something?" Her sister's pillow was a mess. It looked like she'd drooled all over it and her face. There was gunk on the corners of her sister's bleary eyes. "Come on, it's 6:10. Mother fixed your skirt."

Despite not liking her sister, June felt a certain closeness with her now that she'd been yelled at by their mother. Now the animosity was distributed equally between them. Now the relationship between them was fair. Still, it had felt weird to be defended by their mother, who never took her side. June almost felt bad for Alegría, who was experiencing their mother's coldness and quick temper for the first time. June felt like playing the part of a gracious angel. Yes, her skirt had been torn, but she could overlook that in this simple moment of solidarity.

June helped her heavy sister get dressed, brushed her hair in the bathroom mirror at the end of the hall. While her sister tried to put her hair up in her usual ponytail, Marisol called June to the living room and instructed her to make sure Alegría washed her face and brushed her teeth. She gave her a light pink lipstick with which to paint her sister's mouth. Rolling her eyes, June took the lipstick and did as she was told. These past few weeks, her mother had talked to her more, but she seemed to always be asking her to do something. June almost wished her mother would go back to ignoring her.

She pulled her sister's hair into two braids and drew the lipstick better than Marisol would've done. A twinge of sisterhood tugged at June's heart.

When the Cana family finally left for Crecimiento Elementary School, it was 6:33 p.m. Alegría speed-walked to the school auditorium, daintily holding the rose-patterned skirt up by its hem. Miss Turtle scolded her for her lateness and attributed it to her upbringings in a half-Prudento household. Alegría accepted the scolding and found her place on the vinyl steps, next to Bo, for the opening musical number of the play, *One Woven Thread: The Tragedy of Verónica Socorro and Raúl Banderas.*

Metal foldable chairs were set up all over the auditorium. Those near the front were filled with a few teachers, parents, and community members who'd come early to show their support or to save seats for friends and relatives. Alegría checked the entrances and exits for her family. They were nowhere to be seen. It was near show time. Alegría's earlier anger dissipated in her apprehension for the play. Parents waved at their performing children from their seats and the children waved excitedly back. At that moment, all Alegría wanted was to see her family waving back at her. She searched through the growing number of faces staring back at Miss Turtle's second-grade class. There was the slippery librarian and Josefina applying a fresh layer of Vaseline.

There was the Flores family in the second row, the son Hector shuffling cards in his lap. There was even Aunt Teresa with her dentist husband and eleven children in the very back. But Daniel, Marisol, and June Cana were noticeably absent. Alegría felt the tears she'd swallowed earlier come back up so she squeezed her hands together, held her breath, and shifted her attention to Miss Turtle standing in front of a microphone stand on the left side of the stage. Miss Turtle tapped the microphone in her hand and waited until the audience had quieted. Josefina whisper-shouted one last "She did, I tell you!" to the librarian. And then the curtains closed and the play began.

The class sang a song about the dangers of the revolution and the new hope of the Mantecanos, Raúl Banderas, stomping their feet on the steps to imitate the marching of the troops. Then they marched out the right exit doors, where they were met by Miss Turtle backstage. The black curtains opened to reveal a proud, arch-backed Raúl Banderas wandering about the streets of Manteca and a shy Verónica Socorro weaving a shroud for her dying parents by a chipped fountain. The two met and it was love at first sight. Raúl left with the promise of return on his lips.

Searching for her parents behind the curtain, Alegría almost missed her cue to go on stage with her basket of *tortillas*. Verónica with the pink ribbon in her hair clasped her hands together and told Martha all about her wondrous encounter with the dashing Raúl. In turn, Martha gave her a good lesson on what to look for in a man and urged a quick marriage with Raúl before the civil war took a turn for the worse.

Alegría sang well, with no accidents, if a bit distractedly and with a smile that didn't reach her eyes.

In the second act, Paolo as Pantaleon the Prudento hurt the benefactor uncle Verónica had been living with and forced her into poverty. He scrunched his shoulders inwards in imitation of the smaller shoulder-width of Prudentos. Someone from the audience booed.

Soon, the play was over with another musical number in which the girls twirled in their skirts and the boys stepped forward and back with a hand behind their backs. Miss Turtle walked to the middle of the stage with microphone in hand and gestured to her students. At her cue, the students bowed and the audience erupted in applause.

But the action was only just starting.

June stood up from her seat in the ninth row, where she and her parents had snuck in just in time for Alegría's solo. Her parents turned to look at her the same way they would look at a two-headed hippopotamus. "Parents, faculty, Mantecanos, my name is June Cana and I am a student at Enrique Delgado Middle School. My father is a Prudento and my mother is a Mantecana." Daniel cringed and shifted in his seat farther away from her. "I wanted to talk today on the injustice between Prudentos and Mantecanos. For many years, there's been unfounded enmity between our two communities. What you saw today was an example of this. You all saw how Prudentos were villainized. And we all accepted it, thought it funny, even. But it's wrong. And we must not stand—"

"Sit down." Daniel spoke through his teeth and tugged on her arm forcefully. It was then June became aware of the eyes staring up at her, of her mother's horrified owl eyes, of the pursed lips, crossed arms, and indirect side-glances of others. The audience felt uncomfortable being told that the production they'd just seen and enjoyed was wrong. Unfounded enmity towards Prudentos was wrong. Of course it was wrong. But Mantecanos' enmity was not unfounded. That would make Mantecanos bad. No, Mantecanos were not bad people. Their enmity towards Prudentos was righteous, having its start in the meddling, lazy men who had sought to take away Thomas Delgado's scored bread empire away from his family. Watching the play had reminded them of the cruelties Prudentos had inflicted on them during the civil war. Hearing that small portion of June's speech had refreshed their memories on the ability of Prudentos to twist truths to suit their needs. Prudentos always made themselves out to be the victims.

Hector's friends and the other members of the PM Club took June's pause as the end of her speech and clapped blindly. They began passing out slips of paper with the PM Club's information. By this point, the audience had started loud, angry chatter, which club members took as a sign that they were initiating a discussion, raising awareness and a new point of view in Mantecanos. They gathered their children and filed out of the elementary auditorium irked and offended, leaving Miss Turtle still on stage holding the microphone with a crick in her neck and her mouth gaping like a fish.

Alegría was glad to find her family, though she knew from the air that something was wrong. It felt warm and humid and heavy. There was electricity in it, like the Big Painter in the Sky had rubbed balloons against his canvas and left them there, suspended by static cling. The air hung, peaceful yet charged, carrying with it a sharp smell like Aunt Mary's chlorine solution.

23.

At eight o'clock on the eleventh of August, the sky fell. Probably, the Big Painter in the Sky had caked on too many layers of puffy whites and baby blues trying to hide the ugly charcoal grays exhaled by the people. For a moment, his fruits had borne labor. The air had been still. Stray alley dogs had ceased barking. Park swings by the Circle of Elites hung in suspense. Josefina's wind chimes calmed their clinking chatter. But nothing lasts. The gray weighed down on the canvas, bleeding through the white and blue patches, remaking the sky into clouds of cumin. Globs of paint leaked from the sky, splattering the trees and roofs below. They sank the canvas, dripping with deadly urgency. The Big Painter in the Sky gathered his tools and swatches, leaving his canvas to cave in. All he could do was wait.

By the rocky banks of the Mipared River, angry gang members vagabonded near the arch concrete dam. Certain of their brothers had been incarcerated so that an old Mantecano could keep his pride. They saw a peculiar trickling of water coming from the top of the dam; it was narrow and high-pressured, like the round of a water gun. The workers of the Estandar Company took shelter inside the cereal factory. Over the rushing of the river, a cracking sound. Sharp as a blade in a gunfight, the water broke through the crumbling concrete. Water spilled over with incredible power.

A fissure formed straight down the middle of the dam, the pop of a skull hitting the pavement. The gang members held their breath as tiny leaks formed. Pressure mounted. Pure. Beautiful.

Gang members ages fourteen to thirty-five whooped and hollered. ¡*Que barbaridad*! What glorious atrocity was the crashing of an empire, the fall of the Mantecanos' dam by their own hand, their own river. As the reservoir water went off, the gang members could not help but look for rocks and sticks to throw in the frothing fountain, to see them splintered and swallowed up in the water, to witness that immense power. The younger members edged to the front, trying to prove themselves to the elders by their recklessness.

"Get back." The dam shattered in two, hitting the sides of the river like the doors of heaven. Teal water foamed white as it pushed the fragments of concrete down the river. The river roared louder. It struck the chiffon-white rocks at the edge, dissolving the clove-colored land on which they lay and climbing up all over them until they became part of the river. The gang members' awe faded from their faces. They ran back up towards Prudent. Water swelled behind them, waves crashing with the beat of the river. It rolled forward, making their shoes wet and the ground muddy. In the distance, the wheat fields lay unaware. To the right, flat houses squatted, providing familiar safety. Knocking on doors, they alerted the people of the dam and the river.

Down in northern Manteca, Prudento farmers amassed at the Estandar company's terminal elevators (which looked like a stack of women's hair rollers), protesting their offered prices as too low for the value of their wheat. The workers of the terminal elevators said they just followed orders; the bosses must've thought the long rains had damaged the quality of the spring wheat. The Prudento farmers defended their wheat and their worthy labor, raising strongly worded signs on sticks and stomping their feet.

When the news reached the farmers and factory workers at the terminal elevators, the disputants looked east towards the river. The blue jewel of the earth stretched over Manteca, reaping in rocks and sticks and bushes. No clove-colored land could stand up to it or absorb it. "Get to a shelter, get to the hills," said the news reporters, the meteorologists, the watchdogs. But harvest didn't end until September. If the water had traveled that far into Manteca, then it could easily travel to the hard red spring wheat fields of Prudent. Then the farmers' livelihoods would be destroyed, and the bosses of the Estandar Company would have to pay more for the existing stored wheat.

"*¡Ay, caramba, mi trigo!*" said a Prudento farmer under his breath, throwing his sign on the ground. The rest followed his example and made their way to their rusty trucks, hoping to get to their wheat and their families before the bridge went under. The Mantecano factory workers contacted their loved ones as they re-entered the terminal elevator, gathering belongings before heading home and to the hills.

Meanwhile, the wind picked up speed, propelling the river forward towards the main road bridge. By then, the waters had turned shades of foamy pink and purple, the colors of melted rainbow sherbet. Uprooted trees and large boulders rammed into the thick, concrete pillars. The parallel, gray symbols of Mantecanos and Prudentos' unity stood firm against the thrashing of the Mipared River. The usually quick road stood clogged up with the traffic increased by news of the dam and flood warning. Vehicles honked and sputtered gray smoke on the rumbling road. When the waves crashed against the road's railing, spraying windshields and side-view mirrors, some people unclicked their seat belts, threw open their doors, and ran in-between cars, trying to get somewhere on dry land. Incessant, the river set the bridge quaking. The more pillars, the more surface area the trunks and debris hit. Finally, with the same cracking of the dam, the pillars snapped in two like fried chicken feet. Like a horse with one too many legs, the bridge collapsed. Vehicles fell to the sides. Both Mantecanos and Prudentos flew into the river, some tumbled, trapped inside their cars.

Without winking an eye, the sherbet-colored water continued expanding, gorging itself on the metal and rubber and skin. The few fish and creatures that had survived the dam were drowned by the rumbling water. Their open-mouthed bodies sank under and were thrown back over. On land, piles of fire-ant rafts took to the waves. Stray dogs whimpered and growled at the water, running further inland to escape; those domesticated tied to posts quivered and paced, unable to escape as the cold water hit them, thrashing them against the current.

As the mammoth water grew stronger, it moved further inward. The park where the old Mantecano lay concussed was submerged in the river. The swings were flipped up by the wind and caught by the water, which had turned darker and acquired the smell of hard-boiled eggs and sewers. The wall around the circle of elites was thrown down; trees, poles, and metal rods pierced the windows and faces of the beautiful, brick houses.

The river was coming, and it would leave no man, woman, or child untouched.

24.

In the lower heart of the pumpkin house, Marisol and Daniel Cana both sat on the couch like two fighting cocks trapped in a *palenque.* Daniel had gotten home a few minutes earlier, left muddy footprints down the stairs, flung his jacket on the couch, left his work backpack an eyesore in the middle of the living room, and plopped down on the couch, next to Marisol, who'd been watching the television. He reached for the remote on the coffee table and wordlessly changed the channel. "Where's my dinner?"

Marisol had purposefully ignored the slam of the door when he got home, for then she'd have to confront him over Teresa's phone call. She kept her eyes trained on the annoying glow of the screen until the pixels enlarged and dimmed before her eyes. Daniel was too close to her on the couch. She angled her body slightly right to avoid contact.

"Where's my dinner?" He raised his voice. Holding the remote control, he put his arm over the backrest, like he owned the couch. Marisol's shoulders twitched and she leaned forward. "*Oye, no seas grosera,*" he said, lines of irritation appearing high on his cheeks. His tone was deliberately soft and pleading, condescending, as if he were begging an unreasonable child. Curly, disheveled hair in need of a haircut. Sweaty navy blue jacket. Ripped washed-out jeans. Daniel was laughable.

"*¿Yo, grosera? Tú eres el inculto,* leaving your dirty shoes on and changing what I was watching."

He pointed to the television, which showed newly discovered

pocketbooks from the civil war and invoked again his saccharine understanding voice. "I work all day to pay for that television. When I get home, I want to relax, just for a little while. You get to watch television all day. For the precious time that I'm home, I want to watch what I want. May I do that? Just for a few hours?" Her husband wasn't really asking her permission and he didn't really know her. He hadn't done what he'd claimed, what he'd promised in their youth. He was lying.

"That's not fair. I could've worked too if—"

"If you hadn't married me. Yes?" Daniel growled and muted the television. "Mari, it's always the same with you, isn't it? I'm sorry I don't have the job I'm supposed to, the one I studied for, the one no one in this cursed place will hire me for. I'm sorry you got stuck with me." And he went on victimizing himself, eyebrows stretched to his hairline in mocking sympathy.

Daniel's words faded into white noise and the yellow, grainy walls blurred into one. The room fell cold and empty. Marisol felt nothing, simply wanted to shut down, and hide away in her memories. Daniel pushed off the green couch, making the couch on his side slide against the cement floor. The broken springs protested. "What I say doesn't matter. I don't matter. I'm heating my own dinner."

For Marisol, the living room came back into focus. "Where were you today?" She followed him to the kitchen, standing just behind the yellow-checkered kitchen table.

He took a plate from the cupboard, letting the door slam, and served himself spoonfuls of cold rice and beans from the pots and pans on the stove. "Working."

Marisol felt her heart drop. "How's the company?" Running her hands along the back of a poplar chair, she willed him to tell the truth. Then they could pretend lines of communication still existed between them.

Clicking open the microwave, Daniel inserted his food, closed the door and pressed a two and two zeros. The microwave beeped and began humming. He was stalling. Drawing out the vowels, he said, "Fine. Simply fine." He crossed his hands behind his back, sniffed, and rocked slightly on his heels. Daniel wouldn't look at his wife.

The blood drained from Marisol's face, leaving it the color of dried refried beans. "Teresa called." A ripple went through her husband's back as he tensed. He stopped rocking.

"Oh? What'd that prying busybody want? Hasn't she got enough problems with her children as is?" His voice was strained and sneering, as if he were talking through a reed.

She looked at him, weary. She seemed to have aged lifetimes. "Daniel, is it true? Did you lose your job?"

He swallowed hard and his mouth became a thin line. The microwave beeped thrice to announce his food was ready. He could not say anything.

Marisol ran a halting hand through her knotted, wavy hair. She could not remember the last time she'd brushed it. "Daniel, how could you? After last time you promised. You said you wouldn't do anything." Marisol should've known. Her family had been right, she couldn't trust him. She shouldn't have trust a Prudento, ever.

Daniel's eyes tightened and he flared his nostrils. Cracking his knuckles, he shook his head. "They were discriminating against me, Mari. They wanted to pay me less than the other Mantecanos simply for being a Prudento. After what those rats did to Vernon." He grabbed a towel hanging off the oven door and slapped it on the counter behind him. "What they did to Tim—"

Marisol looked at him with unpitying, piercing eyes. "We needed that job. Think of the girls. I mean, what are we to do?"

"I'll get a new job. I'll do some bookbinding."

"Again with your bookbinding. That was never going to work. It was a stupid, nonsensical dream." She emphasized her words, trying to drill them into his head. Exasperated, she felt like ripping her hair out or throwing a chair.

"It will work. Trust me."

"Trust you? That's the last thing I want to do. You've ruined this family." She remembered the overdue bills, the stressful trips to the grocery store, the missed baby showers of Teresa because she couldn't afford to buy gifts, the embarrassing trips upstairs to borrow cleaning supplies from Mary because she had nothing to clean her kitchen with. She remembered scouring the kitchen cabinets looking for any remnant lentils and rice to feed her daughters, returning Christmas and birthday gifts to get money for groceries, lying to her mother on the phone about her married life's splendor to avoid the deserved *I told you sos*. She had ignored her mother's last plea for a visit and sent her daughter instead, all because she was afraid of slipping up in her fantasy. And Daniel. Not only was he incompetent at manual labor, stuck on a ridiculous whimsy, he was also incapable of saving, spending what they didn't have. Daniel was a fool, but she was a bigger one for marrying him.

"I did not ruin this family. I have been trying to paste it together after you abandoned us." The microwave beeped again. Daniel tore the door open and took out his beans and rice with enough force to make the microwave glass spinning plate wobble. The food was cold again.

"I never. You're the one who's never here anymore."

"Listen to yourself. That's because I actually work, at the job *you* wanted for me." He pointed an accusatory finger at her, then snorted and rolled his eyes. "Or used to. Guess how long it's been since I was let go. It's been two weeks. Two whole weeks. You didn't know, did you?" The acid in his voice was unbearable. He had to be lying, he had to be.

Clenching her teeth, Marisol turned around wordlessly to lock herself in the bedroom. But Daniel was faster. He stalked towards her and yanked her shoulder to make her face him. He took her both shoulders. She gave him a dead stare. He shook her gently, he standing on the terracotta-tiled kitchen floor, she on the cement-finished living room floor. The acid in his expression and voice melted into patronizing sweetness. "Where are you, Mari? Even when you're here, your mind is elsewhere. When's the last time we truly slept together in the same bed?"

She refused to talk to him and turned her face away. His expression hardened again, lines forming on his cheeks. His fingers dug into her. Marisol refused to react. Daniel shook her limp body like a rag doll. "Answer me," he said, opening his mouth wide so she could see his molars. He was a brute.

When she didn't respond, he sighed and took his hands off her. Searching her eyes one last time, he said in a low, intimate voice, "Things are never to get better, are they? *We're* never going to get better, are we?"

Daniel slipped past her and into the hall. Their bedroom door slammed shut. Then Marisol floated back to the couch, where she picked up the remote her husband had left on top of the backrest. She put it back on the coffee table and left the television on the channel her husband had chosen. Marisol sat on the green couch in front of the muted pocketbook documentary, eyes glazed over, adding her fight with her husband to her repertoire of memories she would replay over and over again, sinking deeper and further into them.

Marisol and Daniel Cana's fight reverberated all throughout the pumpkin house so that Aunt Mary sitting in Great-grandma Lolita's rocking chair in the attic and June and Alegría laying on their cousins' mattresses apprehended the ensuing family drama. Once Alegría felt enough time pass for the beating in her heart to subside, she crept out of bed, told June she was getting a drink of water, tiptoed down the hall, peeked in at her mother watching television, and continued on to her parents' room at the end of the hall and to the left. She knocked on the door, tentatively slid it open, and found her father sitting on his bed facing the window. There was an open suitcase on the bed with miscellaneous shirts and pants roughly folded, a toothbrush wrapped in paper towels instead of inside a plastic bag, and his bottle of hair oil.

Alegría asked her father where he was going, to which he

replied he would go visit his brother in Prudent for a while. She asked him why and he said it had to do with adult stuff that she would understand when she was older. Then Alegría bit the bullet. "Did you and mama fight?" she said. He asked if she had heard them fighting and she said yes. He then explained how her mother and he were, indeed, fighting and told her that as soon as her mother had resolved her issues, he would be able to come back.

Alegría asked if he still loved mother. Daniel lifted her on his knee and told her of course, but his smile didn't reach his eyes. She asked if he still loved June and her. He said there was no question about it. Alegría wondered if June and mom and her could go along with him to visit Uncle in Prudent, like last time, as a whole family. Daniel took her off his knee and stared at the floor beneath his feet. Finally, he quietly said no.

"Are you dying?" she asked. Daniel reproved his daughter for thinking of such nonsense.

He packed in some socks, a comb and razor. Alegría filled in the role of her mother, helping Daniel find his missing items where she'd seen her mother put them away. Then Daniel zipped up the black suitcase and took one final bathroom break. When he came out, Alegría was sitting on his suitcase and telling him to please not go. Daniel had to force the suitcase up from under her and pry her fingers off his leg, where she had attached herself like an octopus. Alegría cried and made a scene. She knew she had to stop his leaving at all costs, for there was an icky feeling in the pit of her stomach that told her the family would crumble without him. "Why don't you like me anymore? Why can't you stay?" she said. Feeling trapped, Daniel made multiple assurances in his reedy, strained voice, saying he would come back soon and that he'd call the next day.

Overpowering her for a moment, he ran out the door and bounded up the stairs.

In the living room, Marisol heard his struggle with Alegría and knew he was leaving. She felt swamped and helpless. She had no money of her own, no education, no job. Without Daniel, she was lost. A hidden fear crept up in her river of memories: the leaving of her own father. Part of Marisol wanted to run after her husband as he went up the stairs, but she was trapped in the memories of her father, how nice he'd been and how suddenly he'd left. That old fear resurfaced that there was something wrong with her, that she held some sort of responsibility for her father leaving and for her husband's leaving as well. Marisol was trapped by the past, sabotaging her own happiness through a self-blame that predestined her for tragedy. The keys jangled in the door as her youngest daughter cried by the bottom of the stairs.

Daniel opened the door and stepped into the raging storm outside. June went barefoot on the stairs to bring the inconsolable Alegría back to their shared bedroom. Marisol lay on the couch, leaking tears on the armrest, watching the pocketbook documentary, feeling scared and alone.

The morning after Marisol and Daniel Cana's big fight, Alegría and June rose up by themselves and warily walked into the living room. Their mother had already gone back to her room. They made themselves a breakfast of cereal. Alegría got the spoons and the cereal, June got the bowls and poured the milk.

The silent tranquility between them was broken when Marisol walked in the room. She asked June to get her a cereal. *"Con rapidez."* Marisol had transferred her irritation with Daniel from the night before to Alegría and June. She asked June for a glass of water, the annoyance in her voice showing. Her bad mood was catching. Soon, June began to feel indignant at the vexation in her mother's voice, directed at her but caused by her father. She felt she had nothing to do with her mother's bad mood and shouldn't have been a victim of it. However, in the current state of the house, June knew she couldn't tell her mother as much. Unable to speak freely in the pumpkin house made her feel trapped, suffocated. She wanted to go outside and breathe.

After breakfast, June announced she would be going outside

to discuss important matters with the PM Club. She was rinsing the used dishes in the sink while Alegría spread the dirt and crumbs farther apart on the floor, sweeping the way she'd seen her mother do.

"You will do no such thing," said Marisol turning on the green couch in front of the television to look at her. "There's a storm brewing outside. It's too dangerous." The finality of her words increased June's desire to rebel and go. She closed the faucet and dried her hands with the same green towel her father had slapped on the counter the night before.

"It's not that bad. And you can't make me stay." She challenged her mother with her look. After the fight last night, Marisol felt weak and frail. To hear her daughter contradict her, she grew inflamed but also scared. Her eldest daughter's eyes reminded her of her own, when she had rebelled against Susana in her youth. Time was a cycle, the past an inescapable trap. Her daughter would be just like her, do the same thing to her as she'd done to Susana. For all her realizations, Marisol could not help but want to make her daughter stay. "Yes, I can. I'm your mother."

June ignored her and walked past Alegría, who stood with a broomstick in her hand, unsure of what to do. She picked up her shoes from their spot near the door to the boiler room and put them on.

Marisol remembered wanting to escape her mother's love, which she felt she didn't deserve. Her heart beat uncomfortably in her chest. Her daughter was slipping away. Trying to give her daughter what in her youth she wanted from Susana, she said, "*Como quieras*. Leave. Why should I care? It doesn't matter to me," and turned back around to watch the television. If she had spoken to Alegría, her youngest daughter would've come running back, her bluff called. But she had spoken to June, who had learned not to back down.

Marisol's words had bruised her pride, realized her fears that she wasn't wanted. "I know. I'm going." June's face was shadowed like a storm cloud. She stalked to her room to pick out a jacket from her closet.

Marisol's heart skipped a beat. The broken springs of the couch bothered her. "Wait, where are you going?" Panic rose in her voice.

"You said you didn't care." June talked from the hall, where she was putting her gray jacket on.

It was a repeat of yesterday, of her husband leaving. "Wait. Come back." Marisol stood up from the couch and followed June to the hall, who was halfway up the stairs.

"No."

They were on the small square second-floor landing of the front door. June clicked the locks. Her hand was on the door knob.

Marisol's palms were sweaty. She swallowed the stuttering, fluttering feeling of trepidation inside of her and used the voice that had silenced countless others, enunciating every word in warning. "*Malcriada*. Come back here now."

Turning her head and lifting it haughtily to match her mother's eye-level, June said, "No," almost goading.

Marisol was desperate. She slapped June. The sound echoed in the house like a firecracker.

June jerked her head back, her eyes wide and smarting with tears, a red splotch on her cheek. Marisol's hand tingled where it'd made contact with her daughter's face. She was stunned at what she'd done. Marisol reached her hand out to touch her daughter's face, to comfort her. June flinched. Harding her eyes, she turned her hand on the door knob and left without another word. Like her father, she slammed the door behind her.

Marisol sat on the second step of the second-floor stairs. Her arms lay limp at her sides, the tingling hand turned upward.

From the bottom of the stairs, Alegría witnessed her sister's leaving. She dropped the broom in her hand, put on her rainbow-striped jacket and the pink rain boots she'd been gifted by Great-grandfather Francis, and made her way up the stairs, clumsy in the blocky rubber boots.

Passing her mother, Alegría decided that her sister was in

need of more help. She opened the door, gave her mother one last look, and went after her sister.

Marisol did nothing to stop her. She slumped against the wall and drowned in her memories, asking herself repeatedly what she'd done.

25.

June took off at a run through the tree-lined streets outside of her grandmother's old house, the sting of her mother's hand on her cheek. She was unloved, a plain object for her mother to abuse when she needed her and ignore when she didn't. She clenched her teeth. Hot tears streamed down her face. June didn't know for whom she was crying. Her mother was selfish, careless and didn't deserve her tears. She was silly, sniveling ugly tears no one would care to see.

Heavy raindrops fell from the sky, washing away the salty streaks on her face and soaking into her back, sticking her black jacket onto her skin, flattening her hair around her face so she looked thin and bald. She smelled of wet dog. Her lungs burned and she fell short of breath, but she continued running, relishing the pain as an effectuater of her self-hate.

The wind whipped the rain into sharp shards, making her bones ache with the cold. June didn't care if she got sick. Maybe she would and then her mother and father would feel bad, guilty, and remember her. Yes, she wouldn't take care of herself, get deathly sick, die, and leave her parents to clean up the mess, knowing her death was all their fault. Maybe then they'd care. Or maybe not.

"June? June!" A squeaky voice called out behind her. She took a quick left, hiding behind the shabby fence of the corner house. Her heart beat quick in her ears and her chest. She didn't want to be found. She didn't want to go back to that hideous house with her hideous mother, who'd never bothered to buy new mattresses like she'd promised nearly a year ago. The voice called out again, farther than before. June swallowed hard. She stood and took off at a sprint, hating the squelch of her shoes on the puddling pavement. She crossed two streets without checking for cars like her father had drilled into her, and followed the lines of the sidewalk, bypassing drummed-on garbage cans and an ugly shrub left at the end of a driveway.

June had lied to her mother about the PM meeting. There was nowhere to be, no one that wanted her. She took two rights and a left, pushing past the dull houses and stupid driveways. She forced her eyes open, allowing the tears to well up in them so that the road swam before her. All the grays and browns melded into each other until she couldn't see. Good. June didn't care if she couldn't see and fell. A scraped knee would be welcome.

A stitch dug at her side and her legs wobbled like jelly. The piercing pain in her lungs slowed her down and she had to take a breath. Opening her mouth, a wracking sob escaped. She sounded like a ninety-year-old man, wheezing and whimpering uncontrollably. June stumbled to the floor, the cold rain seeping into her pant legs, as it had into her shoes and socks. The cement pavement tore her palms, drawing blood. Rain, apathetic as her mother, pelted her head. She shifted onto her back, whimpering worse than a lost, pitiful puppy. June was no better than Alegría, breaking down into a slobbering mess. But she couldn't help it.

She was humiliated. She didn't think her mother had hit her. Of course, her mother didn't love her. No mother who actually loved her child could physically harm her. But for a trivial second, Marisol had defended her, spoke with her, taken her side and June had been foolish enough to hope. Now she knew, her mother was simply using her while she took a break from Alegría.

June was the replacement, not Alegría. Her nose ran; she wiped it on her black jacket, what Cousin Stacy would've called dirty. She didn't care anymore. She *was* dirty and bad and black inside.

Her tears subsided and her sobs turned to occasional gasps and sniffles. The rain continued its attack. Everywhere was cold and wet. She shivered violently. June felt tired of life and tired of herself. June hated her mother but even that was hard to hold onto in the wake of the rain. Mostly, she felt numb, dull like the mark on her cheek.

"June?" A different voice called out from in front of her, deeper and smoother and boyish.

She was cowering at the edge of a vibrant green, manicured lawn in front of the grand Flores' house, with its four floors and two driveways. The golden glow from the Christmas party was gone, leaving an ordinary house standing against the torrent of rain. Hortencia Flores was carrying Concepcion in her arms, tucking her into the baby car seat. Forty-eight-inch Paolo ran after his mother, diving under her arms, trying to wedge himself in the seat below her. He pulled at his seatbelt, clacking the metal tongue with the buckle, hands shaking, unable to properly lock the belt. Jonas Flores was already in the driver's seat, adjusting the mirror from when his wife had driven the car, and checking behind him to see that the driveway was clear; his shirt and face were spotted with water. The car radio was turned on, a static voice mumbled evacuation procedures and listed the red hills of Manteca as a safe haven for those in the danger area. Hortencia chafed Concepcion's chubby legs with the seatbelt, making the three-year-old cry; her usual mask of tranquility was taken down, in place a worried woman with dark circles under her eyes and sagging cheeks. Hector was on his driveway, stretching his hand out towards June. His hair, usually a stylized pile of curls, hung like a dead flower, dipping into his eyes and down his face.

"Hector Flores, you get inside right now," said Jonas, the glowing patriarch.

For the first time since the third-grade, the middle-schooler talked back to his father. "Wait a moment, Dad. June's here." Hector prodded June up, then he had his arm around her shoulder and was guiding her up his driveway. The rain beat down hard on their maroon Toyota van, the model from last year. From somewhere beyond the house, a rumbling sounded, growing in size and decreasing in distance.

"Get her in here then, son, now. The flood's almost here." June and Hector half-walked, half-traipsed to the car. Hortencia had gotten Concepcion buckled in and slammed the door shut on the passenger seat. Like a gentleman in the midst of the world ending, Hector held onto the top of the door while June went inside; she sat in the second backseat of the van, an intruder in the happy, dignified Flores family. Hector crouched inside the door and yanked it shut, following his father's orders to hurry. Before he had sat down, Jonas Flores was backing out of the cement driveway.

They were driving down the street when the flood arrived in southern Manteca, sloshing in between houses and shaking trees down to their roots, picking up play toys, coolers, inflatable pools, lost house keys, potted plants, anything left abandoned on neighbors' doorsteps. Raindrops plopped into the water, creating small craters in the moving mass. Around them, other neighbors had already left, evacuated close to an hour ago. Luckily for June, the Flores' had spent time packing valuables into their van, waiting until the last second to leave.

From the window two doors down from the driver's seat, June looked past the streaming, distorting rain. A red wave was moving behind them, like a river of blood, gorging itself on everything it touched. It stretched out a filmy hand, just grasping the tires of the maroon van.

Jonas Flores stepped on the gas, trying to evade the water. A white car left parked at the end of a dirt-brown house's driveway ten houses behind, was surrounded by the water, which rose until it was at the level of the door handles. Then the white car began rolling backwards, until it was carried by the river and hurtling towards the maroon van of the Flores'.

It was then, seeing the monstrosity of the river, that June

remembered her mother, her sister, and her father. She didn't know where they were or whether or not they were okay. The tinge in her cheek was forgotten. She had left her family in the middle of the storm, though her mother had warned her not to. Their father had taken their only car, the jean-blue sedan, and there was no way for her mother and sister to reach safety. "Stop the car," she said, "I need to find my family."

"They're probably already at the shelter, sweetie," said Hortencia Flores, keeping her eyes locked on the side-view mirror.

June had heard a voice, a squeaky, small, annoying voice, that drooled when it slept and shifted multiple times a night until morning, that liked princesses and monkeys and asking insignificant questions about everything. That voice had been outside, looking for her and she'd ignored it, hid from it even in her petty, selfish tantrum. A tree gave into the flood, carried behind them on the current. Another's branches trembled, giving out one last shudder before raising a spray of water as it crashed into the flood. The water smashed the trees against the sides of houses, breaking their trunks into jagged pieces like the spines of unprotected women. "No," said June, "let me out."

"We can't go out! There's a stupendous flood moving down there," said Paolo, pronouncing stupendous as "stoop-it-toes" ("stupid-us"). He waved wildly with both hands in the air for emphasis. Concepcion wailed her support for Paolo. Hortencia leaned in between the two front-seats to reach her three-year-old in the back. She held her foot and shushed her.

"It's better if we don't stop. Or else we risk putting the family in danger," said Hector, putting his hand on June's hand in her lap. He was sitting in the middle backseat next to June.

"No, you don't understand. My mother and sister don't have a car."

"They'll find their way out." Jonas Flores set his hands firmly on the wheel. The wall of red water was not far behind. There was no way he was turning the car around. So June complained and pleaded and tried whatever she could, but there was nothing she could do. The Flores' van would continue moving north, to the muddy hills surrounding the border of Manteca.

Alegría walked the path she'd walked in her dreams many nights ago. Only this time, the bordering houses and trees had ceased disappearing, and the ground beneath her feet slid not backwards. Strangely, the sky was there, a mixture of dark, shadowy clouds hiding the sun away for good. And a heap of rain, sprinkled down as if it were the Big Painter's last. Alegría went right, for she felt she needed to go there. June was nowhere in sight. Alegría walked outside, not too far behind June. She called her sister's name but the sound seemed drowned out by the pouring rain. The ground was wet and soggy. The ladies from the neighborhood were leaving in their cars and trucks and vans, heading towards higher ground.

From the street she was walking on, Alegría heard her the jean-blue sedan sputter into view from around the corner. Her father was driving back the way she'd come, his wheels cutting a white path through the dark road. He was yelling and with one hand signaled his daughter with a waving up-and-down motion, though she couldn't tell if he wanted her to come closer or go back. Alegría stood there until her father had reached her on the sidewalk. "Get in," he said.

Alegría did as she was told, but asked about June and where she'd gone and Uncle Tim and where he was. The radio played broken static in the background. Daniel Cana ignored her questions.

"The roads leading up to the hills are packed, we'll have to stay in that cursed house while the storm passes."

"And June?"

Daniel Cana squeezed the steering wheel before pulling up to the driveway. "Go check inside and see if she's returned."

Alegría wasted no time in unbuckling her seatbelt, pushing the door open and running up the front steps. She opened the unlocked door and called out her sister's name. Marisol was still sitting on the second-floor steps facing the door. Aunt Mary wasn't yet home. "Mama, is June back?" Marisol didn't answer, so after a quick look around, Alegría ran outside, telling her father June wasn't yet home. Daniel said to go back inside while he searched for June.

Alegría was scared. The things she'd seen outside and the hard expression on her father's face let her know something was wrong with the situation. And June wouldn't come back and her mother was a cold stranger. And it wouldn't stop raining, heavy, angry drops. Alegría needed comfort. She wanted her parents to wrap their arms around her and tell her everything was going to be okay. She wanted her mother to stroke her hair and sing her a song of joy, a song of peace; her father to carry her and remind her she was a big girl now and could handle anything; her sister to joke around about the proper way to be a lady and complain about her loud chewing. She wanted someone she could talk to because then, she wouldn't feel so alone, holding onto the railing, peeking around the corner at the door and her stranger mother inside the three-story pumpkin house where her grandmother had left without saying goodbye.

Hanging her head, Alegría trudged to her bedroom, where the weight of her limbs was calling her. With sadness came a kind of tiredness, except she was old enough now to know that sleep didn't bring rest and good dreams, and that when one woke up, no curses were lifted and no dragons were slayed and nothing changed for the better.

Mama had hurt June. Except Mama was hurting, too. And she and Dad were mad at each other. Alegría didn't want to sleep in her own bed. She didn't want to be herself, who was always tired and grumpy and annoying. She didn't want to be the girl who Mama needed to buy expensive medicine for and who needed to be coddled. She didn't want to be the Alegría who disappointed her grandmother and couldn't make her family happy. So the eight-year-old girl pulled back the deck-of-cards curtain and lay face-down on her sister's bed.

Moving her head over the edge of the bed to give herself breathing room, Alegría noticed a bump where the bed covers had been tucked under the mattress. She let her arm hang limply down the side of the bed to smooth out the hanging covers and poked her left index finger on two very pointy corners. Sucking in to make sure she wasn't drooling on June's bed, Alegría got up to investigate. Lifting the asparagus-green covers, she saw two pieces of paper sticking out. The first was the photo of Grandma Susana with her late daughter in the hospital. The second was a crinkly paper with June's fourth grade acrostic poem, praised by her teacher with an "Excellent!" mark in the top right corner. The poem read:

> *Juniper flowers*
> *reqUire*
> *kiNdness like*
> *aquilEgias*

With Alegría's underdeveloped reading skills and June's blocky handwriting, she skipped the second line and read the poem as "June likes Alegría." At that moment, Alegría knew her sister loved her even if she didn't say it. Smiling, she stood up with a dazzling determination to find her, whatever it took, which is why she almost didn't notice when the too-high-up basement window began dripping.

The window creaked as more water began seeping down through the cracks in the casing like one of those fancy fountains in the Street of Shops. "Mama!" she said. Going upstairs, she told her mother about the leaking window. Marisol didn't respond. Heading back downstairs, Alegría saw the kitchen window was dripping, too. So was her parents' bedroom window. Holding her head, she thought and thought until her brain hurt, but the only solution she could come up with was to put clothes and towels and buckets where the water was falling. But she was running from room to room trying to sop up the mess and it was only getting bigger. The carpet where the water fell was soggy and the tiled floor slippery. Alegría ran back upstairs to update her mother on the situation. "Mama, what do I do?"

Marisol slipped out of her reverie long enough to say, "Unplug the appliances." But Alegría didn't know how to do that. Her heart beat in her ears and she was scared. Water was starting to seep in from under the front door and a thin layer of water had developed downstairs. Alegría went back to get June's photo and poem and Mateo the Monkey, her favorite from on top of her bed and Great-grandfather Francis's before joining her mother on the second-floor steps.

Instinctively, she laid her arm around her mother in a side-hug and offered her the stuffed monkey, both of which Marisol refused. Alegría stayed there, sitting on the steps while the water seeped from the doors and windows. Then the front door creaked with the pressure of the water from outside. Something was wrong. Alegría took hold of Marisol's hand on her lap and tried to run upstairs. Her mother resisted. "Mama, please." Reluctantly, the mother climbed upstairs with her daughter.

The door burst open. A swirling blue-and-pink wave reached in like a tentacle, claiming the basement and moving upstairs. They passed Susana's pink and yellow-tiled kitchen and the dining room table where she'd broken down in front of her eldest daughter. From the clear patio door, they could see the ground had risen four, five feet and turned a murky seething mess of timber and clothes. And yet the sky continued falling. Alegría and Marisol went down the hall, the hungry water hot on their trail, skidding from side to side of the hall and sloshing up the closed bedroom doors. At the end of the hall, Alegría scrambled up the staircase, momentarily letting go of her grip on her mother. They were almost to the attic. Alegría could see Susana's blue crates and colorful bookcases and aged wallpaper. Behind her, Marisol moved as in slow-motion, dragging her feet as if she were turning into wood. "Come on! We can make it." Stepping onto the floor of the attic, Alegría turned around with one hand on the railing to offer a hand to her mother. The big wave lunged at the bottom of the stairs, broke, and reassembled. Rearing high in the air, near the ceiling lights, it coiled around Marisol's foot, throwing her off balance so her left hand slipped from the railing. Alegría reached down and caught it, trying to pull her mother up to safety. But the blue-and-pink water climbed up over Marisol, who hung like dead weight. Alegría crouched on the poplar floor, wrapping her knees around the railing. Her arm felt like stalks of cilantro being ripped in two. Only the mother's head and arm were visible. Alegría's back hurt and she felt the floor beneath her shaking. The water tugging at her mother, swallowing her whole. Marisol looked at her daughter with a shining, indescribable look before letting go of her daughter's hand, closing her eyes and falling into the water.

In the mother's mind, she still sat on the second-floor steps of the pumpkin house, going over and over the things she'd done to her mother, her sister, her daughters, her husband. The words she'd said. She could not escape the timeless loop of regret. Staring at the white front door, scuffed where her husband, Daniel, had kicked it closed with his work boots numerous times, discolored where Aunt Mary had rubbed off the paint with her homemade cleaner, and burned gray where two family parties ago, Muriel and Uriel had discovered the power of matches.

After a while, her eyes dried and the white colors blended together so that the doorknob looked like the pear nose of her mother, the peep hole looked like twinkling, knowing eye of her smile, and the square patterns looked like the horse teeth in Susana's mouth. The white became Christmas lights in the distance, out of focus, and the room blended together.

The Mipared River had coursed through the street, hunting and sniffing at the Circle of Elites, at Crecimiento Elementary, and at the houses of the neighborhood ladies, like a bloodhound searching for a particular corn-flour scent. It'd slammed into the pumpkin house, trying to bring it down. Attacking its foundation, it'd seeped into Susana's dead flower pots and broke the planks of the white-washed, vine-encapsulated fence, throwing them asunder like splintering chew toys. Going up the front porch steps and making a pool out of Susana's dead grass, it burst through the front door, seeped in through the cracks in the windows. Marisol, in her mind at the second-level stairs, was taken, not by surprise as an eight-year-old would be, but by the blue familiarity of coming home. She'd been engulfed by the frothy, debris-filled waters of the River, encircled by pinks and purples, and then falling. Falling. Falling and flying and spinning in infinite circles.

It was at that cardinal moment in time that Marisol Cana disappeared off the face of the earth. She was transported into the past. In between waves crashing, she could see images rise up like the unburied dead. To her left, amidst the frothy brown mist of clove-colored sand, she saw the moment she drowned her sister, her eight-year-old fingers beckoning Ría to the pool while their mother's back was turned. Above her in the eyes of a dead chicken, she saw the moment she left her mother, holding a plate of *piña empanadas*. She saw the funeral of her sister, saw her mother accepting Josefina's condolences. Below, inside the billowing emulsion from a nearby gas station, she saw her husband leaving, saw their prolonged fights and heard their strained conversation.

Marisol had fallen into the waters of yesterday, wandered and drifted into the past she had wrapped around her like a maze. She'd become nothing more than the memories she'd accumulated.

In Grandma Susana's attic, Alegría had little time to process the fall of her mother. The floor started rocking and swaying. Crawling to the cyclops window and avoiding the sliding crates and toppling bookcases, Alegría saw the world bathed in water. Roaring waves ripped the pumpkin house off its foundation and carried it down the river that was Manteca. Through the window, Alegría saw four-legged starfish and wide-mouthed rats and wild-eyed cows, and creatures with jagged teeth unknown since the beginning of time. Easy as snapping a toothpick, the waves ripped the trapezoidal roof off. The smell of a thousand year-old porta-potties intensified. Still, more rain fell.

Alegría needed to find shelter, to move to higher ground. But there was nowhere to go. Everywhere was water. She had only time to wonder what had become of her sister and father before the murky, rainbow-colored water picked up her small body and claimed it as part of the river. The water was shocking, numbing, so cold it felt like lava. Trapped underneath it, Alegría knew she must hold her breath. She tried flailing her arms to stay afloat but the rolling waves pushed against her. The water was yellow, blue, and red. Her heartbeat thrummed behind her eyes and in her ears. She pursed her mouth, stuck in her body. Her lungs hurt from holding in her breath. She must not breathe. There was no escape. Her limbs grew heavy. She couldn't move them. Her shivering sub-sided into a contraction of her muscles. Like at the Flores' Christmas party, like when she hugged her parents on Christmas Eve, like when she practiced her solo during the school play, her body had turned to a lead prison. All around darkness settled. Her insides were ready to rupture. She must not breathe. She must not breathe. Alegría's spirit was waning, receding from her limbs into a hidden nook inside her heart. Her body took over, exhaling a breath and involuntarily inhaling in. Her throat felt like it had a million paper cuts and she was swallowing a bucket-load of lime juice. Her vocal chords spasmed and she stopped breathing. Alegría was too weak to fight any longer. A soporific stupor washed over her. Somewhere in a different world was another Alegría, bobbing up and down in the water, struck with sharp branches and the wings of a dead bird, who had a mom and a dad and a sister to find. But that Alegría wasn't her; she was far away. The only thing that mattered was succumbing to the cold. Cold and sleep.

Out of the churning blue and berry, a hand, bathed in an ethereal glow, stretched out towards Alegría. Then she was flying upwards, the dead fish and branches tossed all around her. With the surge skyward, Alegría's purpose returned. She crawled out of the hidden nook in her heart and burst out of the water.

Fiery, burning light erupted all around her. It consumed her making her feel weak, she raised her right hand to shield her eyes. When Alegría's eyes adjusted, she found her left hand enveloped in the warm hand of Grandma Susana. The grip felt natural, like home, and she knew that whatever came, her grandmother would always be there for her.

"Hello, *mi Grillita*. You've wandered a long way, wouldn't you say?" She smiled her horse-teeth smile with the twinkle in her eye that meant a laugh was close by.

"Where are we going?" The two were walking, hand-in-hand, on a filmy white lake, the color of milk in tea. In the distance were hills of sugar. All around were bread houses, fluffy and airy, floating like sponges. Trees with leaves of shredded coconut sprouted from the lake. The air rumbled, as if there were seashells taped to Alegría's ears, and it smelled sweet, like *arroz con leche*. They were on a version of the street just outside the pumpkin house, where she'd been before the river took her.

"To see *mi cielo*, over yonder."

Alegría's eyes lit up and she swung her hand in her grandmother's. "You found her?" "I never lost her." Susana's mouth curled in a lopsided smile.

"But you said. When you were walking."

"Then I must've. Though I don't remember."

They arrived at a sugar hill, the grains crunching under their feet, climbed up to the top, where two walls of sugar cubes rose up from the ground, partly hidden by bushes of coconut. Walking in between the sky-high walls, Alegría and Susana entered a walled enclosure. Inside were boxes of all shapes and sizes, built out of toasted amaranth seeds held together by honey. Each box had its own little house at its head, made up of arches, pillars, obelisks, tablets, domes. Some were simple, no more than one or two foot tall, while others were extravagant, about six or seven feet, with protective statues for the people inside. The smell of ginger and wood danced around the tombs. All around were *merengue* flowers in light hues of pink and green, purple and orange, yellow and blue.

Alegría felt an itch deep in her throat, as if she'd forgotten something. She scratched at it and coughed twice to make it go away.

Susana walked a path she knew as well as her *empanadas* recipe. After clearing her throat to get rid of the itch that was starting to burn, Alegría followed her grandmother into the amaranth maze, past a tomb shaped like a swan and another shaped like a train, to a white box beside its twin, surrounded by little, white candles. Engraved in the seeds was the name "Alegría Ramos" and the epitaph, "*El cielo es para siempre.*"

"Grandma, is this your sky?" She rubbed her throat and pointed to Ría's plain tomb. "No, *mi Grillita*, my sky is my loved one—"

Alegría frowned, looked down, and rubbed her pink boot across the sugar. "The other Alegría?"

"*All* my loved ones, and that includes you." Susana smiled and held out her hand for her granddaughter to take. "Love is unfathomable, wonderful in all its colors and flavors, and the kind I have is more than enough for the two of you." She swung their interlocked hands playfully. At first, the little girl brightened, smiling wide as the moon. But after a moment, her smile disappeared and her brow furrowed.

"What's wrong, *mi Grillita*, aren't you happy?"

Alegría coughed and scratched at her throat. She felt oddly parched. "It's just … what if I can't be happy? Mama, she's sad when I'm happy. Because I have this thing. That makes me sleepy. And the happy makes it come back. And Mama, she—she gets sad, and then she's not Mama anymore." Quick as a spark, the little girl remembered her sister's poem, her grandmother's laugh, and her parents' song. "But it's okay. Once I get better, then Mama won't be sad and Dad won't get mad and we can all be happy." She set her mouth in a determined line, nodded once, and swallowed her itch.

Grandma Susana patted Alegría's hand with her date-colored one and looked straight at her with her chocolate-brown eyes. The tombs behind her caught golden in a sudden ray of light. "Now you listen well, *mi Grillita*, what you have isn't something as easily cured as a cold. It'll stay with you until you're good and old. Nonetheless, that doesn't mean you can't have joy. For all her recent distress, I can assure you, your mother loves you no less. Remember how she stayed with you when you couldn't sleep? The same accompaniment is all she needs."

"But then she gets mad. And I'm tired. When I'm awake, she doesn't talk to me like before."

"Simply keep loving her to the best of your ability, without expecting the same in return. And I promise you, no tossing tempest, no myriad of dreams can break the bond between you. Alright?" Susana smiled at her granddaughter with a twinkle in her eye, her salt-and-pepper hair flowing in the crisp wind that had picked up.

"Alright." And then it all came back for her, images of water and the disappearing roof and her mother. Her mother. Alegría's eyes widened and she let go of her grandma's hand. She turned to run back towards the lake, where she knew her mother was. "Grandma, we have to go. Mama's in danger." Her footsteps were the only ones on crunching on the sugar. "Grandma?" She turned around. Only the amaranth seed structures and *merengue* flowers remained. Beside the white tomb that read *Alegría Ramos* was a sister tomb reading *Susana Ramos. True joy comes from love.* There was no time. The little girl took off at a run. Her grandmother would be there as long as she needed her, but her mother couldn't wait. Past the sugar cube walls and coconut bushes, Alegría saw the milky lake stretching over everything, soaking through the bread houses. There, over there, hanging on to a few crumbs of a house was her mother.

The girl half-ran, half-slid down the hill and directly onto the lake. Her lungs burned and the itch in her throat returned worse than ever. "Mama, I'm coming." The lake rippled with her every step, revealing the burnt amber color of tea underneath the film of white. She was almost to Marisol, who was splashing the lake trying to get out. "I'm coming." Alegría rasped, her breath rattled wet inside her. The pain spread into her limbs, stiffening them, making it hard to push forward. If she breathed in again, she would break down in coughs, so she held her breath. "Coming."

The rumbling in the air grew louder, morphing into a sucking sound all around her. From the lake rose up lopsided, faceless monsters, the creamy thin layer of the lake melting off them in globs, like hot wax. They fell forward, trapping air into the water, and rising up again in fluid forms, shuffling towards her.

Although her insides burned and she was weak from lack of oxygen, Alegría ran faster. The blood pounded in her head. The edges of her vision blurred and blackened. If she could just get to her mother, everything would be okay. Marisol had stopped struggling and was disappearing into the lake, which had changed consistency. No longer could Alegría ran across it, for it pulled at her legs like thick *cajeta*.

Marisol, within reach, saw her. Her mouth opened and she began struggling anew. She reached out her hand, within an arm's grasp. The lake congealed into glue. The shuffling things were closing in. Frantic, Alegría lunged forward, fell hard on her knees, stretched out her hand. Her heart rate was like a hummingbird's. Her fingers scrambled in the air until they interlocked with her mother's.

The fluid monsters lunged at them, cold and sticky milk and tea dousing them. Marisol and Alegría were whirled around, whipped and walloped from head to toe. In the breathless chaos, Alegría was sure of one thing only: her mother's hand wrapped firmly around hers.

26.

Out in the calming waves, June spotted a rainbow-striped jacket hanging on the edge of a wooden rafter. "There," she said, pointing Great-grandfather Francis in the jacket's direction. She'd been in the Flores' van when it was picked up by the river. Jonas Flores had instructed them all to unfasten their seat belts. The van had been pushed against one of the earth-colored houses and they'd all climbed out of the vehicle onto its roof. They'd been in the process of trying to climb into the house through a open second-story window when the all-knowing *chaman* had arrived in his *bolillo*-shaped *barco*. He'd thrown them ropes and lifesavers and with his crew, consisting of Josefina and the people from the cement houses, gotten them safely inside the boat. Daniel Cana had already been rescued. The two had reunited, with June asking all the while where Alegría was. They'd been in the midst of looking for Marisol when they'd seen Alegría carried off into the river. In her mind, June heard her mother's words, "Catch her!" just as she'd heard them the day her younger sister had tumbled down the stairs.

The boat docked near the remains of the pumpkin house while June and Daniel helped Great-grandfather Francis unload the lifesaver tied to a rope. Daniel put on a life jacket and waded into the river, putting the lifesaver around Alegría and lifting her into the boat, where June and Josefina were ready to catch her. Daniel hoisted himself up into the boat with Jonas Flores's help. The rains and winds had quieted down.

Alegría was limp. She had a bruised right eye and various cuts and scrapes all along her face. *"Grilla? Grilla!"* June held trembling hands over her sister's body as Josefina lifted her from Daniel's arms, head supported at a weird angle. Her sister's legs dangled like two pieces of string, one foot bare, one pink boot waterlogged. She was placed on her side on the soft, wet planks of the boat. Her left knee looked wrong, facing her right one at an awkward angle. Alegría looked like a slack marionette crushed, lifeless.

June didn't know what to do. She couldn't touch her sister, or else she'd somehow harm her. Her sister was fragile, still, with closed lids, wet lashes, and a partly open mouth. If not for the bruises and thin hair pasted all over her face like scribbles, she could be sleeping, maybe even drooling. How June wished Alegría would drool, see the familiar goopy puddle at the side of her sister's mouth and the steady rising and falling of her chest, just to know she was alive.

From far away, a hoarse voice called out "Where's Mari?"

Josefina yanked the plastic water bottle off her neck and set it down on the floor, the chain and keys clanking against the hard bottle as it tipped over and rolled away on the undulating floor. With thick knuckles, she turned the little girl up and tilted her head back by lifting under the jaw. Then she put her ear next to Alegría's mouth and nose. Josefina couldn't hear anything. Alegría had been abandoned inside the pumpkin house and had had to weather the flood alone; she'd been colorless in the water for who knows how long.

June grasped her sister's wrist, forcing her hands to stop shaking. It was cold, fingers curled inward, no pulse. Josefina smacked her lips, interlaced her right hand's fingers with her left's and placed the heel on the center of Alegría's chest, above the zipper of her rainbow-striped jacket. She pressed down and up, down and up, her green grocery store vest flapping up and down with her.

There was the splash of a person with a tube going into the water. Voices shouted directions and encouragement. Wood creaked.

Alegría let her chest be pushed. She didn't whine or ask questions or call out for June as she'd done earlier. Before the streets flooded and the sky and land became one, she'd gone out to look for her older sister. And June had heard her and hid behind a fence on purpose. She'd left her sister alone in the house with her mother because she'd been hurt. But she'd only been thinking of herself. At the time, she simply didn't want to be found, but she hadn't thought her dumb little sister would keep looking for her. June was stupid and selfish, and although she'd accused her mother of being selfish, she was exactly the same. And now Alegría wasn't coming back. Her chest was moved up and down, up and down. Somewhere, a hoarse voice called out "Mari." People with blankets and Great-grandfather Francis's rain jackets were gathering all around in a circle, talking and fidgeting as they had when she'd gotten lost at the store. But they didn't matter. June's vision darkened at the edges and spun as the boat rocked. She raised her shaking hands to her lemon-shaped mouth. It wouldn't stop trembling. Alegría lay still as paper jerked up and down, up and down. She wasn't annoying or bright or lazy or sad. She was nothing. Stupid.

Stupid. *Malcriada*. The water and everything it'd touched smelled awful, like unclean bathroom stalls. June smelled awful, sticky patches of dried water all over her. A disgusting odor rose in the back of her throat. She felt the same guilt Marisol had felt when she'd witnessed her sister drowning.

What if Alegría didn't wake up? If June hadn't left, she could've helped her sister avoid the water. She could've been there for her mother and sister, could've held their hands, could've held onto the house and waited for rescue. She could've helped them get somewhere safe, could've pulled them onto a roof, built a raft from the rafters. She could've told Alegría, who couldn't swim, to hold her breath underwater. If she hadn't left, she could've at least done something! Anything. June pulled at her hair. Frustration and helplessness dribbled from her in quivers and jitters.

If only Alegría could wake up. If her pallid face would twitch, if she'd just move. Please, if she could breathe, if she could live. Up, down, up, down. A crack of thunder sounded just over the Mipared River. Alegría's body spasmed. Her eyes flew open and she half-raised herself, choking out water. June and Josefina turned her on her side, while she vomited.

From behind, "Mari?"

"We got her, we got her."

Josefina called out, "Francis," beckoning with her left hand for help.

The waves whispered all around them, knocking on the sides of the boat. They swirled in shades of green and gray. The plastic water bottle rolled towards them. The sky was dark and grim as soot. But holding onto her little sister's shoulder, there was hope.

27.

Alegría opened her eyes, disoriented by the bright light of the hospital room. The ceiling's squares danced in her vision. A ringing echoed in her ears. Her mouth was dry, and her throat was sore. Somewhere was itchy, and then a dull ache in her muscles returned, somewhere below. Alegría scrunched up her eyes before the room came into focus. She was in a warm room, on a bed with green covers. To her left was a wooden table with a fake shrub and a computer screen showing colored lines and shapes. Next to it was a brown, polka-dotted couch. Through the unshuttered window above it, she could see the tops of the autumnal poplar trees, honey and ginger and yam-colored, grown quick and strong after the flood. Their leaves rustled in a cool, salty breeze from the south, where the Mipared Dam had once been. Far away were the clove-colored hills where Mantecanos and Prudentos had once united and a backdrop of cement houses, old and new in the yellows, reds, and purples of maize. Up above, the Big Painter in the Sky sprinkled his canvas with no more than a hint of cream of tartar, stretched it open and unknown.

Alegría looked to her left, where her daughter rested swathed in white and pink blankets on a clear plastic bed. Fuzz on her head with the same pear nose as Susana, she lay sleeping, serene and beautiful.

The door creaked open. In came her husband, his smiling eyes like two grains of black sweet rice under his thin, blue glasses; behind him, her mother, smiling wide looking all over the room with glossy eyes and her hair done up in humongous curls, supported by her father, who, with his slicked back hair, had stood by her all these years. Then came in June with a fitted green jacket and a white purse, smiling crookedly and lifting her shaped eyebrows over fixed, clear eyes. Before she closed the door, Grandma Susana sneaked in wearing her frilly white apron, come straight from preparing a dinner in the other world.

With the click of the door, Iris began crying. Alegría's husband clucked his tongue and rushed to pick up his daughter. As he rocked her on his shoulder, Grandma Susana settled down in the wooden rocking chair near the foot of the hospital bed, arms crossed in her lap and leaning back.

After nodding at Susana and greeting her family, Alegría told her husband, "Let me see her." He handed the baby off and tenderly watched the two of them rest. Because of the pregnancy, Alegría had stopped taking the slumbering brew and all other medication to help her stay awake during the day. Thus, she had to be especially careful not to fall asleep while taking care of her baby. And Iris was her baby. Her very own. And it was hard to believe that someone so small and precious could be entrusted to her care, and that she could love her so much in so little time. Seeing her shining face, Alegría felt a powerful love and happiness bubbling inside her wanting to burst out.

And it was the same love Marisol had felt for her and Susana had felt for Marisol, an unconditional bond that meant she would nurture her in the best way she knew how.

Sitting on the soft, cushioned hospital bed in the rainy season of Manteca, protected in the lilac light of those she most loved in this world, Alegría tenderly caressed her daughter's hairless head and breathed in the scent of new life; she bid Grandma Susana farewell and, in that moment, experienced incandescent joy.

www.ingramcontent.com/pod-product-compliance
Lightning Source LLC
Chambersburg PA
CBHW020548020726
47494CB00006B/1968